# The Dawn of Nia

# The Dawn of Nia

by Lauren Cherelle

Resolute Publishing
Louisville, KY

ISBNs: Print 978-0-9973211-0-4 | Ebook 978-0-9973211-1-1
Library of Congress Control Number: 2016933525

First Printing

Cover Copyright © 2016 L. Curry
Editors: Andrea Hayes; Nik Nicholson, final content editor

Acknowledgments: V. N. Jones, L. Hankins, C. Oglesby, A. Brown

Resolute Publishing, LLC
P.O. Box 1833
Louisville, KY 40201


www.respublishing.com
info@respublishing.com

# 1

I DON'T KNOW how much more of this funeral I can stomach. The minister is eight minutes into the eulogy and still begging for a thunderous hallelujah or soulful amen. "Ain't no party like a Holy Ghost party," he screams. Obviously, he doesn't know a damn thing about Pat.

She would look him squarely in the eyes and say, "I didn't ask for this party, fool."

Aside from an occasional cough, the congregation is as lifeless as Pat's body while the minister is in the pulpit hovering over her closed casket, pleading to souls to rejoice in her death. The organist tries her best to follow his highs and lows, adding crescendo whenever he falls flat. His efforts, however, are subpar to the energy Pat radiated on any given day.

I admired Pat, especially in her last days. Although I was with her almost daily as she fought cancer, nothing prepared me for the night she lost her battle. As a nurse, I witness the debilitating stages of dying. But no amount of experience or preparation could have made her passing easier. My mornings have been absent and the evenings long. I'm already missing her understanding and infectious laughter.

I tune the minister out with memories of Pat, holding back tears as I recall our last conversation. "Don't cry for me," she said, her arm resting on mine. "We've had too many good times for you to cry. I should make you smile."

Jacoby takes my hand as mascara blemishes my cheeks. I almost laugh out loud at the idea of the eulogy boring me to tears. The humor fades when I notice Pat's sisters peering over their shoulders to the rear of the sanctuary. I look back, with dozens of eyes, curious to see who just walked into this homegoing service almost an hour late. A woman stands before the closed sanctuary doors, clutching her purse and scanning all eyes that meet hers.

"Can I get a amen?" the minister pleads for our attention.

Friends of the Carter family turn their heads back to him, apparently unfamiliar with the woman. The eldest women of the Carter family keep glaring with disapproval under their wide brimmed church hats.

Are their hostile stares due to the woman's tardiness or white dress? The lightweight material trails her like smoke as she makes her way up the center aisle and checks the cramped pews for a place to sit. She passes my row unconcerned with probing eyes, her dress sweeping the carpet.

"Who is that?" Jacoby whispers.

I shake my head. I don't know. But she looks like a family member. Her high cheekbones and blush lips resemble Pat and her sisters' faces.

She stops four rows ahead and waits as a mourner creates barely enough space for her to squeeze onto the pew. Then she sits down and disappears from my view. I'll definitely ask about her later.

With the temporary distraction over, I look at the memorial program in my lap and read her name again: *Patricia Ann "Pat" Carter*. I turn the page to the obituary and focus on the sentence that soothes my grief. *PAT CHERISHED HER STUDENTS AND WILL BE FOREVER LOVED AND MISSED BY NIA ELLIS*. At first, this sentence surprised me because I'm the only non-relative identified by name in the obituary. I'm grateful that the Carters acknowledged my friendship with Pat.

At the minister's closing remarks, two funeral directors push the service along. They move the lavender standing sprays away from the casket and proceed down the aisle. The pallbearers follow in their footsteps, marching to the pulse of the piano, swaying to the hum of the choir. I drop my head as they approach with the glossy black casket atop their shoulders. It's a procession suitable for royalty. I find comfort in Pat's spirit and the adoration that so many attendees share for her. I lift my head as the bereaved family approaches. Pat's mother and three sisters walk proudly and greet me with smiles. As proprietors of a long-established funeral home, they spared no expense on Pat's homegoing service.

Row by row, the pews empty, and the woman in white walks by as expressionless as before. Jacoby and I join the slow-moving line through the vestibule to the parking lot. I lose sight of the woman due to the crowds and commotion of cars.

I step from the pavement into a patch of lush grass that's shaded by a tree while waiting for Jacoby to return with his overpriced gas guzzler. I feel lighter in the shade, like I can finally breathe without cries tugging at my throat. The short breeze and alone time are calming until Pat's aunt assaults me with a hug.

"It'll be okay," the over-dressed woman says, squeezing my hand too tightly.

What the hell is okay about never seeing Pat again? This is why I didn't ride to the funeral with the Carters; why I didn't sit in the front pews with them; why I'm not riding to the burial with them. Condolences irritate me. When I don't respond, she drops my hand and compliments my dress and heels.

As Jacoby pulls up, I step aside and watch the Carters load into three family cars, just as dark and immaculate as the casket. I open Jacoby's heavy SUV door, almost free from the discomfort of my aching feet until someone calls my name. "Are you riding with us?" Pat's youngest sister, Cookie, asks.

I politely decline and climb inside the SUV.

"Are you sure?" Jacoby says.

"They'll smother me. And Kayla may be in there."

He pulls into the procession without further question.

I latch the seatbelt and tug at my A-line dress. Though the hem stops right at my knees, I feel sparsely dressed. I replace my heels with flats and smile. Pat begged me to "gussy up" sometimes. "You're too cute and young to look so drab all the damn time," she'd complain.

Today, I'm honoring Pat's wishes.

~ * ~

The cemetery tent is too small to shelter everyone from the harsh July sun. I stand with Jacoby in intense heat, shifting from one leg to the other. We're in the middle of nowhere, suffering through day three of a suffocating Tennessee heat wave. The air is so thick and stiff that sweat is creeping down my thighs. The surrounding dead bodies bother me, a harsh reminder of the permanency of Pat's passing. I'm not the only one on edge, though. Children are whining. Men are fidgeting. Women are dabbing their sweat-smeared makeup.

The only person who seems content is the woman in the white dress. My curiosity about her helps distract me from the heat and folks' constant sniffles. I've watched her closely. I wonder why she isn't as antsy as the rest of us. She stands alone, arms crossed, on the opposite side of the crowd, a few feet from the tent. She's standing around like this is a pleasant day and occasion. Only two family members have spoken to her. Their interaction was quick and cautious. Even the family members with longstanding grudges briefly smiled and hugged one another at some point. But no one has touched her. Every few minutes the immediate family members swap whispers before cutting glances her way— like she's a mistress that overstepped her bounds. I've watched all of this long enough to know she's related to the Carters in some way.

"Stop staring at her," Jacoby says. "She'll think I'm staring at her too."

I use the handkerchief I stole from Daddy this morning to wipe sweat from my chest. Then I bow my head for a painfully long prayer. After a wave of amens, I open my eyes to watch her again, until Pat's niece approaches and blocks my view.

I want to step away from Kayla. But where would I go? We're in a cemetery. There's nowhere to disappear. I roll my eyes and say, "I was hoping we would keep our distance."

"Given we're at a funeral, I figured we could be cordial," Kayla says.

Me? Cordial to my ex? Cordial to a woman who lied and manipulated my reality for the majority of our three-year relationship? During my rocky break-up with Kayla seven months ago, Pat served as peacekeeper. With Pat gone, I don't have to remain civil. I'm ready to place as much space between us as humanly possible. But Kayla will not let go of our relationship. She won't accept that she's gone from lover to public enemy.

I need to set the record straight with her: we are not friends and there will be no more contact. But damn, I can't. This isn't the time or place.

"I'm so over this heat," Kayla says. "It's making me sick."

She's determined to make me talk. I don't want to engage Kayla, but she's the opportune Carter to probe for specifics about the mystery woman. I have to be flexible for a minute. "Well, she was smart."

Kayla follows my gaze to the woman, still standing alone. "Guess we should've worn a light color, too," I add.

"Ugh, she's so wrong. We did not agree on white."

"She didn't get the family memo?" Jacoby asks.

Kayla rolls her neck in his direction. "Boy, please! I'm surprised her tacky ass is here."

Tacky? This woman is far from tacky. The sleeveless white dress complements her camel-colored skin and nicely accentuates the contours of her frame. She is captivating. Feminine. Poised. She caught my eye at first glance. Only the blind or envious would deny her appeal.

I'm not going to share these thoughts. Besides, with Kayla riled up, I can pop the burning question. "Who is she?"

"Ladies," an elder says to hush us.

Kayla hesitates out of respect for her great aunt, but she never retreats from blathering about someone else's affairs. She's a pampered princess whose only talents are gossiping, shopping, and gossiping while shopping.

After a moment she proceeds as expected. "Girl…" She leans forward. "She's the best-kept secret in this family. That's Pat's daughter."

The three of us exchange glances.

I've heard Kayla say some awful things to initiate and spread rumors. Still, I can't believe she would make up something like this at Pat's funeral, and then call it a secret. Jacoby has been my friend for seven years; he knows my history with Kayla. She isn't credible enough for her words to stand unchallenged. So I look to him for assurance that Kayla is bullshitting, again. But he's shocked speechless. He loosens his striped tie and stares at the grass. I study Kayla for a hint of dishonesty, except she's still and silent— a sign of sincerity. Damn. Daddy always said funerals are a family's worst enemy, an occasion where secrets are slain by death. I guess he's right.

"Ashes to ashes, dust to dust," the minister says.

After Pat is lowered into the ground, I head to the car to avoid more hugs and chats. "Take me home!" I order at Jacoby.

"What about the repast?"

I turn around to address him so quickly that he accidentally bumps into me— one hundred eighty pounds almost knocking me off my feet. He grabs my arm to break my fall. Then he notices the effect of Kayla's words across my face and takes a step away from me. Loud and clear, I'm mad. I need some space. And I'm on the verge of crying. I'm not in the mood for food, conversation, or more condolences. I'm sweaty and conflicted, and I need a shower. I prefer to sort my emotions at home.

Pat was a second mother— the cool, younger matriarch I turned to when my natural mother was too set in her middle-aged, Baptist ways to provide unconditional support. I can't fathom why Pat would omit someone as important as her own daughter from every heart-to-heart conversation we shared during our six years of bonding. How could she hide her for so long? And I don't understand how a family that accepted me with open arms could cast out one of their own. Why is this woman in white their black sheep?

# 2

I STARE at the butcher knife in Caroline's hand and hold up my copy of Pat's house key like a peace offering. I've used this key so many times, especially after Pat started her second cycle of chemotherapy eleven months ago. I didn't think about ringing the doorbell or knocking before letting myself inside.

"Why didn't you say something before walking in this kitchen?" Caroline asks. "You scared the crap out of us." Her face relaxes as she places the knife in the drawer. She steps forward to hug me, her floral fragrance reaching me before her arms. Once free of her person and perfume, her mother—whom I've nicknamed Mama C—beckons me with an outstretched hand. I cuddle her wrinkled fingers and take the seat at the kitchen table between Mama C and Pat's middle sister. Mama C pours me a glass of tea and says, "Why didn't you come to the repast?"

I've been rehearsing a response for four days. "I had to go home." I shake my head for effect. "It was too much, and the heat made me sick." A half-truth stolen from Kayla is better than a whole lie.

Mama C touches my hand again, her aged but taut face content with my explanation.

"You and me both. I thought I was gone pass out," the middle sister says, slouching in her seat. She whips the fan in her hand with so much force that hair brushes my forehead. I move back to dodge the breeze. Yes, the weather was brutal that day, but what did she have to complain about? She sat pretty in the center of the shaded tent the entire burial with the same Carter Funeral Home hand fan she's using now.

"We should've had the repast first," she goes on, "and waited till after seven when it cooled down a bit before we stepped foot in the cemetery."

"I ain't surprised that's your idea of a better funeral 'cause you're sixty-pounds too heavy," Caroline spits in her speedy-mouthed manner.

"Look, don't start with me," her sister warns, pulling the box fan closer.

"Somebody needs to! Keep eating all that salt, fat, and sugar and you're next. Sad part is, Pat ate like a rabbit. But you suck up food like a pig."

"Caroline," Cookie intervenes with her soft voice. "None of us want to lose another sister, but that's uncalled-for."

"Says who? Let's be clear, you're just a Twinkie away, too."

At this point, "Loca Tres"— as Pat affectionately called her sisters— are an unstoppable force. Usually, their escalated inter-action irritates the hell out of me. Now, I'm enjoying their mingled voices, the pungency of oak cabinets and fresh potpourri, and Mama C's sweet tea. It all creates a harmonious mix of quasi-normalcy. This feels like my second home again.

In these moments, Pat would intervene. She would chide Caroline for being the eldest and pettiest. Then she would scold all three of her sisters with profanity and demand that *they* apologize to Madear for *her* disrespectful language *and* their spat. After this, she'd sit back in her chair with crossed arms and dominate the conversation.

I look left, longing to see Pat at the head of her table, only to see a bare seat. No one dares sit there. Instead, we all sit in our usual places pretending she's present.

Mama C slams her hand on the table, taking all of us by surprise. "Let's do what we came here to do," she orders, slapping us across the face with reality.

Pat asked us to sort and donate her belongings. With the exception of jewelry and photographs, we have to deliver all material possessions to a pre-designated halfway house for women.

Silently, the sisters stand and walk into the living room. Mama C and I follow and wait for direction. Bossy Caroline takes the reins, assigning her sisters to separate rooms. "I'll stay in here with Madear," she says. Then she pulls the seniority card and assigns me the master bedroom. "You good with that?"

Hell, do I have a choice? In a way, I understand her motive. Pat's bedroom is the most difficult to clear. She charged me with the toughest area because I knew Pat for the least amount of years. I don't have the standing to resist. Before parting ways, Caroline instructs us to create three piles: a donation pile, a sister pile, and a stuff-you-want pile.

I don't want anything but the artsy, aqua-colored bracelet Pat wore almost daily. She told me the bracelet was "just a habit." Her understatement amplifies my sadness. In having her brace-let, a part of her will always be with me.

I search high and low, combing through every drawer, pull-ing everything from under Pat's bed. I rest on the floor to admire her hidden treasures. I start with the jewelry box that's filled with colorful seashells taped to airline stubs, and move to the shoebox stuffed with weathered handwritten letters dated between '88 and '90. I read the pages, noticing distinctions in the handwriting among the heartfelt messages and racy poetry from boyfriends. The doodled hearts and flowers in the margins make me think about the conversation Pat and I had a few months back.

"I was in love once," Pat said. "I mean real love. Not that

desperate shit. I'm talking about transformative love. Love where consequences didn't exist. The type of love where all voices— except his— fell on deaf ears. His name was James. And girl, I would've married him in a heartbeat."

She reclined in her wicker chair, her body exhausted from the short walk from the living room to the patio. She slowly sipped the chai tea I prepared for her. Her hands trembled, but she didn't spill an ounce of it.

"That was a long time ago," she added with a smile. "It's your turn now."

"You want me to be in love?" I asked.

"Not just in love. I want you to *know* it."

I remember looking up at a clouded, crescent moon, trying to make sense of her words. "You mean fall in love?"

Pat pointed at me. "That's it! You act like your feet are covered in concrete, but I really want you to experience how good it feels when you're on the way to knowing love. The falling. I want you to be hit with the moment you know that you *will* love. 'I'm in love' is a destination. I want you to experience all the good stuff that happens before you get there."

She gazed over to make sure I was listening. I can still see the pit fire dancing in her eyes. I can still feel the satisfaction in her face slaughtering my spirit. She wanted me to find the love she had once, but I couldn't care less about my status with Cupid, then or now. Didn't Pat see that I was heartbroken, or how I could barely look at her face without tears attempting to hijack my eyes? I had to force myself to focus on the ruffled neckline of her nightgown or the aqua bracelet hugging her wrist. Anywhere except her face.

"That's easier said than done," I told her and pulled my blanket tighter.

"Well." I'll never forget the way her breath curled into the chilly night air. "If you won't do it for yourself, Nia, know love for me."

Love? I throw the letters in the shoebox and fight my tears. I'm mad about the loss of her love and madder about the growing donation and sister piles next to me. My stuff-you-want pile is empty. I get off the floor to keep looking and sorting.

I hope Pat cleared out any unmentionables before her health took a turn for the worse. I can't bear to run across something phallic or anything that vibrates. It was one thing when we talked about self-pleasure. It's a whole different animal to see her intimate products in person.

Eventually, I open the closet door to pull her clothes from the racks and built-in drawers. "Why didn't you answer my calls, young lady?" Caroline asks. She steps in the closet and inspects my progress.

"I needed a little time."

I ignored calls and texts for two days after the funeral because seclusion was comforting. But now, I need more time. I'm struggling to balance my grief as I remove Pat's clothes. Certain blouses and pairs of shoes invoke specific moments of happiness with Pat I can never experience again.

"You know you're part of this family," Caroline says.

Really? I stop myself from saying, "Then why didn't I know about your niece before the funeral?" I need to handle one emotional load at a time. Plus, I feel betrayed by Pat for not telling me she had a birth child. Everybody else in the family kept her secret, too. As long as I don't verbalize any resentment, I can keep my feelings at bay. I throw an armful of clothes into a box and listen as Caroline admonishes me.

"Don't feel like you can't come to me or my sisters just 'cause Pat is gone. We care about you. Okay?"

I shake my head in agreement.

"I'll be back with some tape for these boxes," she says.

Moments later, I hear footsteps in the hallway, fully expecting Caroline to walk into the bedroom with tape. I turn to the door to see a copycat of her face staring back at me— her daughter, Kayla.

"What is it?" I ask and snatch clothes from hangers.

"I'm here to help," Kayla says.

"Find another room. The kitchen is free." I exit the closet to toss more clothes onto a mounting pile on the floor. "Run, skip, jump, or walk away. I don't care how you leave, just do it." I don't have time for Kayla's antics, mind games, or pleas for my time or sympathy.

She stalls before leaving with a grin on her excessively made-up face. Now that Kayla's here, I need to wrap things up.

I leave the room to retrieve tape for the boxes I've packed. Whatever we didn't complete today can be postponed until tomorrow. I have the entire week off from work anyway. Loca Tres agree that we should call it a day. I help load each sister's car to capacity. As they pull out of the driveway, I go inside to get my keys from Pat's bed. Just before I flip the bedroom light off, Kayla steps in the doorway.

"Can we talk?" she asks.

I ignore her and proceed to slide by until she crosses the doorframe.

"You can't keep avoiding me."

"We don't have any business, so how am I avoiding you?"

She sighs. "I can't keep acting like this shit doesn't hurt, Nia. I lost you because of my choices, but I didn't choose to lose my aunt. You know how much Pat meant to me." She drops her head to suppress the pain, but can't hold back the tears. "The three of us were close. I don't understand why we can't push aside our baggage to be here for each other." She wipes her eyes before pulling her long, wavy extensions into a ponytail. "The least you can do is look at me."

Once again, I stand before Kayla under rare circumstances. Her sincerity is so real that I can't ignore her tears or the compassion I lack for her loss, too. In an effort to be somewhat of a decent ex-lover, I invite her to sit on the bed with me.

I can't stand to look Kayla in the eye, but I listen as she talks. She repeats herself a few times. At first, I don't mind the long-windedness. "I still can't believe it...Just two weeks ago we were watching TV with Pat and things were fine."

"No, they weren't," I finally say.

"You know what I mean."

I do. But, I can't fight the urge to disagree. "Pat was dying. We were counting down the days. Things were *not* fine."

"Are you saying I'm in denial?"

I blink.

"*We* took her to appointments," she says, gesturing between us. "We brought her home. We cooked and cleaned for her. We made her comfortable in her last days. You and me!"

"Look, I'm not trying to upset you."

"Then don't say shit like that...like I'm not aware of things." She drops her head and sobs.

I feel bad for her tears and my compulsive need to argue with her, so I hug her. I want Kayla to know that I care. As we hold each other her breathing settles. The familiarity of her embrace comforts me. A tiny part of me doesn't want to let her go.

"Why don't we ever hang out?" Kayla asks, holding me close. "I miss you sometimes."

"Sometimes?" I laugh and release her to guard my vulnerability. "You know I'm the best thing that ever happened to you."

She smiles and takes hold of my hand. "I'm serious. I can't stand your ass, but I care about you...I always will."

My eyes creep up to hers. I've avoided her deep brown eyes because they're a gateway. A gateway to our past. Every time I look in her eyes I'm reminded of our intimacy. Her betrayal. But right now, her gentle gaze doesn't reflect betrayal. I keep telling myself to snatch my eyes and hand away, but I can't move. Her touch is too soothing. Since Pat's funeral, I've fooled myself into believing that I don't need anyone to console me; that being alone and tucked in my bed helps me cope with Pat's death. Kayla attacks every syllable of those lies as she rubs her soft hands up my arms. Although I'm well aware of whose hands now stroke my back, and whose tongue caresses my neck, I don't stop her.

I sit still in the midst of an out-of-body experience. I see her lifting my shirt and exposing my skin. I hear the rustle of the comforter beneath our bodies. I watch her sit in my lap and pull her dress above her head. I assumed Pat's home and family were enough to make me feel regular. But this house and their presence didn't work. I've longed for days to feel normal and bury my distress. Pat's death ripped me into pieces. Lord knows I want to feel whole again. So all I can do is stare at the dresser as Kayla's kisses subdue my body and this yearning to feel like myself.

My mental and physical states reunite once she pushes me onto my back. I'm present now, moaning as she pushes her fingers inside me, filling the emptiness I can't escape. I didn't know sex was the only behavior potent enough to elicit a natural high capable of numbing my grief.

The shame of fucking in Pat's bed, the disgust of feeling I will never do any better than Kayla, the embarrassment of reneging on the no-bullshit attitude I displayed with her less than an hour before— all were a fusion of emotional masochism in exchange for a transient moment of peace.

# 3

I step off the elevator and proceed down the art-filled hallway in search of Maria, one of the hospital's mental health professionals. Last fall at a co-worker outing we established a solid rapport. Since then, we've become hallway friends. She always encourages her colleague-friends to reach out whenever we need "mind, body, or soul help."

I sigh with relief when I run into Maria near the Radiology corridor. We chat before I pull her to the side to ask for an "appointment." With no area for privacy surrounding us, I turn to the wall as familiar faces walk by.

"You can stop by anytime today," she offers.

During my lunch break, I head to Maria's office, a space large enough for a small desk, two chairs, and a bottle of water. As soon as she closes her office door, I feel self-conscious about sharing my business with someone outside my core group of friends and family.

"How can I be helpful?" she asks and sits. A hint of a Puerto Rican accent lingers in her voice.

I focus on the accent to control my emotions. I want my words to answer before my tears. I inhale deeply to force the crying away. "My...my mentor, slash play mother, slash friend died almost two weeks ago from breast cancer." I exhale deeply, satisfied that I've taken the first step to initiate therapy.

"Oh, I'm so sorry to hear that, Nia. How are you feeling?"

"Not good. I…" I asked Maria to meet with me to talk about my feelings, but I don't want to address my feelings right now, especially feelings of fear. The fact that Pat died so young bothers me more now than it did two weeks ago. She was only forty-eight. I've read the reports on how breast cancer pops up earlier and more aggressively in African American women. I know it happens to us. But to witness someone I love crumble to a statistic is… unexplainable. I've gone to bed for a week fearing death. And I'm starting to think that I'm moving toward paranoia.

I need to finish my sentence, so I skip those feelings by explaining to Maria how Pat and I met and the significance of our friendship. "I never expected my nursing professor to become a good friend, that I would develop such a fulfilling relationship with her." I replay what I said. "I'm not saying it was sexual. It was *nothing* like that. Things got sexual with her niece, though. We were in a relationship for a while, but that got messy…And last week we had sex in Pat's bed." Now I feel like Maria's a preacher and I'm a sinner.

She examines me and I look away. It seems like five minutes passes before she speaks again. "How do you feel about all that?"

Feelings, again? I exhale. I don't want to waste Maria's time. I have to open up a bit. "Like I've fallen off the deep end. This is my first significant death. I've never lost someone this close to me." I stop to reflect and redirect. "And I've got to get my shit together."

There's only one colleague at Methodist East Hospital aware that I'm living with my parents: Jacoby. I bite the bullet and explain to Maria that eight months ago I was living the high-life in a four-bedroom house in the 'burbs with Kayla, paying the mortgage and bills, blowing my disposable income and time on her. Unaware that Kayla was plummeting my credit with her shopping addiction while I focused on Pat's sickness. I also didn't know

she was ruining our relationship with her cravings for "O.P.P."
When I dropped Kayla, I sold the house and everything except
my clothes and car. I didn't want a single item I shared with her.
I decided to start over by moving back home with my parents. A
hard decision, but I needed time to pay off creditors and save,
again, for furnishings and a down payment on a new home. I also
needed time to smother myself in the embarrassment of being a
single, broke professional. By sleeping night-after-night in my
childhood room, I'd teach myself a serious lesson about dating
an emotionally and spiritually immature woman.

"That sounds like a lot to deal with in such a short time
frame," Maria says. "Did Pat's cancer spark a sense of urgency
for you?"

"It made me think about what I wanted out of life. That's
when I realized I was fooling myself with Kayla. She was crip-
pling me."

"You blame Kayla for your current situation?"

"Hell yeah!" I smile a little, surprised at how comfortable
I've become with Maria. "But I know it's not all her fault."

I was a bit immature, too. I was in my mid-twenties, spending like I made twice my salary. I partied most weekends, treated myself with too many expensive trips, and purchased too many
virgin weaves and handbags. I thought having fun with Kayla
was the same as loving her. And her love soaked my ass dry.

"Besides coping with Pat's death and being deflated by Kayla,
what else is happening with you?"

"Pat never told me she had a grown-ass daughter," I blurt
out. "She's like my age. Maybe older."

"Wow. Are you mad at Pat for keeping such a big secret?"

"More confused than mad at this point."

Maria nods. "Have you talked to Pat's family about it?"

"Not yet. I don't know if I should."

Maria crosses her legs and stares like she's waiting for me to say something else. "So, you want me to tell you what to do?"

"That's why I'm here."

"It's not my job to tell you what to do. I can say there's nothing wrong with how you feel. You're grieving. That takes time. Just try to surround yourself with people who care about you. And don't spend too much time alone because life keeps going. Thoughts can run wild when you spend too much time by yourself. That's my professional stance.

"Now, on a personal note, you need to ask some questions because the daughter thing is crazy. And you had sex with an ex. So what? Lots of people have sex with their exes."

I tap my fingernails on the arm of her off-balanced chair.

"I don't feel like I'm telling you anything you didn't already know," Maria says. "Look, there's no fairy dust. You know your problems and solutions better than me. So I know you've got this. Just remember that I'm here if you get stuck and need to process."

"Thanks…People pay for this shit?" I tease.

She smiles. "Good thing I like you."

As soon as I leave her office, I decide to take the advice from my free therapy session. I need to stop wallowing in my loss and my missteps with Kayla. I head to the elevator in search of Jacoby— the only person within a ten-mile radius who knows and cares about me. I'm ready to move forward and let the people I care about back into my emotional space. Jacoby will force me to rise from my slump and act like me again.

# 4

I PARK ALONG THE CURB and zigzag my steps through Jacoby's driveway to miss all the puddles left by heavy August rains. He opens his front door and cuts his eyes. "I should charge you a late fee."

I push him aside. It's too misty outside to stand around with my hair uncovered.

I get together with my best friends Tasha and Jacoby on most weekends for breakfast. This has been our ritual for two years. It's a chance to hash out problems, tell secrets, and lend advice without work, family, or relationship interference. We usually rotate between each other's homes. Lately, I've been enjoying our get-togethers at the Cherry Street Diner a little more since I'm out of rotation. I'm starting to get jealous whenever I step into their houses.

The host is responsible for buying and cooking breakfast, but Jacoby only buys and eats the food. So I help Tasha cook while he slouches on the couch watching a profanity-laced movie and eavesdropping. Most of the cookware in his cabinets originated from Tasha's kitchen or mine. And if it weren't for his long-gone, interior decorator ex-girlfriend, he wouldn't have that nice couch to lounge on or a home suitable enough for Tasha and me to regularly visit. We're the women who transformed his cheap, black and silver bachelor's pad into an inviting, mature haven. Once in a while, someone that Jacoby is stringing along with false promises adds an expensive household item to the mix.

"Can I have this?"

He looks over at the standing corkscrew I'm admiring. "Hell to-the-no. Somebody just gave that to me. And it better be here when she gets back."

Whatever. I can't have the gadget, but because he's a lazy host, I'm definitely going home with the bottle of '91 Riesling I spotted on the baker's rack.

"You been missing for a month," Tasha says. "What you been doing?"

A month? I roll my eyes at the exaggeration and sit at the counter.

She steps beside my bar stool and removes a flask from her purse, adding a shot of clear liquor to her orange juice. "What?" she asks as I stare. "It's been a hard week."

"Girl, it's nine thirty," I remind her.

"You have your days. I have mine. Now answer my question."

"Stuff." I'm actually devoting my free time to house hunting. I won't share the news until I make an offer on a property.

"You still sleeping with Kayla?" Jacoby asks, pushing me to give a lengthier explanation.

When I first told Jacoby about my quickie with Kayla, I was too embarrassed to admit she seduced me. Instead, I told him that I slipped and fell into Kayla's cookie jar. Her treats were too good and warm not to eat. "I grew blue fur and googly eyes," I said. Unfortunately, he mistook my slip-up as a revolving door.

"I've talked to her a couple times," I confess.

Since our blunder in Pat's sheets a month ago, Kayla hasn't stopped calling me. Pat's death is such a fresh wound that I have to spare her feelings. I don't have the heart to curse her out and hang up— yet. The compassionate side of me agreed to meet her tonight for dinner *only*. I take a sip of water to clear my mind of the nauseating thought of Kayla pursuing me.

"I hope you're not sleeping with her," Tasha says. "You can do way better than a heifer passing out STDs. She needs to close shop."

"Thank God we're here instead of Cherry Street with you shouting my business out. I did *not* have a STD."

I had a urinary tract infection. After it cleared up, I cleared Kayla from my life. I didn't need her cheating to lead to something I couldn't remedy with water, baking soda, and amoxicillin.

"Change the subject," Jacoby suggests to keep the two of us from arguing.

"Fine. Y'all still coming over tonight?"

I forgot that I committed the evening to Tasha, but now I have a valid excuse to postpone with Kayla. I really need to heed my good senses and keep her at arm's length anyway.

Jacoby fidgets with his phone as we continue to cook. I can only imagine what's brewing in his head. As long as he doesn't press the issue with Kayla, I don't mind focusing on Tasha and sobering her up a little with water and conversation. The more her mouth moves the less she drinks. So I purposely ask about her new crush, K.D.

"She's dragging her feet," Tasha complains. "Maybe I can get her drunk and lure her to my bedroom."

I love Tasha, but she doesn't wear single well. When she gets lonely, she gets desperate. It's funny how we are today. Fifteen years ago you couldn't pay us to have an open conversation about our girl crushes. Talking was too risky. We didn't even share our crushes with each other. Instead, we buried our secrets deep inside until our twenties. Back then, talking, even to Tasha— who liked girls just as much as I did— would have made my feelings too real. Talking would have made our boyfriends a

Lauren Cherelle

complete lie and sham. Just knowing that she sensed my true feelings, and vice versa, was comforting. It brought us closer. Someone else, someone I loved and trusted, shared my suffering.

We're out, full-fledged lesbians now, but that doesn't make dating any easier. I've already given her tips to garner K.D.'s attention and affection. I guess my suggestions were too lame or lengthy. "Don't be scandalous," I say.

"Maybe she thinks I'm fat," Tasha pouts. She pinches off and nibbles on bacon. "Shit, I knew I should've lost fifteen pounds by now. Next week, fuck breakfast. Let's go to the park and walk."

"You can take them thunder thighs to the park," Jacoby says. "We're good."

She counters with her middle finger. "Since you don't have nothing to contribute other than your big mouth, does K.D. think I'm fat?"

"How am I supposed to know?" He stands and walks to her. "We don't talk about you. But, every now and then, she lets me look at an official copy of The Stud Handbook. I remember reading on page fourteen that a fat ass always trumps a fat stomach. Too bad your ass is flat."

We laugh as she attempts to punch him in the stomach. "So what? This is fat," she says, pointing between her legs.

I shake my head. Tasha's tactless and pushy at times, but she's a supportive and steadfast friend, alongside Jacoby. Now, if I can wiggle Kayla out of my circle, without unleashing the beast, it will be a remarkable feat.

# 5

I DODGE MY NOSY SUPERVISOR and meet Jacoby at the west wing entrance. He suggests that we spend our lunch hour outside of Methodist East and I instantly agree. So far, the workday has been fast-paced and stressful. Each I.V. took double the time to insert and every patient has been unnecessarily difficult.

He starts south along the sidewalk and I follow. After weaving through three blocks of slow moving pedestrians, he asks, "So?"

Why would he wait two weeks to ask a one-word question with a ton of implications? "Kayla wants to keep in touch, but I'm cutting ties."

"What did she do?"

"The same old thing," I explain. "I made the mistake of finally going to dinner with her and offering to foot the bill— only because I wanted to smooth things over with one last meal. This female ordered a sixty-dollar steak!"

"You know your wallet is her true love. I thought you would make better decisions when it came to Kayla. But since you haven't, it's clear you're meant to be single. Look at me, I wear singlehood like a badge of honor."

"You're single because you're a womanizer."

He laughs. "I'm single by choice. I know my strengths and weaknesses. I'm weak when I'm playing house. I'm strong when I'm single and free to mingle. You need to accept that we're birds of the same feather."

Sometimes, Jacoby is insightful. He verbalizes the truths I can't confess. I'm single by choice, too. Unlike him, however, I haven't completely given up on what the future holds. I don't expect much because my relationships have failed to date. But that's no reason to fall prey to his predatory vision of my reality.

"Anyway, where are we going?" I ask as we leave the hospital district.

"Chuck E. Cheese's."

This brings a smile to my face. I need to relieve the strain of twelve-hour shifts and my unfruitful house hunt with a little child's play.

First up, air hockey duels. Jacoby is a sore loser so we switch games and shoot flying ducks. Next, we challenge each other to hoops. But the best tension reducer is smash-a-munch. Yellow lights flash as I bang the purple-haired munches with joy. Jacoby stands by my side, guarding my growing chain of tickets, waiting for his chance to beat my high score. His reflexes aren't as sharp as mine, so he'll never defeat me.

As he strikes munch heads, my eyes bounce to the games we haven't played today, landing on the water shooter beside skee-ball row. My interest in game play vanishes when I spot a familiar face.

"Hey," I say, elbowing Jacoby. "That looks like the woman from the funeral."

Jacoby finishes the game and glances through the center in her direction. He grabs his tickets and turns to me. "You ready to go?"

Is he crazy? I'm too curious to leave right now. I don't plan on speaking to her, but I've got to get closer. Something about seeing her after the funeral makes her real. This really is Pat's daughter.

As soon as I raise my foot, he tugs my scrub top and says, "Hell no!"

I snatch away from his fingers to proceed across the room. I park myself at a skee-ball machine and reach into my pockets for tokens. I look to my right as she stands beside me assisting two children with chunky plastic guns.

Jacoby steps next to me wearing a death stare, warning me to keep my mouth closed. I'm not bold enough to approach a stranger without cause. I didn't come over here to interrupt her. Standing here satisfies my desire to see her up close and in action.

I watch her out of the corner of my eye, but I can't linger for too much longer. I hand Jacoby three tokens so we can both play skee-ball. I'm on the verge of inserting my tokens when she says, "Excuse me."

I turn to her in amazement. Something about this poor plan of mine actually worked.

"Do you mind if the children play these two? The *children*," she says. "The other one isn't working."

I blink in disbelief.

"Not at all," Jacoby says.

When he reaches for the tokens in my hand, I pull myself together and insert the golden coins into both functioning machines for the kids. "Have at it."

The little boy and girl wait for her permission to step forward. She nods and tells me, "Thank you."

"No problem." I step aside with my eyes glued to her face.

"You want your tokens back?" she asks.

"Nah, I'll pay it forward."

She gives me a quick once-over. "How cheap."

Jacoby and I laugh, caught off guard by her sassy reply.

"Are these your kids?" he asks.

"Maybe. Do you plan on hogging more games from people

under thirteen?"

"Maybe," he says and glances at his watch. "We have eighteen minutes to spare."

I have to think fast. I haven't talked to Kayla or reached out to Loca Tres about their secret family member, so I'm excited to prolong this chance encounter as long as I can. I dig in my pockets and place a handful of tokens on the broken skee-ball game. "Cheap?"

"Leave the tickets," she insists.

"Gold digger," Jacoby mumbles under a cough.

"Pardon me?" she asks, side-eyeing him.

"I'll be back," he says to me.

Once he's out of sight, I apologize. "He forgets to use his filter sometimes."

She crosses her arms and turns her back to me.

I try to think of something to pique her interest, to continue the exchange. I feel around my pockets again, but I don't have anything to offer except lint and a pen.

I step away and stand by another arcade game to wait for Jacoby, but my eyes remain on her. What can I say to re-engage her? I can't believe Jacoby blew my opportunity to chat with Pat's offspring. Or maybe it's my fault. Maybe I made a bad first impression. This morning I should've ironed a newer pair of scrubs and pulled my undefined coils into an up-do.

Nearly two months have passed since Pat's funeral. If I don't act now, I'll possibly never have the opportunity to speak with her again. So I'm still thinking about what I should say to her. I'm also thinking about how she doesn't sound like me. She has a regional accent. Northeast, maybe. An accent too clean, rushed, and choppy for a Southerner. And she appears shorter without a dress to elongate her legs. I'm slightly above five feet and she's barely taller than me.

I decide move to another waiting place to see her face again. I walk by skee-ball, taking her in with each step, but not walking so slowly that I look creepy.

Her sandals expose short toes with French tips. The top of a black and gray tattoo peaks above the back collar of her blue tee. She looks just as good in blue as she did in white. A cute silver bracelet dangles from her wrist. Her ring finger is bare.

When I stop at the dinosaur blaster, she looks up, locking eyes with me. "What department do you work in, Nia?"

"Whoa!" I say and throw up my hands. "How do you know my name?"

Her eyes fall to my chest. "It's on your badge, silly."

I touch my badge and giggle in embarrassment. Then I wonder whether my name jogs her memory. I'm sure she saw it in Pat's obituary. I wait a few seconds to see if she'll mention this. When she doesn't, I respond. "That's what a hard morning will do to you."

"Has it been that bad?"

"Cardiology is rough. My day is better now that I'm talking to you."

I can't believe I just flirted with her. But this is a window of opportunity for the answers I want. This way, I won't have to deal with Kayla or quiz her family. If my approach backfires, I'll tuck my head down and run away.

"Hmm," she says. "I'm flattered."

"Do you come here often?"

"The question is do *you* come here often?"

I chuckle. "I should." I want to flatter her more. "Never know where I'll find that someone special."

"Dang, slow down. I don't like to rush," she says and smiles.

My attention drifts to the tiny diamond in her left nostril. Then her shy dimples. Dimples just like Pat's. A few minutes ago, she was meaner than a junkyard dog. Her smile completely diminishes her cold exterior. Her smile confirms the physical attraction I wanted to ignore.

And the attraction obliterates my reasoning. I could disregard the butterflies, but she's given me a green light to proceed. "Maybe one day we can meet each other here, alone."

"I'm not into women who play children's games. But, you're in luck. I have a soft spot for women in uniform."

My increased heart rate interferes with my ability to make a careful decision. This is Pat's daughter and she has no clue I know this. I could hold my tongue and tell her later. Or, I could walk away, attributing our chance encounter to a blip in fate instead of bombarding her with questions. Really, I want to seize the moment, taking advantage of our mutual attraction to solidify a future conversation. Pat's daughter or not, she's beautiful and I want to see her again.

"I'm into adult games, too," I say. "I know a few grown folks' places we can chill."

~ * ~

Once the pedestrian signal switches to walk, Jacoby and I cross the bustling boulevard and head for the hospital quad. "Where did you go?" I ask.

"I had to piss like a racehorse. It's that damn organic tea you gave me," he complains. "So, what did Ms. Get-y'all-grown-asses-out-of-here say when I left?"

"Nothing really. She was real quiet. Maybe she'll loosen up when I call her."

"What? You ran into her and assumed she was gay?"

"I didn't assume anything. My gaydar actually went off at the funeral."

"That's bull. And speaking of funerals, did you tell her how much she looks like Pat?"

I look into oncoming traffic.

"I guess you're gonna wait and tell her at the same time you say 'I live with my mommy and daddy'?"

Jacoby is wrong for poking fun at my living situation, but has every right to remind me that this woman obviously didn't notice, or remember, that we were at the funeral, too. She has no idea we're connected by only one degree of separation.

After much consideration, I say, "When I talk to her, I'll bring it up."

Jacoby checks the time and picks up the pace. He's often late for work and doesn't have any demerit points to spare. I jog to keep up with his stride. He dashes into the side entrance of the hospital and swipes his badge in the nick of time.

Now in the clear, he says, "What's the pretty lady's name?"

"Deidra."

"Dee—dra," he says. "Sounds like trouble."

# 6

THE THOUGHT of cold-calling Deidra makes me anxious. I haven't pursued anyone in years. Kayla led the efforts when first dating me, and before Kayla, I rarely beckoned the attention of those I found attractive. Instead, I substituted pickup lines with the twinkle in my eyes and bounce of my hips. From there, it was an easy ride. I stepped outside of my comfort zone with Deidra at Chuck E. Cheese's. That moment was do or die.

I table the effort for thirty minutes before considering the call again. What if she regrets sharing her number with me? What if she answers the phone and brushes me off? What if we sit on the phone listening to chirping crickets, unsure of how to foster a conversation? Before I'm consumed with more bad scenarios I decide to just call. Ultimately, I won't know what happens unless I call. It has been four days since we met. I shouldn't postpone another hour.

I close the bedroom door so Mama won't randomly walk in during the call. I feel fifteen again, locking the door and cutting off the light to pretend I'm asleep so I can stay up late talking on the phone with my boyfriend. I can't wait to have my own house! After accompanying my realtor to over thirty properties, I've settled on a recently built condo that suits my extensive preferences and limited finances. I pray morning, noon, and night that my inspection and closing will soon come to an end.

When Deidra answers my call, I can't think of anything to

say other than, "Hey, this is Nia." I should have given her something sexy and confident. I stand from the bed like I know the call will end soon, like I know I'm about to unlock the door and head to the kitchen for snack food.

"Why'd it take you so long to call me?"

I smile with relief. Then I tap the speakerphone icon and answer, "Work has been kicking my ass. How are you doing?"

"Good. I'm in Mississippi hanging out with my pops and his crew."

I smile again. I hang out with my dad sometimes. I hear voices and the vocals of delta blues in the background. I desperately want to pry into her relationship with her father, but it's too soon to meddle in her personal life. I also want to ask why she has a Virginia area code except I stick with the basics. "What part of Mississippi?"

"Hold on a second. I need to move. I can barely hear you."

The noises sifting through the receiver parallel a storm as Deidra searches for a peaceful place to talk. First, hissing wind and buzzing, a loud pop, scrapping against a hard surface, a slamming door, and then her pleasant voice. "You know we can get a little out of hand during spades."

I agree and prop my feet on the footboard of the bed. I lie on my back and stare at the dim ceiling. This feels oddly familiar. I recall talking on the phone in this same bed and position with a girl I secretly crushed on in eleventh grade.

"To answer your question," she says, "Cannon."

I'm sort of familiar with northern Mississippi. She's about forty minutes away from the heart of Memphis.

"So," she says, "how was your day?"

"My day was uneventful but okay. I'm keeping a low profile this weekend, spending time at home."

"At home alone? Are you in a relationship?"

I skip the first question. "I'm single."

"Any stubborn exes?"

I bite my lip. Is Kayla a stubborn ex? The break in conversation is a great moment to be upfront about my past with Kayla, her blood-related cousin. I can even disclose my relationship with Pat and her family, except I don't want to sour the conversation. And I don't want to turn her off given I know a deeply personal fact about her while she knows nothing about me. Plus, the information doesn't seem appropriate over the phone. Some matters are better suited face to face.

"I'm a free agent," I tell her.

She likes my response because she proceeds by summarizing her day's activities. She assisted her father with killing and gutting a hog that weighed a ton. "I'll never do it again," she says. After the massacre, she washed grit and tiny, unidentifiable creatures from a truckload of turnip greens, shucked at least two acres of corn, and baked three of the best homemade sweet potato pies ever created on this side of heaven. I enjoy the lofty storytelling as she recounts her day. "Six hours of slaving for ten minutes of eating." She chuckles. "It was worth it, though. It's been a while since I've spent a day with my dad."

I imagine the young man who impregnated Pat. He's lean and handsome with smoky brown eyes and shimmering white teeth. A smooth cat that swept Pat off her feet.

I can't help but to share a day I recently spent with my father, fishing for small mouth bass in the St. Agnes River. "Did you scale the fish?" she asks.

"Yeah. I'm not afraid to get my hands dirty. So when are you coming back to Memphis?"

"I haven't decided. But I really can't handle being in the boonies for more than a few more days."

An indefinite time frame. Does this mean she's temporarily

off from work or permanently unemployed?

"Where are your parents from?" she asks.

After I explain that my parents grew up in ridiculously rural counties in eastern Arkansas, we drift into conversation about our childhood experiences in the nuances of rustic living. One of her most vivid childhood memories is eating red dirt, the thick clay-like kind dug from the sides of hills. "I really can't say if I liked the taste or just the idea of eating dirt."

I glance at the timer on my cell phone. We're approaching an hour and seventeen minutes and I need to pee. But I won't let the pressure in my bladder intrude. I roll out of bed and unlock the door. I amuse myself by tiptoeing down the hall like a sneaky teenager, muting the phone as Deidra recalls more food-related oddities. I quickly relieve myself, splash water on my hands, and dash into my room by the time it's my turn to speak.

"Did you eat pigs' feet?" I ask.

"Ooh, no. They scared me. They still do. I couldn't touch them earlier today. Did you?"

"I couldn't go to the corner store without buying one. I grew out of that. Thank God."

"Yes, Lord," she laughs. I like her laugh. It's a hearty, genuine laugh that creates instantaneous false trust— as if this talk will lead to future ones about things more personal. In the meantime, we reminisce about other country shit we hate but will never erase from our pasts.

"Nia," she says before we end the call. "I really, really enjoyed talking to you. This may sound strange, but I needed this conversation. Your call was perfect timing."

Her voice is so warm, so new. I don't know how to respond.

"Are you there?" she asks.

"Yeah... I'm glad you feel that way. Let's do it again, soon."

"How soon?"

"I pull a lot of overtime, and I work a third-shift gig on the weekends sometimes. So…" I can't mentally pin a free period in my schedule for the next week.

"Why are you working so much? You got mouths to feed or something?"

"No. I…" I'm uncomfortable with the real answer. I'm not ashamed about living with my parents. I'm doing what's needed to move out. But I can't tell her why I'm living here. "I guess because I'm single."

"Well, how about this? I'll call you, and if you're free, answer my call. Okay?"

That's such a simple question, but it makes me feel so desired. And the anticipation of talking to her again is alluring. I notice I've taken teenage reminiscing too far when I catch myself twirling in my curls. I drop my hand and say, "Scratch that. Call me tomorrow."

## 7

THE SLAP OF MY SANDALS syncs with the beat of the bass drum as we approach the entrance of the jazz lounge, Gillespie. After a string of conversations, I agreed to meet Deidra at the corner of Fourth and Market for an evening of live music and Dezza Reign— the fire spitting, spoken word, one-woman-show extraordinaire.

Deidra's demeanor is different from our initial encounter three weeks ago. Now, it matches the casual tone she conveys over the phone— no side eye, no neck roll.

I considered mentioning Pat before today, but struggled with a definite decision. On one hand, I wanted to wait until Deidra was in my presence. On the other hand, our conversations have weakened my burning curiosity about the extent of her relationship with Pat. Their kinship is a factor, but not my first concern. I'm more interested in *Deidra*, the woman who tickles my ears with humor. I'm a sucker for witty women with a sprinkle of bad attitude and a generous portion of sex appeal; women that tease my fantasies with a smile alone. Since our third conversation, whenever I close my eyes at night, visions of her nude body cloud my mind. I haven't fooled myself into believing I can let Pat sit on the backburner for too long. This evening, however, is reserved for just the two of us.

The Gillespie hostess greets us and requests identification. "How many times are you going to ask for my ID?" Deidra says.

"I'm not getting any younger."

"Don't play, Dee," the hostess says. "You know the deal." Deidra reaches into her purse and pulls out a red wallet. She un-latches the wallet and flashes her identification so quickly that only a person with supernatural ability could check it. Then the hostess looks at me. "I know she wouldn't hang with an underage woman, but I need to see yours, too."

After she verifies I'm of legal age, we move to the far wall to make room for entering patrons. I wonder why we haven't entered the lounge, but figure Deidra has a plan. After all, she suggested this place.

"How often do you come here?" I ask.

"Once or twice a year."

"I haven't been since it opened."

"That was about three years ago."

"I know. I work too much. I should get out more."

"I'm sure you will," she says and shifts her attention to the older gentleman approaching us.

He introduces himself to me and escorts us through the dark and crowded lounge to a private, U-shaped booth with a direct view of the stage. He hands us menus, shares the drink specials, and insists we order whatever we please. I glance around while considering my options. Looks like we're the only VIP folks in the building.

Deidra requests sweet tea. I ask for sangria. When he leaves, I ask, "You got it like that?"

"Girl, I wish. That's my cousin's husband. They owe me for watching their spoiled-ass kids."

I've met all of Pat's nieces and nephews and most of the Carter clan, so he must be a paternal relative.

As the minutes pass, the sangria sparks an urge to scoot closer to Deidra, narrowing the two feet between us so our pheromones can mingle as we talk. I want her to flirt like she did the day we met. I want her to reach over and touch my leg while throwing her head back in laughter. Instead, she's guarded, keeping her bubble away from mine. Really, she's more into the music than me. And once the saxophonist coasts into a passionate solo, it's like I'm no longer present. Deidra's adorable face is relaxed, but from her eyes, she's drifted to another location. Somewhere far from this building. Somewhere serene and romantic.

When the solo fades, she shifts her focus to me. We talk and share potato skins until Dezza Reign takes the stage with a monologue about women's oppressed speech. Dezza's words are swift and distinct. Her hand motions are seductive. She captures the audience through call and response. It's nice to be away from work and home, surrounded by others with a similar interest. The delicious food, good spirits, and new company are welcomed. However, there's one little problem.

I can't shake the nagging feeling that I'm being observed. I look left to find Deidra shamelessly staring at me. Minutes ago, she acted as if she was sitting alone. Now, she won't take her eyes off me. "Your cut is nice," she says, acknowledging her own gaze. "It fits you well."

I rub along the waves of my newly shaven and chestnut dyed hair. "I wanted something different. I haven't had a cut in years."

"Caesars are sexy on women."

I'm unsure how to take her compliment. She said it so casually that I can't take her seriously. On the phone she's sugary sweet. Now she's lukewarm and unconvincing, and I can't determine whether she's feeling me. I can't figure her out so I turn my attention to the show.

The drummer cues the band and Dezza exits stage right for a brief intermission. I bob my head to the tempo of the lively jazz quartet and scan the venue for other cute faces during the wait.

Dezza returns shortly after to engage the audience again. She ends her set with a mix of spoken word and scat before stepping off stage. She makes her way from table to table, greeting admirers and posing for pictures.

Deidra stands when she approaches us. "You were on fire, as usual," she says and hugs Dezza.

They talk for a moment before Dezza greets me. "I enjoyed the show," I say.

"Aw, thank you, love. I appreciate you coming out."

"She didn't have a choice," Deidra states.

Dezza's eyes return to mine. "You don't know what you're getting into with this one." She shoots me a quick smile and gives Deidra a farewell hug.

Was I just forewarned, or was Dezza kidding? Deidra doesn't seem the least bit offended, so maybe I shouldn't over-react to a light-hearted comment. I don't want to assume the worst because we have plans to visit the state fair after this. I have to spend at least another sixty minutes browsing the fair with Deidra. If the remainder of our time together doesn't go well, at least I've blown my Saturday evening with fresh off the factory conveyor belt eye candy, a woman whose figure eight and full D's put my shallow hips and false C's to shame.

As soon as we exit the building, the aroma of heavy rain envelops us. The gray blanket of clouds advancing from the east ruins our plan for the fair.

"I really wanted that funnel cake," Deidra whines.

"Right. We don't have to go our separate ways. You're welcome to come to my place."

The sound of 'my place' satisfies my ears. I'm so proud of finally having my own home that I want a guest to confirm it's real. I've only been in the condo five days, but I've already purchased enough furniture to make it livable and presentable.

Deidra responds with a blank face, making me wish I could renege on the offer. My intentions were good, though. She's good company. Why call it a night on account of poor weather?

Deidra reaches into her oversized purse and pulls out a lighter and pack of cigarettes. She props a cigarette between her lightly glossed lips and ignites the flame. She takes a long drag while staring into the distance, pinning the smoke in her lungs for several seconds, as if the fumes will help her make a wise decision. She releases the white haze, letting it float at her face before she looks at me and says, "Where's your car?"

"A couple blocks over."

She puffs again. "Lead the way."

"What about your car?"

She flicks ashes to the concrete. "I didn't drive."

I consider the risks of inviting a stranger over *after* we're in my car. I don't care for smokers, and for all I know she could be insane. Maybe that's why the Carters disregard her. My eyes slide to the passenger seat. She's looking out the window, slightly moving her head to the ballad on the radio. For just one evening, I want to hang out with someone other than Jacoby or Tasha— and I really want to poke into her life— so I push aside all reconsiderations.

By the time I arrive at my new home, the sun has fallen below the hazy horizon. I haven't interacted after dark with a woman other than Kayla since March. It's October and I feel out of practice. I hope my instincts will awaken and lead my actions. I don't want to seem uptight, only to make her too uncomfortable to loosen up with me. Even if I don't raise the subject of Pat, our time together is a stepping-stone and has to go well.

"Hey," she says when I unlock the car doors. "Give me a minute. I need to make a call."

I leave Deidra in the garage and go inside, placing my keys

and clutch on the entry table. I sit in the living room as she talks. Traces of her voice make me wonder who's on the other end of the call. Maybe she has a girlfriend, or maybe not. She wouldn't have introduced me to multiple people if she has someone exclusive in her life.

While waiting, I go upstairs and replace my sandals with socks. When I return, she's sitting on my couch looking at her nails. I sit near her and ask whether she cares for a mixed drink.

"No, thanks. I don't drink."

A smoker who doesn't drink? I almost laugh out loud. "Well, I've got soda, water, and cranberry juice. I can make some chocolate milk."

She grins and turns down all the options as I walk into the kitchen. I scan the frosted shelves in the refrigerator for something to calm my nerves. The thought of mentioning Pat unsettles me. I place ice cubes in a shaker and pour a three-to-one ratio of pineapple juice to mango rum. I top my glass tumbler with a lime wedge to salute a good evening.

"I noticed that you glanced at my license," Deidra says once I step back in the room. "What do you want to know?"

There is so much to ask I don't know where to begin. We've shared casual facts during phone chats, but nothing about who we are in the present. So, I start simple. "No offense, but I assume you're older than me... I'm curious about your age."

"How old are you?"

My birthday is only three weeks away so I round up. "Twenty-eight."

"I'm four years older than you. Is that all right?"

I nod while calculating. Pat was fifteen, maybe sixteen when she gave birth to Deidra.

She looks at the broken-down boxes in the dining area and the artwork propped against the wall. "You just moved in?"

"Yeah, Monday."

"And you've unpacked and cleaned up already? Were you expecting me?"

"Does daydreaming count?"

She laughs. I finally said something to encourage her beautiful smile.

She drops her eyes and scans the parallel lines I vacuumed into the rug protecting a section of the hardwood floors.

"I like a clean home," I state.

"Or, you like to make a good impression before sex."

Excuse me? I'm already trying my best to keep my eyes above her neck while taming sexual feelings, which are growing stronger with each swallow of rum, and here she is inciting my desire. We look at each other and smile, sparking an opportune moment to straddle each other. I keep my hands and mouth to myself and she does as well.

I mention Dezza and this seamlessly leads to conversation with less pressure. With each passing minute, Deidra becomes more comfortable in my presence with welcoming body language. She increases eye contact. She relaxes her back to rest against the couch. She uncrosses her legs and leans in my direction. The likeable personality I experienced on the phone begins to surface. This is a horrible time to bring up anything Carter related. I feel selfish holding on to this secret, but I like where we're headed. She's warming up to me.

As the night sky turns violent with thunder, we drift deeper into conversation. Before I know it, my glass is empty. Again, I ask whether she wants anything to drink and she accepts the offer. I hand her a bottle of water and mix myself a cocktail with less juice.

I can't pinpoint what's transpiring between us as we talk about our most frightening weather experiences. We don't have the rapport to deem our chemistry romance. This interplay of attraction is fast camaraderie and instant lust, and the latter is undeniable.

My noiseless condo amplifies the pitter-patter of raindrops on the living room window seals. The storm massages my ears and spirit. I enjoy the stories we share and the fact that no performance, music, or people can distract me from Deidra's wandering eyes and flirty smiles.

When I grow quiet, she says, "Am I making you nervous? You've stopped looking at me."

I lift my head to meet her gaze. "You're kind of direct."

"Kind of?"

"Very…and that makes me…"

"Self-conscious?"

I ask myself whether that's a fitting term.

"It can be hard to spend time with a woman who keeps it real when you're accustom to pretense," she adds. "Just be yourself." She leans forward and rotates the overturned pendant on my necklace. The warmth of her fingers forces chills from my chest to the shielded space between my legs.

"I am," I respond, just as she rests her hand on my leg.

"If that's the case, are you glad this isn't a daydream?"

I bite my bottom lip to control my excitement. "Absolutely. You know I'm attracted to you. Who wouldn't be?"

She slides her hand up my thigh, her finger tips an inch away from where I want them to be. "It's okay to show me."

What? This can't be happening to me. I've never received what I desired, from whom I desired, when I actually desired it. Except now, I'm sitting in the comfort of my own clean home on the brink of a best-case scenario— a good first date and some ass from a nice-looking woman who hasn't presented as crazy. What should I do next? Which part of her should I touch first?

On second thought, this is too good to be true. I gently take her hand and move it back to her lap. No need to postpone the inevitable.

She smiles. "You're moving in reverse."

I stall by consulting with myself. This internal discussion thing is involuntary behavior I can't control when I drink liquor. The rum insists that certain parts of my body move forward, quickly. She wants me closer, and I don't need to appear afraid of touching her. The sensible part of me that's still swimming above the rum fights back until she touches my leg again.

I abandon my thoughts and place my glass on the ottoman to sink into a pool of lust. I rub the honey-coated calves I've marveled at all evening and trace my fingers to the hem of her dress.

She remains still as if her body is high-value cargo, watching my hand to see whether I'll handle her with care. I'm too tipsy to care whether I pass or fail. I pull our chests together and press my lips against hers, and then pause like I'm allowing someone else to capture the moment. Maybe myself. She prods me forward, her bottom lip parting my lips, waiting for my tongue to explore this new region.

The passing of our tongues, my elevated blood-alcohol level, and the soothing rain are more than enough reason to thump the good angel from my shoulder. Even the residual smell of her cigarette incites my carnal desires. And I want this. I've thought about this for days. And apparently, I've done something right because Deidra has transitioned from keeping me at arms length to caressing dangerously far up my leg.

My tiered metal earrings chime when she pulls my hips closer to massage the nape of my neck with strong kisses. She blows on my moist skin, triggering the most sensitive part of my body to prick my panties. The piercing tension is pleasing but begs for mercy. Accordingly, I stop and pull Deidra to her feet.

She follows me, hand-in-hand, up the stairs to my bedroom. She stands in my dark room as I kick a box out of the way and then pull the comforter to the foot of the bed. I step to the window to open the shutters a bit. I want to see her without the invading presence of overhead lighting. The full moon softens the shadows of my room— the perfect mood lighting. We kiss until we join my crisp, new sheets.

She touches me, deliberately— preceding her kisses with the stroke of her fingertips along my neck and chest. I like her hands. Fresh hands. Free of infidelity, bad communication, and letdowns. I miss the excitement of unknown touches. Fresh hands exploring all over, trying to figure out what pleases me.

When Deidra reaches my navel, I stop her. She can't know this hot spot just yet. I take hold of her hand and kiss it once. She smiles. I've never experienced this level of sensuality during an initial sexual encounter. I let go of her hand and she removes my shirt, lifting the hem up my torso until I stop her again.

"What's the matter?"

I'm nervous but I can't tell her this. I don't want her to think I'm reconsidering sex. I'm all go for fucking. I'm stalling because I can't stop thinking about how I'll look once my pushup bra is removed. I exhale. This is not the time for insecurity to surface.

"I won't do anything you don't want me to do."

She rubs my legs and hips and I begin to relax, letting all the tingles of arousal lessen anxiety about exposing my body. "No worries," I say.

She kisses my lips while pulling up my shirt. I stop breathing when she unhooks my bra. The straps fall from my shoulders. The first reveal is always the most difficult, but I have to get it over. I pull the straps down my arms as she nibbles on my neck, emitting a poison that paralyzes me onto my back.

She travels south to savor my breasts, sending waves of anticipation through my core so strong that I moan and squirm my hips. She mounts my lap to keep me still and suckles my breasts like they're bountiful gifts. She explores wherever she pleases until I sit up to meet her face to face. Unaware that she's lifting her head, too, our foreheads collide. She giggles and rubs my forehead before touching her own.

"Is this a bad one-night stand?" she asks.

I'm tipsy and clumsy and could enjoy staying on my back until morning. But, I don't want Deidra to feel she'll be the sole top tonight. I roll her over in preparation of what I want next. This also gives me a moment to pull myself together. "You're not a one-hit wonder," I answer and pull down her panties.

Lightning flashes, illuminating her silky skin as I trail down her midsection with licks and kisses. She strokes my hairline, reminding me how much I love being touched by a woman, also teaching me the joys of this new hair cut. When I reach her pussy, I take a moment to take all of her in: the warmness of her inner thighs, the hypnotizing smell of arousal, and the wetness coating hairless folds of skin. I push her knees farther apart and kiss as closely as I can without grazing her most sensitive zones. She responds to my teasing kisses with deep breaths.

Month after month, I devoted myself to Pat's diagnosis and increasing sickness. Her slow and physically debilitating death reinforced the importance of *living*. So, I choose to indulge in Deidra's body without considering tomorrow morning or possible consequences.

# 8

MY WORST FEAR is standing on the opposite side of my front door. I place my eye at the peephole again. Kayla grips her purse strap and knocks three more times. I pull away and wait a few seconds. I knew the risk of letting a mutual friend serve as my realtor. It didn't take her long to leak my new address to Kayla. I want to tiptoe away and pretend I'm not home, except my open garage and car have exposed me. I wait a moment longer to see whether Kayla will take a hint and leave. She calls out my name while ringing the doorbell.

I flip the deadbolt and crack the door open. "What is it?"

"I was in the neighborhood. Figured I'd stop by." We stare at each other. "How long do I have to stand outside in the dark with bugs?"

I should have known that forty freaky minutes with Kayla would result in her poking in and out of my life without my consent. With Kayla, there are no boundaries. She has no regard for the meaning of *ex*-girlfriend. I switch on the porch light to attract more critters.

"Seriously? Nia, let me in!"

"Scream all you want. Nobody's paying attention to you anyway. Why are you here?"

"To talk about the bitch who's stealing Pat's estate."

Those words grant her instant access. I follow Kayla through the foyer to the dining room, which now has a table. She rests her hand on a chair as her eyes explore the kitchen and living room. "Nice place. How much did this run you?"

"Stay on topic."

"I cannot believe Pat gave *everything* to that low-down ass daughter of hers. Can you?"

Really? Did Pat actually have a relationship with Deidra? "That's Pat's business. At this point, I'm liable to believe anything given I just found out about her two and a half months ago."

She crosses her arms and considers my words. "But didn't you at least expect Pat to include us in her Will?"

I couldn't care less about the fate of Pat's stuff. I shift the conversation to what concerns me. "Is she not family?"

"The bitch is blood, but she ain't *never* been a part of this family. Never made an effort to be. So why does she get the house, land, car, and life insurance? You know Pat co-owned the funeral home, so she's entitled to that, too. She ain't did shit to deserve a dime from any of it!"

Kayla can't hold a coherent conversation when she's upset. I need her to simmer down before she begins to interject stuff I'm not interested in. I have questions and can't risk her emotions altering the facts. While she gets comfortable on the couch, I make drinks. I pour us both a glass of orange juice, adding a short pour of gin to hers. I can't give her any excuse to not drive home after this.

I sit across from Kayla and we shoot the breeze. She smiles and bats her false eyelashes as we talk about random nothings— her attempt to prove we can coexist, we can talk without bicker- ing, we can indeed be friends. I know Kayla; she wants me to reciprocate, to laugh until I open my heart to her again. But she has turned my affection to stone and trust to disdain.

Eventually, she kicks off her sandals to sit cross-legged. I push the conversation along when she reaches out and touches my arm while speaking. Her two-second touch is intentional. One touch could lead to a rub that leads to a kiss that results in sex and more hard feelings.

I slide a few inches away from her and ask, "Did y'all know she was the beneficiary before we cleared Pat's house?"

She exhales. "Mama was told that Pat's lawyer would send her a copy of the Will after the funeral so she could go to probate court and file for a hearing. Two days after the funeral, she still hadn't heard from him. So she went to the clerk's office to get a copy herself. That's when she found out Pat submitted a new Will and that she isn't her personal representative anymore. It's public record. Our names are nowhere in that Will."

I'm offended. I've done a good job staying clear of Carter family politics, which is one of the reasons I never asked her or Loca Tres about Deidra. If I want to dabble in other people's mess, I can turn to my bio family.

"Pat asked us to donate her things," Kayla reminds me. "We didn't do anything wrong. But now we can't get anything done because we don't have ownership or access to anything."

"Has anyone contacted her?"

"Mama has, but she won't answer calls or reply to texts."

As I continue to pry, Kayla consistently refers to the 'low-down ass daughter' as *she*. Pat's daughter remains nameless, as if saying her name will validate kinship. *Deidra* almost slips off my tongue twice, but I maintain my ignorance.

To my disappointment, Kayla doesn't know much about Deidra. She gives me gossip instead of relevant details. Prior to the funeral, she hadn't laid eyes on Deidra in nearly five years, and that encounter was in a restaurant by accident. All she expresses is hearsay and animosity. "I think some of the distant cousins keep in touch with her because they went to high school together, but not us."

Really, Kayla's disregard for Deidra is learned behavior. Her condescending attitude is a product of environment. If I want to know the root of Pat's past secrecy— as this is the only thing I inherited from her— I will have to turn to Deidra or Loca Tres. Kayla is a dry well incapable of satiating my curiosities, so I have to kick her out. I press her departure with, "I need to get some sleep. I got a long day tomorrow."

I actually have the day off but she takes the bait. "I'll talk to you later," she says and leaves.

I, however, have no intention of talking with her again. Our short talk confirmed what I've already suspected: Kayla sees confiding in me as an avenue to friends with benefits. Bullshit.

I place our glasses in the dishwasher and return to the couch. I rub my hands across the smooth beige cushion while thinking about last night. This is the cushion Deidra and I sat on when I said, "You have the prettiest brown eyes I've ever seen."

When she laughed and responded, "Your lips are Cover Girl perfect."

When I glanced below her belly button and said, "Your lips fit perfectly on my lips."

When we shed our clothes and straddled each other.

We slid off this cushion and onto the floor for positions better suited on a harder surface. Her distinct taste and textures linger on my tongue.

The blinking notification light on my cell phone catches my attention. I grab it from the ottoman and open a text message from Deidra. Coincidentally, she sent the text while Kayla was here. I slouch into the comfy padding and sigh.

Since meeting at Gillespie four weeks ago, Deidra has visited me three more times bearing sensual gifts wrapped in silk and lace. She's so down to earth I couldn't help but drift into erotic desires. She has become the break in my routine.

I still don't know anything about her other than casual facts and vice versa. But that's okay for now. A little anonymity protects both of us. It only matters that we're compatible, sexually. A single, mutual expectation.

The only problem is there *always* has to be a problem. And this time it's a monumental problem. I've separated Deidra into two people. On one hand, she's the bed buddy who graces me with orgasms worth committing a crime for. On the other, she's the core of Carter family drama and the cousin of my ex.

I pick up my phone again to reply to Deidra's text. I've invited her to Tasha's house party. She wants to know what time she needs to get here tomorrow. After texting her, I place the phone face down and close my eyes. I enjoy Deidra's company, but it's time to strike deceit from my agenda.

I've created a deep dilemma for myself. Where in the world is the rope to pull myself out?

# 9

THOUGH IT'S THE FIRST WEEK of November, the weather is warm enough for Deidra to flaunt a short hem and plunging neckline. She isn't afraid to show off her all-natural assets—clothed or unclothed. Her streaked hair isn't pulled into the bun she usually sports. Her barrel curls smell like almond conditioner and bounce of her shoulders. She looks like she's ready to have some fun. I tuck those thoughts away and focus.

At first, I was reluctant to pick at Deidra's privacy. I didn't feel right digging into her personal and familial worlds while guarding my secret. Now, I'm hungry for details and ready to move past our sex-only association.

To start, I want to know about her car situation. She never drives herself to my place. And when she's ready to leave, I'm the one who drops her off at a fairly decent house in a working-class neighborhood on the opposite side of town. No questions asked until now. "Who brought you here?"

"My sister."

Sister? Interesting! "Why didn't you call me? I would've picked you up."

"She passes your exit on the way to work."

"Well I'm glad you didn't ride the bus. You don't need to be on anybody's bus dressed like that. Someone might mistake you for a street walker."

"Do I look slutty?"

"No, you look high-priced."

"Watch yourself," she says and laughs.

She has the prettiest smile, the type of smile that brightens her eyes and my day. I'm okay with the jokes and careless chatter, but my patience is thin. I have to pry. "What's your sister's name?"

"I'm not giving you any more money, Juanita. You're getting on my last nerve, Juanita. Take care of your kids, Juanita. Clean up sometimes, Juanita. Jua– ni– ta," she sings the syllables.

I chuckle. "Do you live with her?"

She nods.

"How old is she?"

She stiffens her back. "Why do you ask?"

"I'm just killing time." I wanted to guide the conversation to other leaves on her family tree, but apparently, I'm too nosy for her.

Deidra keeps staring at me. As she assesses my aura, I do my best to not set off alarms. I don't want her to sense that I'm nosy for a reason. I keep my calm expression steady and let the moment go by grabbing the remote to surf the channel guide.

She ends the silent interrogation and says, "Tell me about your friend."

Tasha is a bank teller who moonlights as a bartender with her aunt's catering company; my best friend since meeting in middle school; the sister I always wanted. She's the kind of friend that rarely holds her tongue, will never let me go without, and loves when I'm happy.

"She's good people," Deidra says. "I look forward to meeting her."

# 10

THE DRIVEWAY AND CURBSIDE PARKING at Tasha's town-home is lined with cars. I make a U-turn to find an empty space farther down the poorly lit street. Tasha lives in a questionable neighborhood. The former middle-class community has a shrinking tax base and increasing mentions in the news. I grab Deidra's hand and quickly lead us along the sidewalk.

"You look really nice, Nia. Blue fits you well."

Her approval makes me proud of my decision to wear a tailored, two-piece cropped pants suit. "Thanks. I rarely dress like this. I feel weird when I'm not in scrubs."

"Maybe I can change that," she says and smiles, almost stopping me in my tracks.

This isn't the first time Deidra has made a statement suggesting influence over me. The statements are strange because they imply us being in a relationship— us being more than fuck buddies. I can't decipher whether the statements are an extension of her personality or an undertone of her intentions with me. She never seems to mind that I don't respond, so I ignore her and pick up my pace.

The night sky is clear. The humidity is subtle, and the bugs are sparse. I thought Tasha would take advantage of such a good night, but the backyard patio is empty. We enter the kitchen through the back door. Several women are congregated over a card game. R&B and fried food fill every inch of the space.

"Hello, hello, hello!" Tasha says. She passes her cards to a lady on her left and approaches us. She welcomes Deidra with a hug and two disposable plates. Then she looks at me and says, "You're late, again."

"You said ten-ish," I remind her.

"I meant nine."

"We're right on time then."

She thumps my arm and chats with Deidra while I look around at all the new and familiar faces. My friend lives for cooking, entertaining, and partying. Tonight, her house is at least fifteen occupants overcapacity. And she loves when half her houseguests are strangers. But it isn't a true house party unless a third of us have nowhere to sit.

"Why are we crammed in here?" I ask. "Why didn't you take the party outside?"

"Girl, I ain't trying to sweat tonight." She winks. "Not yet."

When Tasha leaves to tend to new arrivals at the front door, I make myself a drink and pile assorted wings and veggies on a plate to share with Deidra.

She bites into a celery stick and says, "Thanks for the wings, but I only eat animals with gills."

"You don't drink alcohol or eat chicken, but you smoke." I've developed a habit of calling Deidra out on her nicotine addiction, especially whenever she steps to my garage or patio to soothe her cravings.

"Chickens, pigs, and cows are equally filthy."

"You want me to get you something else?"

"No, thanks, Nurse Nia," she says and then laughs. 'Nurse Nia' alludes to the last time we had sex, the first time we role-played during foreplay. Wherever my patient complained of pain, I applied a slow, sensual remedy. She stands from her stool. "I can't wait to get in your bed tonight," she whispers in my ear.

We share a kiss to confirm tonight's role-play. "Do you know any of these people?"

"I know a few faces. My cousin Shonda is here. And Jacoby should be here soon."

"Jacoby? That's your playmate, right?"

I laugh and summarize the history of our adult relationship. We were in the same nursing cohort during undergrad. Post-graduation, we worked at different hospitals before he transferred to Methodist East. "Chuck E. Cheese's has kept us sane for two years." I hope by sharing more about myself she will begin to do the same— saving me the trouble of asking.

The Coke and rum I'm sipping is ready to exit, so I excuse myself and head to the bathroom. When I return, Deidra isn't in the kitchen. I'm pretty sure she stepped outside to smoke. I make myself a bowl of chips and queso and join the folks at the table, squeezing onto the bench next to my friend.

"Where's your girl?" Tasha asks as she sorts her cards.

"I don't know. Where's your future wife?"

She shrugs with disappointment. "I'm texting her if she's not here by eleven."

"Speak of the devil."

Tasha looks up from her cards, eyes widening as her crush draws near. K.D. prides her boi-ish charm, firm physique, and licentious reputation. The trio is a seductive weapon. And Tasha willingly steps in the line of fire. "Here, play my hand." She flings her fist to my face, nearly scrapping my nose with the cards.

She escorts K.D. to the refrigerator, opens a bottle of top-shelf liquor, and pours a strong drink without a chaser. Everyone, including Tasha, drinks from cheap disposable cups. Tasha, however, gives K.D. a glass from the cabinet. I shake my head. The first phase of her scheme is in motion.

I give my seat to a stranger at the close of the game because

I haven't seen Deidra in over thirty minutes and want to confirm she's in the vicinity. I find her in the living room, sandwiched between two women on the couch. They're staring at the screen of a cell phone, engaged in intense-looking conversation, as if they've known each other for years. She appears content so I leave her alone.

On my way back to the kitchen, the Coke and rum presses me again— a symptom of a social drinker. I bypass the card game and cut the corner for the hallway, colliding with Jacoby.

"Damn, you stepped out sexy tonight, huh?" he teases.

I push him to the wall and hurry to the bathroom.

On my way back to the kitchen, he's waiting for me and ready to vent. "I called Tasha this morning and told her not to invite Melissa. She told me 'I don't talk to that hoe.' Why was Melissa the first fucking face I saw when I walked in here? Did she say something to you?"

"No," I say, though I actually greeted his ex to avoid an awkward stare. Melissa was Jacoby's last real relationship; the woman who made commitment the eighth deadly sin. Since breaking up with her, Jacoby only talks to folks with no-strings-attached attitudes. "Anyway, you see Deidra? Cute as hell."

"I did, but I didn't speak. She rubbed me the wrong way on day one."

"Do you remember what you called her on day one?"

"Look, I should've said something when you first told me she would be here tonight, but I'm not comfortable being around her. You need to tell her about..." His eyes leave mine.

I follow his gaze past my shoulder and realize why he stopped speaking.

"Good evening," Deidra says. "Guess you couldn't say hello to me earlier."

"I didn't notice you. You look a lot younger today."

Ugh! Why Jacoby, why? I'm not dressed to referee tonight.

Deidra steps forward, her heels barely bringing her face-to-face with him. She places a hand on her hip and shifts to the right. "You mad, bro? You mad you blew the opportunity to fuck me? You mad I chose Nia instead of you? Remember, *you* blew the chance to taste my pussy. Not me." She stares Jacoby squarely in the eyes, challenging him to a duel.

"Did I miss something?" I ask.

"Nah," he says and walks out the back door.

I cross my arms. He's hiding something.

"Hey, you know if there's any bottled water in here?" Deidra asks, like the last twenty seconds didn't occur.

After a moment, I move my feet and locate a pack of water in the pantry. Deidra thanks me for the water and disappears again. When I turn around to find a seat and process what I just experienced, I notice Shonda staring at me. "What the hell was that?" she asks.

I sit next to my closest cousin and shake my head. "I have no clue." But I will surely address the issue as soon as I can.

"Are you with her?"

"No, we're... we're just friends."

"Ha! Girl, you don't know the definition of just friends. And them some midget-ass shorts she wearing. Take three stitches out and they'd be panties. Your friend is on a mission to land in somebody's bed."

"Mine," I say without much thought.

"Ooh, okay. Somebody's being a little territorial over a..." She raises a hand to her ear. "What was that? A friend?"

"Shonda, shut up!"

"Don't get loud with me. If you like it, claim it."

"I don't know her."

"Whose fault is that?"

Hands down, mine. All I've shared with Deidra are friendly conversations and late-night fucks. The sex is good and growing better by the week, but I don't know anything about her besides where she lives and how she performs in bed. My ignorance— in addition to her questionable statements and words with Jacoby— has morphed into a thorn in my side. With sex, I've put the cart before the horse, but it isn't too late to demand clarity on the status of our supposed friendship. If Deidra can't clear the air about where we stand, I'll yank the chastity belt from under my bed again. I can't march into another week risking murky waters because emotions *always* spill into sex. And I can't avoid the subject of Pat any longer. The thought of all this has me feeling irresponsible. I didn't leave a bad relationship just to walk into a careless, sex-crazed adventure with no purpose.

Shonda and I table the conversation because of the commotion brewing across from us. Seven or so women are in a heated debate about lesbians with children, a topic that stalks lesbian circles. One woman— whom no one seems to know— is offended when a frequenter says, "Women who use'ta fuck wit' men don't trust real lesbians. They always waitin' on dey kids' deadbeat daddies to do somethin' fa dem. I'm more uva man than they will eva be. But she can't stay down wit' me dough." Her opinion pleases some and infuriates others.

Tasha is intoxicated yet sensible enough to lift the lid from the pot before the dispute spews over. "Go outside and cool off for a minute," she advises a friend.

I've seen one too many near-confrontations for the night. I need to clear myself of this space, so I ask Shonda to accompany me outside. We stand in the driveway admiring the sprinkling of stars while ignoring the passing airplanes. Shonda updates me on the latest family news, including our alcoholic grandfather, our philandering second cousin, and my incarcerated brother. She gets most of the scoop from my mother. "You moved out and abandoned my auntie."

True. My mother is a mild allergy; she sometimes irritates the hell out of me. I love her, but we function best with distance. "I may go by and see her next week."

"You may? Girl, you need to stop play—"

"Nia," Jacoby shouts. We look back as he marches out the house. "You need to go in the backyard and tell your new friend to stop flirting with K.D. before your old friend walks her drunk ass outside and kicks your new friend's ass."

The quickest route to save Deidra is through the house. I open the back door to find her and K.D. in close proximity, both smoking a cigarette. K.D. touches the hair along Deidra's shoulder and briefly strokes her arm. K.D. drops the ear-to-ear smile when she realizes I'm watching them. "Let's head out," I say.

Deidra looks at me hard, like I don't have a right to make a demand. "Nice meeting you," she tells K.D. Then she follows me along the perimeter of the house. "Are you okay?"

I open the metal gate. "Yeah, it's just time to go."

"Okay, I need my purse. It's in Tasha's bedroom."

Shit. That's the last place I want to hear. I ask for details about her purse's exact location and hand her my car keys. "Lock the doors," I warn.

As soon as I walk upstairs, I hear Tasha ranting behind her closed bedroom door. I try to enter, but something or someone holds it closed. I knock and Jacoby sticks his head out. "What's the password?" he asks.

"Now!" I answer.

He checks to see whether Deidra is nearby before letting me inside the room.

"Where is she?" Tasha's cousin asks. Tasha stands next to her mean-mugging me.

"We're leaving."

"Then why are you in here?" Tasha says.

"I just came to get my purse." I walk to the opposite side of the bed and pick up the bag at the bottom of the nightstand.

"That ain't yours," her cousin says.

"Damn, are you Tasha's watchdog now?" I say and make a dash for the door.

Tasha sprints forward to block my exit. "If she wants it tell her ass to come get it!"

I plead with Tasha to chill out, but it's a useless plea. She responds the way any jealous, intoxicated person would respond. "Give it here!" she orders, attempting to snatch the purse from my hand. Her drunken fury takes me by surprise.

We play tug-of-war with the purse strap until Jacoby intervenes. He grabs her waist, lifting her off her feet and onto the bed so I can finally leave.

The only voices in the car rise from the rear speakers. When I merge onto the southbound expressway, Deidra looks at me. My condo is in the other direction.

"What's wrong?" she asks.

"Let's just call it a night." Though frustration is written across my face, she doesn't question my demeanor or the change in tonight's plans.

~ * ~

I've been in bed for three hours, but I can't fall asleep. My mind won't stop replaying my encounters with Deidra over the past eight weeks. I want to figure out what's happening. I'm so desperate for an answer that I'm starting to compare us to a cake. A cake that baked too fast. The outside browned. It smells good. A pinch from the top tastes good, but the middle is undercooked.

An hour later, I start to unpeel the layers of my dissonant feelings, finally reaching the core of discontent. How could I lend intimate parts of myself to a woman who shares substantially less in return?

Tomorrow, I will end this unrest.

# 11

DEIDRA AGREED TO COME OVER at 3:00. In an hour, I won't be the woman she talks to occasionally and pleasures into the wee hours of the night. I don't want to shatter the fantasy we've formed. But I can't continue to ignore this burden I'm carrying.

I don't know how to initiate a conversation about Pat. How do I let it spring forth naturally to avoid forced statements like 'you been to any funerals lately?' I have to say something less prepared, more sincere than that.

Maybe I can complain about how my mother still hopes I will come to my senses and marry a man. How she disregards that I've completely stopped dating and sleeping with the opposite sex. Then I'll ask, "Does your mother do shit like that?"

As each minute passes, I add bad alternatives to my scrambled thoughts and reach a point where I can't keep track of the ideas I've considered. I need an outlet, now. A way to unwind.

I lunge out of bed and head downstairs. I pull the vacuum cleaner from the laundry room to the living room and plug it into the nearest socket. The droning appliance steadies my mental pacing. I come up with better options while brushing crisp lines across the rug and around the perimeter of furniture.

In round two, I reach a solution. I'm not convinced this is the best solution, but it ranks higher than the others. I head to my bedroom closet for the shoebox stuffed with unfiled bills and other important documents. With Pat's funeral program in hand, I run downstairs and place it on the end table, nested between the covers of two lifestyle magazines. I'm optimistic about this course of action until I loop the power cord of the vacuum back in place. Something about the circular motion helps me recall the advice I gave Tasha during breakfast. Her plans with K.D. backfired, so why would a let-Deidra-discover-it strategy work for me?

I scratch that idea and resort to plan B, opting for an amateur detective tactic. I'll pluck Deidra with a ton of questions until I strike a harmonious cord.

The mental prep is taxing. I stretch out on the couch to rest with less than thirty minutes to recharge.

~ * ~

Deidra's hair is tucked away in her customary bun. The modest hairstyle emphasizes every inch of her exposed skin. Her floor-length halter dress is an outright tease, an easy-access outfit. She smiles and says, "I thought you only liked me at nighttime." Then she steps inside my house, grazing her hand against my stomach while passing. The appetite in her eyes is tempting.

I want to follow her lead and allow my thoughts to escape to our sensual safe zone. I indulge a bit, trailing her ass as she walks to the living room, the fresh scent of bath soap wafting from her skin. She's prepared for more than conversation. When she sits on the couch and places her jean jacket aside, I remember that sex-first-secrets-later is not on the agenda.

"You drove here?" I ask to break the ice.

"Did you assume I don't drive?"

"I don't know a lot about you. I have to make assumptions."

"You don't have to stay in the dark. It's my sister's car. What else would you like to know?"

Her amicable mood and gentle gaze are welcoming, leading me to believe we've formed a connection wide enough to cross into new territory. This good start boosts my confidence in plan B. I make a strategic decision to begin with the obvious. "What exactly did you mean when you told Jacoby—"

"Wait. I guess your friend didn't 'fess up?"

Apparently, I'm not the only one who has some 'fessing to do in here.

"The day we met," she explains, "I was at your job with my sister and her kids. My baby niece was there for a minor procedure. I was dying of boredom and decided to take the other two to Chuck E. Cheese's. Jacoby was standing around when we walked outside the hospital. He got my attention and tried to unload his game. Blah, blah, blah. You know how men who think they're an ounce of attractive do. He asked where we were going and I told him. No big deal. I didn't expect him to stalk us. The two of you showed up a few minutes later, he showed his ass, and the rest is history."

I'm half surprised, half disturbed.

I'm surprised because Jacoby knew that Deidra would be present when we entered Chuck E. Cheese's, whereas I foolishly believed it was serendipity. I'm disturbed because he pulled me along without considering how I would feel about seeing her, and because he never said anything about their prior encounter.

"So, if he was nicer, you would have slept with him instead?" I ask.

"Possibly...But I think I made a good choice."

Strangely enough, her response doesn't bother me. What should I expect from someone who crawled into my bed on the first date?

Deidra has given me a pass to pry, so I jump to a new topic of interest. "You sort of mentioned once that you're not from

Memphis."

"I'm from here. I moved back about four months ago. I was in Virginia for…" She looks to the ceiling to calculate. "Thirteen years."

Those thirteen years are integral to my scattered puzzle. Distance is one piece that separated her from the Carters. "Why'd you move back? Was the move family related?"

"I needed a long overdue change."

Given we're engaged in a private, daytime, and fully clothed exchange, I expected Deidra to elaborate. As usual, she's tight-lipped about her personal life. We sit motionless for a moment. I thought she would take my silence as a cue to proceed with factual and colorful particulars about the overdue change. I want her to shower me with specifics until I'm drenched with information. Instead, she treats me like a tour guide.

I try to remain reasonable by giving her the benefit of the doubt. Maybe she's uncomfortable with this new, unfamiliar style of interaction I've thrown at her. With that in mind, I try again. "So, your dad, sister, and her kids live here. You got other family around?"

"Yeah. My dad's sister, sometimes his mother, my cousins," she answers as if they're minor players.

"What about your mother?"

"Why?"

I control my expression and search for another route. She extended the invitation to venture into her personal life, but this avenue is off limits. Her buzzing phone distracts me, but she doesn't move. She assesses my vibe and tries to penetrate my cloaked intentions. I'm not going to give her the chance to sort things out, so I stand and ask, "You want something to drink?"

By the time she declines, I'm in the kitchen. I take advantage of the next minute to regroup. I return and sit closer to her, hoping the friendlier proximity will kill her suspicion.

"Did you really ask me to come over so we could talk? We could've talked on the phone."

In other words, 'you're not worthy of my presence without sex.' I can't remember a time when anyone, male or female, only regarded me as a bedroom accessory. I take a sip of water to drown my irritation. After a moment, I place the glass aside and address her. "I would love to take you to my bedroom, but we *need* to talk."

"About?"

"About a lot of things! Some things more than others right now."

"We could've talked weeks ago. You could've asked for last name, inquired about my sexual history, showed interest in my zodiac sign. You cared about *one* thing. So why does anything else matter now?"

Clearly, from her point of view, I'm a routine booty call and shouldn't have a problem maintaining the status quo. But even if I could magically erase my association with Pat, it wouldn't change my underlying values. I would pump the brakes on the bump and grind to demand substance. The fact that she doesn't share an ounce of the same attitude provokes my anger. I wanted to handle this tactfully, but I don't care about her feelings now. "Obviously, I don't have a problem fucking you. I have a problem with *why* I'm fucking you."

She tilts her head.

"I wanted to get to know you," I add, "but in the process I got lost in you."

She gives me another cross-examining look. "There's no need to beat around the bush with me."

"Good!" I reach over and grab the funeral program from between the magazines. I hold the front page nice and high to guarantee she sees Pat's glowing smile. "I was at the funeral. Jacoby was there, too."

Finally, I've shed the weight of this secret, but her response unnerves me. She stares at the folded pages in my hand, suspended in thought. I try to wait patiently as she connects the dots, but the wait prods my nerves and I have to speak. I turn the page to the obituary and read aloud the portion that contains my first and last name.

Deidra shifts her weight. "How long did you know her?"

The question reinforces the invisible thread connecting the three of us. "Almost seven years, and she didn't mention you once."

Deidra grabs her purse from the couch and heads to the front door. I race behind her and force the door shut just before she can leave.

"Can we talk about this?" I ask.

She could have pushed my hand off the doorknob, except she pivots to face me. "Open the door," she orders.

When I pull the door open, the chilly breeze smothers the heated air in the foyer. She steps away from me and stands in the doorframe, pulling on her jacket.

"For what it's worth," I say, "I didn't mean to deceive you. I just didn't know what to say."

"How about 'hello, my name is Nia. I was a friend of Patricia Carter. I remember seeing you at her funeral.' That's the first thing any decent person would say."

I exhale. "Deidra, you're right. I'm sorry."

She glares at me like 'I'm sorry' is the meanest thing she's ever heard. "Fuck you! You and your apology can go to hell along with my sorry-ass mother."

In the blink of an eye, I press my hand against her chest and shove her out the door. Her lips are moving, but my anger is deafening. My skin stings as her fingernails sink into my wrist.

The next thing I know, I'm standing inside, alone, and the door is closed. But I don't remember closing it.

My throat burns. My heart races. I can't latch on to my spinning thoughts. My rushing rage is unbearable. I lean against the door and sink to my feet.

I feel a little more present on the hard floor, but I have to escape the frantic energy in this space. I hear a vehicle driving away as I approach the stairs. With each step, my breathing settles and my thoughts decelerate.

By the time I reach my bedroom, I gain a slice of control over my emotions. I sit on the bench at the foot of my bed and clench my aching wrist. The jolts of pain help clear my thoughts. I'm starting to recall what happened.

Deidra's words and her complete disrespect of Pat infuriated me. I can't remember the moment I reacted with force, but I do remember Deidra defending herself. I remember the warmth of her chest on my palm. When I shoved her, she tripped on her dress. Maybe. Maybe she slid off the first step. The confrontation happened so fast I can't recall whether she fell to the ground.

I only know, for sure, that she's gone and my worst-case scenario came to fruition.

# 12

AFTER TWO DAYS, I still feel bad about what happened. I can't stop thinking about how I lost control with Deidra. My mind keeps rewinding to old confrontations, like during high school. During high school, my sometimes feisty temperament landed me in scuffles and in-school suspension. I thought I got my temper under control during college. I had fun, slept around on occasion, kept my grade-point average sky high, befriended Jacoby and then Pat, and received my degree within a reasonable time frame. My peer interactions didn't sour until a year after graduation. That was the year I met Kayla at Pat's birthday dinner. She brought out the worst in my emotional management. Ever since we broke up, I've struggled to find the middle road again. The incident with Deidra confirms I'm traveling too far from the median.

I release the bulb on the blood pressure meter and remove the cuff from the patient's arm. The frail woman has spent the last four minutes sharing her woe-is-me life story. Some aspects were jaw dropping, but I'm not in a chatting mood. I have my own troubles to worry about today. I respectfully wait until she ends a story about her most recent arrest before leaving her bed in search of the attending cardiologist.

I find him in the break room rummaging through the nurse's snack cabinet. "Doctor Moreti, Ms. Reid's blood pressure is low."

He drops a snack cake into his dingy coat pocket and returns the other to not appear greedy. "Hold her meds and repeat the BP in two hours."

I grab my cell phone and coat and sneak out of the department. I have thirty-seven minutes before my next round of monitoring. I go outside to the memorial garden. My workplace getaway. I sit on a cold iron bench facing the road to watch the passing cars and foot traffic.

The rush of traffic carries my thoughts and chills away. I'm frozen in time until a familiar voice calls me from behind. "You wanna get something to eat?"

I don't look back or say anything in response. I just rise to my feet and wait on Jacoby to lead the way. I don't have an appetite, but I can't skip the chance to make amends with my friend. He hasn't contacted me in days, which means he's still ticked off about the incident at Tasha's house party. He must be over it now. Otherwise, I wouldn't be going with him to the cafeteria for lunch.

Jacoby selects the usual: a Coke and plain chips. He insists on buying me flavored water. Then he complains about work and remarks about every somewhat attractive person that walks by our table. He shares a long gaze and wink with one female passerby. There are more random stares before he dives into the latest Methodist East gossip. He has dirt on several nurses and techs in the hospital. His criticism of a particular nurse in the Emergency department prompts me to drop the small talk for more important topics. "Kayla called me twice yesterday."

"About what?"

I shrug.

"Maybe she found out you're banging her cousin," he says.

"If that was the case, she would do more damage than call. And I *was* sleeping with her cousin." I rub my forehead. "That's over and done with."

The last words out of my mouth trigger a wave of disappointment. I feel I wasn't given a fair opportunity with Deidra, like I was bamboozled by coincidence. I can't shake the feeling that fate intended to conquer coincidence— that something meaningful should have matured from my brush with her, even if that something is a short, friendly conversation every now and then. Instead, I altered our path.

"Hey," Jacoby says, pulling my attention to the space between us. "You look like there's something wrong with it being over. She was cute, you fucked her, it was fun, now move on."

I shake my head in disagreement. It's always so simple for Jacoby. Romantic quests are a dime a dozen in his world— an equitable price for something that has little worth in his view.

"Listen," he says. "That *Love Jones*, till death do us part, Cliff and Claire shit doesn't exist. What people think is happiness is only a façade. They're chasing the idea of happiness. Name one couple that's really happy, one couple that can teach you how to achieve bliss."

I lean back, crossing my arms. My parents have been married for thirty-one years, but I'd never mimic their union.

"See, you can't," he goes on. "In reality, people are only looking for that one person that will allow them to use them as much as they use them. And as long as they don't abuse that use, they're happy. Then they sit back and call it love."

Irritated by his confusing logic, I ask, "So what exactly were you trying to achieve with me?"

He leans forward. "Why are you bringing that up?"

I've never mentioned our three-month stint down lover's lane about five years ago, which, in Jacoby eyes, was destined to crash and burn anyway. Eventually, we did hit a wall, and then it took us several months to undo a web of sporadic cheating, explosive fights, and hard feelings. After mending our damaged friendship, I made a pact with Jacoby to bury the episode six feet deep. Then, I did myself a favor. I shed the weight of my confined upbringing and professed I was 99.9% lesbian. He's the last man I slept with.

"Shit, you're the one trying to school me," I say. "I'm my greatest reference." I regret the day we decided to turn one drunken night of sex into a relationship. It was a rash decision, a mistake we should've never taken out of context. "You're the last person I need advising me on the choices I make regarding women."

Jacoby has some nerve! I'm supposed to take advice from a womanizer— the same man who claims he never loved me but always reacts like a scorned lover. This Negro had no problem when Deidra was a one-night stand in overdrive. But as soon as I show the faintest interest in shifting gears, there he sits in the passenger seat, trying to steer *my* journey.

"*That* has nothing to do with *this*," he argues.

"*That* has everything to do with *this*! You've never had anything positive to say about the women I've been with since *that*."

"You a lie. I said Kayla was cute... Deidra too."

"Right. I guess that's why you tried to secure the panties just before Chuck E. Cheese's."

He looks away and forces his lips to not curl into a smile. "That was nothing."

I'm annoyed with his indifference. "That shit wasn't cool. You can live for the pursuit of ass, but I take my interactions with people seriously."

"Is it that time of the month?"

I exhale. He never wants to deal with shit when he's the problem. I really want to curse him out and purge my frustrations, embarrassing him in front of this crowd of people. But my anger tank is empty. I stand up, kick my chair under the table, and then return to my department.

"How was lunch, Nia?" a coworker asks.

I roll my eyes and pass by her computer station without a

word. My silence could lead to coworkers whispering behind my back and accusing me of being an angry Black woman— one more thing I don't need right now.

Just before I place my phone into my locker, public enemy number one calls again. This is her third call in two days. If I don't respond to Kayla soon, she'll send an avalanche of texts and emails. God forbid she rings my doorbell again.

I need at least another twenty-four hours to sulk before I return her call, enough time to clear my plate before she loads it with her bullshit.

# 13

CALLING IN SICK is the smartest decision I've made this month. I'm sure my supervisor can hear the faintness of my cough and clarity of my voice, but she prefers an absent Nia to an irritable one. I end the call with her, toss my purse over my shoulder, and head out the door.

I have an extensive to-do list to complete today, starting with a car wash. After that I'll get a pedicure and stop by Macy's for a pair of jeans. After those tasks I'll shop for groceries because my refrigerator is like Antarctica: cold and deserted.

Four hours later those tasks are completed and I'm in my car again to fulfill task five: parents. I haven't seen Mama or Daddy in nearly a month, which is partially my fault. Every time Mama offers to stop by my place I make up an excuse to postpone. She keeps nagging, so I have to pay her a visit.

I like Daddy a little more than Mama, but he isn't home. "You just missed him. He went fishing with your uncle," Mama explains, "over in Arkansas."

I hope he's actually in the neighboring state fishing for food, not women. Years ago, everyone knew Daddy had a side piece. Mama quit her HR job my freshmen year of high school to stay home and play the good wife to keep him home. It didn't work. Two years later, a woman rang our doorbell with a hump in her belly. Six months after that, Daddy presented Mama with a document disproving paternity. By the time he begged his way back into the house, I was living in a dorm room.

Mama doesn't like to spend her days ripping and running the streets with Daddy, so she stays home cooking food bound to shorten her life span. The meals seem like a snail-paced suicide, though I hate to think such thoughts about Mama. I hate her loneliness. Pat was a godsend, but Mama's irreplaceable—regardless of how ignorant or irksome she is sometimes.

Mama sits on the couch and rubs her aching knees. Her increasing age and weight are nuisances to her joints. She stares at me long and hard before speaking. "You doing okay? It's been a few months since Pat passed."

Her concern surprises me. At the peak of my relationship with Pat, I sort of abandoned my mother. Pat knew it. I knew it. Mama knew it, too. But Mama played the loving mother and hid her jealousy.

"I'm fine," I answer. We stare at each other.

"Well...you wanna plate? Everything's on the stove."

Though Mama is the epitome of a Southern cook, I don't stroll to the kitchen to dive into her cuisine. I want to see what she's stuffing in her body. I lift the lid from a pot of simmering collard greens with chunks of fatback and peak beneath foil-covered pans with magazine-worthy smothered pork chops, baked to perfection macaroni, and mouth-watering butter rolls. An evenly frosted red velvet cake is next to the spread. I almost miss the creamy mashed potatoes and gravy on the counter.

Mama enters the kitchen and pulls plastic containers from the cabinet. Days after Pat's funeral, she filled the same containers with similar trimmings and replenished them for two weeks. I appreciated not having to cook my own meals during that period, though I probably gained a few pounds from her feasts. "Mama, I'm good. I just went grocery shopping."

"You better take this food home. We can't eat all this."

"Then why make enough food for a family of six?"

She huffs like I don't have any business questioning her.

I compromise by taking the three containers from her hands. I return two of them to the cabinet and stuff the biggest hunk of cake possible into the third one. Afterward, I accompany Mama to the living room for her daily fix. She's an old school *Young and the Restless* junkie. Though she prefers to watch the daytime drama "live," she had a doctor's appointment when the show aired this morning. "Thank God for DVR," she says.

I watch the absurd soap opera with Mama, thankful that we can fast-forward through the commercials. It doesn't matter whether we say anything to each other during the breaks. This is quality time for us. Plus, I'm not at work and I'm off my feet. What more could I ask for? After an episode of the chaotic lives of filthy rich families, I want to wash my eyes with soap. Mama turns to the four o'clock news to bore me even more.

Fortunately, Daddy rescues me during the late breaking news story. He walks into the living room with a six-pack of Budweiser, home from the quickest fishing trip in history. He showcases his pearly whites and says, "Are my eyes deceiving me?" I stand to hug him. The beer bottles clink as he throws his long arms around me. "You moved out and decided you don't have to come see me no more? You hiding from me?"

"Of course not, Daddy."

"Oh, you hiding from your Mama," he teases and grins. "Come outside and have a beer with me."

I'm not a fan of Budweiser but make an exception for Daddy. It's a comfortable mid-November day, okay for outdoor idling. Mama follows us to the screened porch. She can't miss an opportunity to hang out with her husband and daughter. If my brother were present, the scene would be picture-perfect.

Daddy reclines on the bench and updates me on his six siblings. He's brief because his family isn't enmeshed and dysfunctional like Mama's. "The family reunion is in Maryland this year," she says. "You going with us?"

"I don't know."

"Why not?"

"Joyce," Daddy says, "she don't know what she'll be doing seven months from now. She could be engaged and planning a wedding by then." He takes a slow swig. "So when you gone find a good woman?"

"Johnny!" Mama says. She hates when he encourages me.

"Daddy, I am happily single."

"Why?" he asks.

I stare into the neighbor's yard assuming this is a rhetorical question until I hear, "I'm listening."

"No prospects," I tell him.

"Bullshit," he says.

"You're getting aggressive," Mama says. "You don't need another beer."

He glances at her and pops the cap on his third can. "Why?" His baritone voice holds me prisoner. I won't break free until he receives a solid reason.

A reply sits at the tip of my tongue so I let him have it. "You didn't teach me who or what to look for."

"You saying I didn't set a good example?"

"Neither one of you did."

Daddy leans forward and Mama peers in the house. It suddenly feels like summer.

"You can't hold down a relationship because of us?" he asks.

"I guess it's in my genes."

Daddy's a smart man. He knows exactly what I'm saying. I've witnessed and experienced too many negatives— including infidelity and distrust— to have faith in romantic relationships.

He places his beer on the patio table, shifting his long frame toward mine. "You're insecure."

I tip my can up to swallow an ill reaction. "I'm insecure?"

"That's what I said. You can blame us for creating your feelings. I'll give you that one. But you can't blame us for keeping 'em. At the end of the day, your love life is not my responsibility or my fault. Me and your Mama ain't got shit to do with that."

I drink again, finishing the beer and holding my tongue. This is an area he needs to tread lightly. My doubt is abundant; like a thick forest where sunlight never brushes its floor. Daddy and I have amicably talked about my relationships before. But he has too many transgressions under his belt to turn a critical eye on my so-called insecurity.

"I don't blame you," I lie, attempting to convey some control and maturity over my experiences and feelings. I push us away from love and relationships by tossing my brother into the conversation. We stay outside reminiscing about fond times with him, pre-incarceration, until the cricket choir begins.

~ * ~

I remove a pair of plates from the cabinet and pop the lid off the cake. "This all you got to eat?" Jacoby asks. "I know your Mama made more than this."

He recently left work and came over to raid my refrigerator, but I refuse to make him dinner. "Take it or leave it," I say.

He extends his hand for dinner. "You called in sick today?"

There's too much cake in my mouth to answer, so I confirm by nodding my head.

"Damn, you got it good," he says. "My boss would never let me call in last minute."

I give him a rundown of my work-free day and mention there's one last thing on my list: call Kayla.

"For what?" He shakes his head. "I don't know why you don't listen to me."

"Eat the cake," I say and dial her digits.

Kayla promptly answers and shouts my name. "Why the hell does it take you forever to get back with me?"

"And hello to you, too, goddamnit. What do you want?"

"We're meeting a lawyer on Monday at three to see what we can do about Pat's Will."

"Are you serious?"

"It's the only option."

Only? Why can't Pat have her last say? And why is Kayla calling me about this? I don't have anything to do with whatever feud they've had or continue to have with Deidra. I am not a soldier in their battle.

"So, are you coming?" she asks.

When I decline, Jacoby waves his hands midair for me to reconsider. Kayla attempts to change my mind as well. "You should be there. You have just as much say as we do."

"If I had clout you wouldn't be meeting a lawyer."

I press the end-call icon and turn my attention to Jacoby. "Don't be stupid," he says. "Somebody gotta defend Pat."

# 14

THREE DAYS OF REFLECTION help me realize that Jacoby is right. I stalled because I didn't want to insert myself in anything that involved Kayla. The friction around this Will is not my problem, but my love for Pat won't allow me to detach from this issue.

I leave work as early as I can and send Kayla a text message requesting the meeting location. She responds with a smiley face and address on the east side of town. The meeting is twenty-five minutes away. There's no way I'll get there by 3:00.

The accident-free expressway and my eighty-five miles per hour driving shave three minutes off my arrival. I pull onto a manicured street with commercial office buildings and spot my destination. The closest parking spaces are two office buildings away. With no time to spare, I choose a handicap spot at the entrance. Then I reach into the glove compartment and pull out Mama's old handicap decal.

Once inside, I inform the receptionist I'm with the Carter party. She directs me to a second-floor conference room. The lawyer pauses to acknowledge my entry. I quickly greet Mama C and Pat's sisters. Caroline has managed to pull her husband into this battle, too. I speak to him and choose the chair furthest from Kayla. "Sorry I'm late y'all."

"That's okay," Mama C says, smiling. Her pleasant face makes me feel a little guilty. She has no idea I didn't come to lend support.

I sit patiently by the youngest sister, listening to the probate lawyer, waiting for an opportunity to throw a wrench in the possibility of legal proceedings.

The lawyer explains grounds for contesting the validity of a Last Will and Testament. There are two stacks of paper on the table before him. Due to my tardiness, I'm unsure whether the Carters have already stated their case, or whether he believes something in those documents gives them standing. We listen as he translates legalese into layperson's terms. Once finished, he reclines in his leather chair and says, "Based off what I've said, why is this Will invalid?"

"Well," Caroline starts, "two years ago when Pat got sick we went through this whole process. Cookie and I were the witnesses who signed the Will. That document," she points, "doesn't have our signatures."

"You believe it wasn't signed in accordance with the law?"

"Right. That document is dated June of this year, three weeks before my sister passed. If Pat decided to draft another Will, she would have told me...us. She for sure wouldn't have appointed somebody else as personal representative and beneficiary of her estate. Nobody in this room knows the witnesses. Courtney Simmons and... What's the man's name?"

"Keith," the middle sister says. "Same last name. Maybe they're married."

"Does anyone know the executrix, Deidra Jamison?" the lawyer asks.

Caroline hesitates, waiting for someone else to respond, except they hold their tongues like they could perjure one another. There are five women in this room who can answer better than me, so I keep my lips sealed.

"She's... family," Cookie admits. "She's Pat's only child."

"Has anyone spoken to Deidra about the matter?"

Caroline takes the reins again. "I've contacted her, but she won't respond. And she had some nerve showing up at the funeral knowing good and damn well she was scheming behind our backs. She came to the funeral to throw it in our faces and we didn't even know it. I'm sure by now the bank accounts are empty. The house and land are next. Ain't no telling what my sister was thinking and doing with all the damn poison those doctors kept shooting up her veins!"

"Lord Jesus, Caroline," Mama C says, "calm down."

Caroline drops her head. The lawyer offers a moment of silence before proceeding. "Is there reason to believe there was undue influence?"

The sisters exchange glances. "Maybe," Cookie answers. "During Pat's treatments, some days were better than others. One day she was herself, the next day she was fatigued and would look at you like a stranger."

The room falls quiet as we reflect on those days that proved Pat was dying.

"Listen," Caroline says. "Something happened. We just don't know what happened. That's why we're here."

"If you want to proceed, I will. But I'll be frank. It'll get expensive. Will contests are challenging."

"Do what you have to do," she orders.

I can't leave without presenting a second opinion and attempting to steer this ship off course. I interrupt the lawyer as he explains the next step in the process. For the past fifteen minutes, I haven't said a word. They expect me to place an additional cause for contest on the table. But, I have one question for this family: "Are you sure you want to do this?"

"Of course!" Caroline says. "Why would we let someone steal everything Pat worked for?"

"What else do you want?" This family doesn't long for anything. Their forefathers left the cotton fields and crossed into the land of the talented tenth three generations ago. Today, they hold advanced degrees, live in gated communities, operate a profitable business, and make hefty contributions to local charities.

"I've been wondering the same thing," the husband states.

Caroline scoffs at the challenge. "Look, I care about you, Nia— and don't even start with me, Melvin— but you don't understand."

"You're right. I don't. But what happens if you can't move forward, if the judge doesn't change anything? Then what?"

"Street justice," Kayla suggests.

I don't waste energy looking across the table in her direction. "If this doesn't work out," I continue, "she'll still have the say-so." I'm careful with my words. This isn't the time or place to casually say Deidra. "It may be best to trust in Pat and put some things to rest."

"Duly noted," Caroline says, rolling her eyes.

They're determined in the matter. I can't alter their group-think on my own. With nothing more to offer, I tell Mama C goodbye and accept a business card from the lawyer before leaving the meeting. They have such a strong offensive line that I'm left with only one option. For defense, I'll have to turn to Deidra.

# 15

I PARK along the sidewalk in front of the one-story house, unsure whether Deidra is home. I keep my foot on the brake with the gear in drive as I go back and forth over whether I should leave the safety of my car. Every time I call Deidra, she forwards me to an automated voicemail greeting. And she's ignoring my text messages. A week has passed since the Carters encouraged the lawyer to move swiftly with their case. I can't wait any longer.

I tap the steering wheel to buy more time, wishing someone inside the house would alert Deidra of the stranger lurking in the front yard. Hopefully, she'll peek out the window, recognize my car and come outside, saving me from knocking on the door.

After two more minutes, I turn off the ignition. I approach the carport door since it's open, stepping over a crushed beer can and jump rope. Seconds after I knock a woman answers. She unlocks the dusty storm door and says, "Come in. What you gettin' done?"

Confused, I ask, "Is Deidra here?"

"Is she here? I guess you just gone stop by without an appointment."

"Appointment? I just need to talk to her."

"Aw, come on."

Deidra favors the Carters but bears a stronger resemblance to the woman I'm following through the house. Their round noses and heart-shaped lips are identical. I guess it's safe to say this is her sister, Juanita. She leads me through a messy kitchen to a cluttered den. She stops at the couch and throws a pillow and blanket to the side. I unbutton my pea coat and take a seat as she disappears into a dark hallway.

There's crap everywhere. Toys. Boxes. Laundry. A pair of shoes by my feet. I'm possibly sitting on someone's bed. Sounds from the television clash with voices from other areas of the house. The same little girl from Chuck E. Cheese's runs through the room like she doesn't see me. Then the woman reappears and says, "She comin'."

I nod. "You're Juanita, right?"

She leans against the doorframe and stares at me as I scan the holes and bleach stains in her tee shirt. "Why?" She tilts her head. Her lazy eyes and delay mirror intoxication.

"I'm just asking. Deidra told me she has a sister."

"Humph, no she don't. I ain't claimin' that bitch today. I ain't…"

I can't decipher the remainder of her slurred words. I have a feeling it would be a bad idea to ask her to repeat herself so I smile and say, "Okay."

Juanita continues to talk and I pretend to listen until Deidra steps into the room. "Can you please go lie in the bed?" she says to her sister.

Juanita stomps and stays in place until Deidra steps closer with a threatening expression. She waits until her sister is out of sight before addressing me. "Are you slow? Did the dead end calls and texts not register with you? Get the hell out."

Harsh words from a woman so pretty. The shimmering bronze tones on her eyelids and lips bring out the gold accents in her dress. Hair swoops across her forehead, flowing into a low-braided bun. Apparently, she has plans for the evening.

I stand. "I just wanna talk. I don't feel right leaving things on bad terms between us."

"I—don't—care."

"Then why are you mad?"

She looks out the window and relaxes her shoulders. "What do you want?"

"Just five minutes."

Deidra takes a moment to decide whether she'll honor my request. "Two minutes, outside." Once we are standing under the carport, she turns to me. "What is it?"

"Caroline reached out to you. You know why she's contacting you?"

"Yes. And you're their do-girl, here to finish your assignment."

Assignment? I'm taken aback by the accusation. She thinks my time with her was due to ulterior motives. "I wasn't spending time with you to get in your good graces. This is not a ploy."

"I meet you, sleep with you, and then find out you were lying to me around the same time Caroline starts contacting me about Pat's Will."

Lying? That's a strong word. "Deidra, I didn't know anything about the Will until two weeks ago."

"You expect me to believe that?"

"Yes! This is all new to me. I don't know what happened between you and Pat, but they're alleging fraud. They're going to paint you as some immoral bitch who took advantage of someone with terminal cancer."

She crosses her arms. "Again, what do you want?"

"I want you to fight back."

She raises her eyebrows, surprised by my response.

"Pat gave you power over her estate," I say. "Hold your ground. That's what she wanted."

"You're concerned about Pat's wishes... not me. Just as I

thought," she says and steps toward the door.

"Wait," I plead, reaching out for her hand.

She jerks her arm away and points in my face. "Don't you ever put your fucking hands on me."

When I consider all the places my hands have been on her, it seems strange that I can't touch her again. The intensity in her eyes shames me. I'm flooded with regret and ashamed of pushing her out my house. I retaliated violently. I hate that she could even believe that I'm capable of doing that again. "Deidra, I'm so—"

"Stop!" she demands and walks away.

I want so badly to make her accept my apology and to keep her from escaping into the house. My wants, however, don't mean anything. I head to my car hopeless about my efforts. I came here wishing for the best, but now, I'm leaving with nothing.

# 16

ONE HOUR into the horror flick, I feel my phone buzz three quick times. I open my purse and glance at my phone, careful not to cause too much distraction since I'm sitting in a theater between Tasha and Shonda, along with my college friend Ebony.

Deidra is the last person I expected to text me. Her message doesn't contain words, just a video thumbnail. I turn the screen off and inch my way down the aisle to exit the theater. I'm eager to see the video she sent six days after dismissing me.

I stand in the empty hallway and press play. During the first eight seconds, the video wobbles and displays blurred colors. At second nine, the frame steadies and I can't believe my eyes. Pat is sitting in a chemo chair, her beloved crochet blanket pulled up to her waist. At fifteen seconds, the frame widens and reveals Deidra on a rolling stool to Pat's right. An older man in a gray suit stands to her left. The video shakes and floats to the right—a sign of handheld camera phone footage. Pat moves an IV line past the arm of the chair. Then the stocky man hands her an open portfolio. She places it in her lap and reads:

"I, Patricia Ann Carter, an adult residing at forty-eleven Landester Road in Memphis, Tennessee, being of sound mind, declare this to be my Last Will and Testament. I revoke all Wills and codicils previously made by me. I appoint Deidra Jamison as my personal representative to administer this Will, and ask that she be permitted to serve without court supervision and without posting bond. If Deidra Jamison is unwilling..." She inhales, wincing at her pain.

Deidra stands, placing her hand on Pat's arm. " Do you need a break?"

Pat rubs her chest. "No, I'm okay." At forty-four seconds, she exhales and continues:

"If Deidra Jamison is unwilling or unable to serve, I appoint Courtney Simmons to serve as my personal representative, and ask that she be permitted to serve without court supervision and without posting bond. "This video..."

Pat closes her eyes and drops the portfolio in her lap. Then she looks at the camera and says, "This video, recorded on June eighteenth, is for my family..." She clears her throat. "While I hope you will never see it, chances are that won't be the case. Deidra has agreed to serve as my personal representative, and she *is* the sole beneficiary of my estate. Don't fight this."

"Damn," I say as tears gather in my eyes. Pat's foresight is chilling.

At one minute and five seconds she says, "Cut that thing off." She hands the portfolio back to the man and the video cuts to black.

This footage confirms three things for me. The Carters are dead wrong about Pat's Will. Deidra and Pat were in contact before she passed. And last, I'm confused about the nature of their relationship. Why would Deidra agree to be her representative and then curse her mother to hell?

I watch the video again before contacting Deidra, hoping she takes my call. "That was fast," she answers.

"Why now?"

"To end the harassment."

"Have you sent this to Caroline?"

"No, that's your job. I'm not doing more than what I've

already done," she says and then hangs up on me.

When I return to my seat, Tasha says, "What's going on?" She's still offended by the Deidra/K.D. incident so I shake my head as if nothing significant happened. Ebony hands over my purse and I put my phone away.

For the next thirty minutes, blood and gore flash before my eyes but my mind is elsewhere. Deidra has turned my phone into a weapon. The video is the ammunition I need to kill the Carter's Will contest, and I want to know why she sent it. Nothing will allow me to believe she's holding her ground only because I asked. She could have nipped this situation in the bud without my assistance weeks ago. While I'm pleased that Pat's wishes will be upheld, the delivery of this video will thrust me into hostile Carter territory.

# 17

Yesterday, I called the Carter's lawyer to inform him that he doesn't have a case. Now— less than twenty-four hours since I emailed the digital evidence— Kayla's at my front door, ringing the doorbell nonstop. No surprise, the Carters have sent their "do-girl" for an explanation about the video.

I leave the peephole and tell Jacoby, "Do not answer the door."

When I return to my space on the couch, I prop my feet on his legs again and we attempt to watch the latest episode of *Law & Order: Special Victims Unit*. But Kayla's rings progress to knocks, which progress to profanity and kicks at the door.

"There's a brick in the car!" she says.

Jacoby and I exchange glances. "She's lying," he states.

I throw the blanket from my lap and step to the window to see whether Kayla will call her own bluff. She closes the trunk of her car and marches to my living room window with a red brick in hand. I run and open the front door as she crosses from the walkway into the grass. "Have you lost your God-given mind?" I yell.

She drops the brick in the grass as I approach her. "No, you have! We can't fight against Pat on video. Why did you do that?"

"Don't ask the obvious."

"Is everything okay?" asks my neighbor.

I didn't notice the elderly woman before. "Everything's fine,"

I say, keeping my eyes on Kayla. I refuse to stand outside and let her make more of a scene. "Go inside."

Kayla marches her way to the foyer. I close the front door behind her, leaving my hand on the doorknob since she won't be inside long. She turns her back to Jacoby and says, "Why do you want someone who never gave a damn about Pat to have every-thing that should go to us?"

I considered the ramifications of my actions prior to forward-ing the video. Deidra definitely isn't fond of Pat. I, however, didn't allow my ignorance about the nature of their relationship to undercut the underlying question: What did Pat want?

"I'm not surprised your materialistic ass can't see beyond the money," I say. "This is about principle."

"Principle! Really? So it that why you're fucking Deidra?"

I blink hard and nearly stop breathing, gripping the doorknob to keep myself steady.

"She finally picked up the phone and called Mama back," Kayla says. "Deidra said 'someone personally asked me to clear the confusion surrounding Pat's Will.' When Mama asked 'who' Deidra said 'Nia.' Mama asked 'how the hell do you know Nia' and she said 'we were kind of dating.' And you know my Mama has damn-near perfect recall."

I have to say something to redeem myself. "The sex was unrivaled, but I wouldn't call that dating."

The last syllable is barely out of my mouth when Kayla lunges at me. Her additional three inches and ten pounds slam me into the door. I grip her wrists to defend myself as Jacoby grabs her arms. "Get the hell off me!" she says and swings around to push him away.

Kayla crosses her arms and takes deep breaths to regulate her temper as she paces the floor. Jacoby sits on the arm of the loveseat, ready to spring forth in my defense at any moment.

Seconds later, she faces me and says, "You nasty bitch. I'm so done with you."

"Please! Don't get it twisted; the last fuck with you was a mistake. You were done with months ago. And this doesn't have shit to do with me. This is about you and your greedy-ass family."

"We're greedy? I told you Pat had a daughter and you went out and found her. And I bet you knew about the Will *before* I came over here and told you about it. You had some nerve stepping into *our* meeting with the lawyer trying to stop us from going to court when you were on the sidelines trying to get your hands on everything we were fighting for! I guess you were going to fuck your way to the golden egg."

I lean against the door to consider my position. I'm in the middle of two relatives who have accused me of playing both sides of the fence. And according to both of them, I'm malicious and devious— downright evil. "Kayla, I spent three years of my life with you. Do you really think I would do that? The thing with Deidra…" I don't know how to explain it. "It just happened. The Will is a completely different turn of events. Don't stand here like you didn't know I would stand up for Pat. You know me."

She shakes her head in disagreement. "The person I know wouldn't go behind my back and sleep with my cousin."

"So she's your cousin now?"

Kayla rolls her eyes. "You and that sneaky bitch have opened a can of worms you'll both regret. But Deidra is feeling the wrath right now. That's why she's running her ass back to Virginia to be with her husband."

"Husband?" Jacoby asks and looks at me. "Damn, she's mar—"

"Jacoby!" I say.

When I initially pressed Kayla for details about Deidra, she didn't have much to tell. Was she holding back that day she dropped by, or is she lying to me now? Whichever the case, Kayla realizes a bomb was dropped on me thanks to Jacoby. I want to slap the look of satisfaction from her smug face.

"Well, well, well," Kayla says with a mischievous grin. "His dick tasted real good, didn't it?"

I muster every ounce of self-control I have left to keep my hands from wringing her neck. *Lord help me* I pray. I'm sweating now— my palms and underarms moist with anger.

My thoughts drift to the rage I exposed to Deidra. I close my eyes and rub my forehead, questioning why I'm giving Kayla the honor of a hands-free Nia. I feel foolish for sparing Kayla, but I can't meet her expectation of an emotional outburst.

I tell myself that I won't lash out. I can do this. I will act my age. I'm better than Kayla. Then I repeat it again. This moment of reflection helps maintain my composure. I open my eyes and walk away from her.

I sit on the couch and rewind the *SVU* episode to the segment Jacoby and I missed. "You can leave now," I say, flicking my wrist and refusing to look in her direction. "I got what I wanted."

I sit back and press play.

# 18

ONE THING I LEARNED about Kayla, not too long after we started dating, is that she doesn't believe in empty threats. I can only imagine what she's said or done to Deidra in the past seventy-two hours. I know Kayla can be vicious from personal experience.

During month six of our relationship, I made the mistake of flirting with a woman after having one too many cocktails while at the club with our friends. I didn't learn until after the fact that Kayla managed to steal the woman's wallet during our flirty exchange. The next day, she located an ex-communicated, criminal cousin and bartered the woman's identity for a $1,200 designer purse. Kayla flaunted that purse for three weeks— a friendly reminder about the repercussions of disrespecting her around friends. Week four, she threw the purse in the trash.

With that in mind, I feel bad for Deidra because I'm partially responsible for any conflict she might experience with Kayla. I express my concern in a brief text message: *You deserve an apology. Can we meet somewhere?*

After several messages, Deidra agrees to meet the day after Thanksgiving during my lunch break at a coffee shop not too far from where we first met.

"You drink coffee?" I ask when she enters the shop.

"Sometimes," she says while avoiding my face. She rests her hands in her jacket pockets and looks away.

"Let's order something. My dime."

Once we're comfortably sitting in our seats, at a small round table in the rear of the establishment, after we've taken a few sips of our orders, I ask whether Kayla has interfered in her affairs.

"She tracked down my sister and told her I'm sitting on thousands of dollars. Now Juanita has waged World War Three." She stares out the window, still not looking at me. "You saw my sister. She's twenty-seven on her good days. Most days she's thirteen. I wanted to be there for my nieces and nephew, but I can't go back right now. And I can't handle another night in Mississippi."

"Are you going to get your own place?"

"No. I may go back to Virginia."

I wondered whether Kayla was honest about the move and spouse. I want confirmation, but I don't feel right directly asking Deidra her marital status. I try a different angle. "You just moved here seven months ago. Why would you leave?"

"I don't have the resources to make this home."

"You mean money? Let's be honest, you have access to plenty of that."

She frowns and stares in my eyes for the first time since arriving. "I don't have shit. I don't want Pat's money or anything else that belonged to her. I'm not touching the estate."

"Then why'd you even agree to be part of the legal stuff?"

"For one reason only," she says, holding up a single digit. "She asked me to."

"So you're gonna ignore it all?"

"That's this beneficiary's prerogative."

Her words remind me that Pat is a huge sore spot so I shift the conversation. I take a sip of my hazelnut latté and brace myself for a heated response to the following: "Are you going back to live with your husband?"

She gives me a hardcore once-over; her eyebrow cocks in an eye half-closed kind of way. "Who told you that I'm married?"

"Take a wild guess."

She lets out a disgusted sigh. "Soon to be *ex*–husband. I have no desire to be with him."

"Then why the move?"

She stares into the heart of the shop. "When I left the marriage, I left *everything* behind. I came here with a purse and suitcase… I can go to Virginia and get back on my feet," she says just above a whisper.

Deidra seems unconvinced of her own words. There's a pressing motive caged behind her eyes, but I'm not in a position to demand complete honesty. So, I move on to something I've wondered about for weeks. "Can I ask you something?"

She nods.

"Do you really not remember seeing me or Jacoby at the funeral? Didn't you see my name in the obituary?"

"No one called me the day Pat died. I didn't know about her death or the funeral until her lawyer followed through on his professional obligation. No one in that family cared enough to include me in any way. I didn't care who was there because no one cared about me. So why would I read the obituary? Why would I purposely look for my exclusion? For me, it's not about remembering. I don't want to remember…" She exhales. "Anyway, I tried to be the bigger person by going to the funeral, even if that meant being late and disregarded. And I tried to be the bigger person when I got involved with the Will. But I didn't move to Memphis for the bullshit. And you've had a firm hand in it."

"If I'm so bad, why are you here?"

She turns to the window. "The second time I came to your house, I felt like you were up to something. I told myself it was just the chase; that obscurity was part of the game we were playing. I ignored my intuition because the chase was fun until you fooled me, until I let you fool me. Pat's folks hit a dead-end road. There's *nothing* they can do about the estate. But you have the upper hand and that doesn't sit right with me. You haven't earned that position." Her eyes turn to mine. "There's something about you that makes me lenient. I need to write you off, but I can't stay mad enough to do it."

We sit still, listening to the steps of patrons and the hum of an espresso machine. Her words keep rolling in my head. I still feel bad for mishandling our interactions. I hate that she feels deceived. I hate that she feels like I used her body as a means to an end. She didn't say that aloud, but I heard it in her words. I would feel that way if it were me.

I also feel bad about Deidra doing as I asked and reaping the consequences. The least I can do is offer a place of refuge. After all, I know what it's like to walk away from a relationship, choosing to leave with nothing. She hasn't shut me out of her world, so there's room for compromise. "I truly apologize for what I did to make you feel that way. It was never my intention to take advantage of you in any way. You are more than welcome to stay with me for a few days until you figure things out. My place is familiar...or at least my bed is," I say to lighten the cheerless mood.

She taps her fingernails against her herbal tea. "Thanks. How about Saturday?"

# 19

THE FIRST DAY, Deidra arrives with a large suitcase and two poorly taped boxes. I grab a box and park her belongings at the foot of the bed in my guestroom as she retrieves the second one. Then I search the kitchen drawers for my spare key.

On day two, I walk into an empty condo without a word from Deidra.

On days three and four, still no word from her.

The fifth day, she shows up after dark with a duffel bag. "I promise the contents are not illegal," she says.

The next evening, I come home to a surprise Italian dinner. "You're letting me stay for free. The least I can do is make you something to eat after work."

Seven must be my lucky number because the sex is unbelievably refreshing. Deidra cradles my hips in her arms, burying her face between my legs, sending me to new dimensions. "I'll see you in the morning," she whispers and leaves my bed for the guest bedroom. I assume she left my room as to not wear out her welcome.

The next morning, I go downstairs not really surprised to find that I'm at home by myself. Around noon Deidra texts: *In Mississippi with pops*. I guess there's a post-sex rule that says 'be considerate.'

The ninth day, I come home after an exhausting day of work to see two suitcases in the foyer. "My plane leaves at nine-forty,"

Deidra informs me.

Her footsteps were so soft I didn't hear her walk into the living room. Nine-forty is shy of three hours away and she's ready to go. She places her purse on the ottoman and sits on the couch.

The overhead light and TV are off. The lamp in the far corner barely illuminates her face. I place my purse on the couch and sit next to her. "When did you decide to leave?"

"This morning. If you wouldn't mind taking me to the airport, I'd appreciate it."

Naturally, I shake my head in agreement. Beyond the reflexive response, a part of me wants to say no. This is the hopeful part of me that now adores her company and smile, the same part of me that has always welcomed her legs around my waist. So why would I chauffeur her to the airport?

I exhale as another part of me— the part that sometimes longs for attention and companionship, the part I suppress— unearths itself and settles in my chest. I want to kill the feeling. It feels like clinginess. But I can't slow the pace of my thoughts.

Has Deidra really affected me emotionally? Is this fear? Did I fear she would eventually leave me high and dry, having to start at ground zero? Why would I even think I should be with her? Do I really feel vested?

I need answers. "Why are you leaving?"

"There's nothing good for me here," she says— a second-rate response.

"We had a good thing… or could have had one." The words feel strange in my mouth, but I can't ignore what's right in front of me. I can't ignore that I want more time with her. I want to know and see what can happen. I'm finally honest with both of us— hours before her scheduled departure. I can't identify what's stirring inside of me. But I'm disappointed that she's choosing the salvation of Virginia.

I look away, unsure whether it's safe to let her backstage, noticing the boarding pass sticking out of her purse. I take a deep breath and release my genuine self, a last ditch effort to keep her here. "Deidra... I have feelings for you. But I know I can't ask you to stay."

She drops her face in the palms of her hands. "Oh my God... That's bullshit."

"Is there something wrong with what I said?"

"Yes! First of all, you don't know me. And please don't let my current predicament influence you. I'm *not* a charity case. And let's get something straight: I'm not here to atone for Pat."

"What the hell does that mean?"

"It means I won't ease your loss or entertain you with an explanation of why she didn't claim me until she was on her goddamn deathbed."

I'm too emotionally vulnerable to feed into her resentment. "I smell bullshit, but it ain't coming from this direction. I'm damn near bearing my soul to you. I won't renege on my feelings just because you won't accept them. And I damn for sure won't let you deny having feelings for me."

I know Deidra came back into my home only because I offered, only because she needed a place to temporarily stay. But, she had a choice— just as she chose to be intimate with me the other night. I haven't been around her long, but I've been around her enough to know the only real influence she holds is the power of choice. And every kiss, touch, and moan said that she didn't doubt choosing me.

"I'm going to lie down," I say, walking away. "You're welcome to stay, if you choose. If not, let me know when you're ready to go."

I get in bed and stare at the rotating ceiling fan. I can't move. I can only blink. The exchange with Deidra numbed me, physically and emotionally. All I can do is think.

And I think long and hard about sex with Deidra. Sex is the most substantial thing between us. Because it's a satisfying act, I do it again and again. I swore I would end it— until the night before last when she walked into the living room wearing only a tee shirt. I thought I gave into my desires due to horniness. But now I admit that I surrendered to her full-body massage because sex has bonded us. It's the only thing we openly share. And the superficial connection has permeated our guards enough to let emotions seep through. The tidbits of information I've learned about her— and the aspects of her personality I've experienced and like— sustain my desire for more of what little we have. This murky concoction of loss, sex, emotions, camaraderie, and drama throughout the past four-and-a-half months has pulled me under. I can't just let her fly away.

While exploring the depths of feelings, confusion, and past actions, I forget to open my eyelids. When I awake, I stretch my legs and roll onto my back— realizing I was never supposed to fall asleep. I stop mid-motion when something other than bedding, something firm makes contact with my arm.

I glance back to find Deidra asleep. Sunshine saturates my room but it's cold. I pull the comforter near our shoulders and stare at her. Her peaceful expression makes me feel like I finally did something right.

I inch closer and touch her waist. Her chest rises, but she doesn't open her eyes. She reaches for my arm and rotates her hips until she's elongated, until I can hold her firmly from behind. She likes to spoon just as much as me. "I'll make breakfast when we get up," she says.

# 20

THE TIME HAS COME to make a trip to the fifth floor of Methodist East. I lean against the glossy paneling of the elevator for two floors and exit at Oncology. The unit receptionist doesn't cut her personal phone call short on my account. After she slams the phone down, I ask whether or not Jacoby's on the floor. She glimpses above the rim of her glasses and says, "Mm-hmm."

I walk by patients sitting with their loved ones in front of a towering, glass-paned waterfall. I hate that waterfall. It's an ugly fixture and failed attempt to ease their anxiety. I open the door to the unit and spot Jacoby sitting behind a computer at the nurses' station. I approach him from behind and thump his ear. "Let me chart this patient right quick," he says while typing.

I don't mind waiting because we haven't seen each other since Tasha's New Year's Eve party. Plus, a colleague is within earshot so I can't say much anyway.

Jacoby pauses mid-stroke and looks up at me as I stand on the opposite side of the desk running my fingers across the slick surface. "Why aren't you rushing me?"

"Dang, am I usually impatient? Take your time."

He places his stethoscope across his shoulders. "Come with me." We cross the hallway and go into EXAM ROOM 3. He closes the door behind us and sits on the exam stool.

Jacoby hasn't visited since the day Kayla showed up and showed out. Since then, our *SVU* viewings take place at his house.

He knows I'm no longer a single woman. However, he doesn't know I've grown to a two-person household.

He pushes the stool to the stainless steel napkin dispenser, looking at his reflection on the shiny box to remove his headband and retie his shoulder-length locs. "You still running errands for Deidra?"

Jacoby happened to call the other day while I was driving Deidra to her sister's house. "That was just one trip so she could finish moving."

"So she's gonna leave the husband and stay in Memphis? Where she move to?"

"Nine-one-seven Mount Cedar Lane."

He swivels around to face me. "You know the U-Haul thing is a stereotype, not a requirement."

No profanity? He's taking my disclosure better than expected. "It was kind of necessary."

"Necessary? Homegirl proves it in the nude and you move her in? That's more like greed, in a sense. And she's greedy, too. She saw a fairly new condo with a two-car garage, brand-new furniture, granite counter tops, stainless steel appliances, contemporary finishes, and then decided she had a new residence."

I stare out the window at the neighboring hospital. I had one thing to get off my chest, and now that it's gone I'm not too concerned with Jacoby's reaction.

"All you had to do," he continues, "was close your legs and tell the truth about Pat. You've let this newfound love shit get out of hand."

"Negro, love don't live here. And now I remember why I didn't tell you sooner. You overreact."

"She ain't got a fucking car or a job," he says, slapping the back of one hand into the palm of the other. "Or a place to live *and* she's married. But I'm overreacting?"

Actually, Deidra does have a job... sort of. I learned more about this source of income when I came home from work earlier than expected one day last week. When I walked inside, she wasn't in the living room or kitchen waiting for me. And she didn't spend time in my bedroom without me. That left the patio, office, or guest bedroom.

So, I walk down the hallway to try the guestroom first. After I knock twice and announce myself, Deidra cracks the door just enough that I notice she's barefoot and wrapped in a short terry-cloth robe. "Hey, give me a minute," she says and shuts the door.

I wait a few seconds and then let myself in the room. I hear Deidra rumbling around the ensuite bathroom as I notice a woman standing in the corner zipping her jeans. She places a baseball cap on her head and silently walks past me.

Deidra reappears immediately after the woman closes my front door. "Didn't I ask you to give me a minute?" she says. She leaves the bedroom in search of her guest.

I stay in place, shocked, trying to pinpoint whether I've witnessed before sex or after sex. The room smells normal, so maybe I caught Deidra before the act.

"And who the hell was that?" I ask as soon as she comes back to the room.

"An old friend. And someone I would like to remain a repeat client. You just can't walk in when someone's getting dressed."

"I'll walk through any door I please under this roof."

"You're a foolish one. She was only here for a body wax."

"If it wasn't for the hint of breasts I would've mistaken her for a man."

"There are studs who prefer to be hairless," she says. Her unconcern irritates me.

I notice the waxing chair in a supine position. This is the same chair Deidra and I maneuvered into my trunk on the eve

Jacoby called— the same day I found out Deidra has a skill other than cunnilingus. She's a trained esthetician. I don't spot an open wax container, but waxing strips are in the trashcan. And the bedspread is undisturbed. I step forward and place my hand underneath her robe. Her hip isn't bare. But from the wiggle of her breasts, she's braless. "Is this your uniform?"

She slaps my arm away and opens the closet door, pulling out a pair of jeans. "Get your mind out the gutter," she says, stepping into the pant leg. "Nothing happened. I'm sorry about bringing her into your home. On any other occasion, I would've met her at my sister's house. But she was in a rush and I'm not in any position to turn down money."

"It's cool," I say, embarrassed by my rash assumptions.

Needless to admit, I overreacted— just like Jacoby.

"She's using the hell out of you," Jacoby says.

I look at him, pulling my psyche back inside the exam room. "Save the judgment. I just wanted to tell you before Tasha or somebody else beat me to it with flat-out lies or exaggerations."

"So what are you getting out of this?"

I cross my arms and return to my focal point outside the window. I'm stumped. I really haven't taken the time to evaluate recent changes in my life. I'm on a one-day-at-a-time journey, taking life in as it happens. "I don't know where things are headed, but I'm glad that I'm in a different place than I was a few months ago. Can you say the same?"

He furrows his eyebrows. Then he opens the door so we can leave. Once again, he avoids discussing his feelings or any significant concerns in his life.

# 21

THE CHERRY STREET DINER is a big square with plain white walls. Mustard, ketchup, and jelly provide the only traces of color. The booths are decorated with napkin dispensers, sugar packs, salt and pepper shakers, and coasters from a closed restaurant. The cooks wear crisp white aprons. Most of the waitresses wear false teeth. Payment is cash only. No bells and whistles, just emphasis on mouth-watering, hip-hugging breakfast.

With three minutes to spare, I slow my car down and search for an open space to parallel park near the entrance. Lateness is typically unacceptable and I don't want to start our breakfast on a bad note. I briskly walk to the entrance, admiring the atypical two-inch snowfall, passing the street-level windows of the diner. In my haste, I fling the diner door wide open. Cowbells ding against the glass pane. I ignore looks from patrons and walk alongside a series of booths. Tasha is prompt as usual, except she's sitting in the booth alone.

"Morning my friend!" she says.

I feel a little guilty for being happy about Tasha's failed love affair. But ever since she detoxed K.D. from her system, she's been in an especially good mood. Her complaints are at a minimum, and she's abstaining from sex and dating, again. I like the mature, I'm-doing-me side of Tasha and I'll enjoy her as long as she's around. Eventually, regular Tasha will emerge singing a sad tune, laying on my couch and rummaging my kitchen, asking me to play matchmaker with one of my cousins or old college friends.

"Where's Jacoby?" I ask, removing my coat. "He's always on my case about being late."

"He's not coming. Said he's hung-over."

That's bullshit. We could've had breakfast at his place. I have a feeling that Jacoby bailed on breakfast because of me. His absence indicates deeper feelings he won't express. He's blowing the Deidra thing out of proportion— especially considering that my status with her has nothing to do with my established friend-ships.

Despite Jacoby's absence, Tasha and I pig out. She has me laughing so hard about her family I nearly regurgitate three scram-bled eggs, two servings of hash browns, and the thickest piece of ham east of the Mississippi.

"Girl, my Mama forwards me a Bible verse through text or email almost every damn day to keep the good book and the good Lord on my sinful, gay mind," she says. "This is the same woman who told my sister it's okay to open her pocketbook early if a man has checked all the right boxes." She grabs her glass and sips. "What about your mama? She still trying to get you to join her church?"

"As long as I go on Friends and Family Day— and don't forget her birthday, Mother's Day, or Valentine's Day— she won't bug me."

"Speaking of Valentine's Day, what you getting Deidra?"

Have I given Tasha the impression that Deidra and I have *that* kind of relationship? A mutually agreed upon and committed relationship? "Nothing. Why would I do that?"

"I don't necessarily like Deidra 'cause she was smiling and smoking all up in K.D.'s face. But you like her, and that's all that matters. You liked her enough to put a roof over her head. But you don't like her enough to buy a gift? Shit, I'll be damned if

I'm giving up the goodies and cooking meals on the regular but can't get a V-Day gift in return. You got eight days. That's plenty of time to find something nice. Not expensive, just nice."

I stare outside at the family of four huddled against the chilling wind. Deidra is far from family. True, I like her. But I haven't reached the point of obligation. "Why now? I didn't get her anything for Christmas."

"That was two months ago! Look, either you want the woman or you don't. Either you grow with her or stop wasting your time. You can't have it both ways. Ain't no in between. Make a decision."

Tasha's a serial dater with much experience and advice to lend on the politics of courtship. I should consider her suggestion to make a decision because I can no longer stand the gray area with Deidra. We're drifting with no direction and I need a target. I know from past experiences that we'll eventually reach an impasse that will demand a serious conversation. But till that day comes, Tasha can't convince me to swipe my debit card for a woman who lingers in the space between black and white.

# 22

JACOBY PROBABLY FEELS BAD for missing breakfast yesterday. But he didn't have to ring my doorbell with no heads up. He comes inside holding a greasy brown paper sack from my favorite cheeseburger dive. I prefer a gift card to a dine-in restaurant, but I appreciate his effort. He hands me the bag and requests a cup of coffee, black. He seems pained around the eyes and he's slumped over, so I graciously make him a cup.

Before entering the living room with the steaming mug, I peek down the hallway. I can't tell whether Deidra's in the bedroom. I was upstairs all morning long so I haven't seen her yet. If Jacoby cared whether she's here, he would've called in advance. On second thought, he didn't call ahead on purpose. Is this an ex-lover, best friend inspection?

I park myself on the loveseat. "What happened to you yesterday?"

He blows into the coffee. "Hangover from fucking around with a stripper from East Memphis. I been turnt up since Thursday."

Jacoby isn't a slight man. He has to drink like a whale to reach the point of sickness. "Why aren't you at home in bed?"

"I needed to get out for a while."

He hasn't come over in weeks. I smell an ulterior motive but decide to ignore the scent. I cover myself with a blanket as Jacoby searches for a movie on a free-for-seventy-two-hours premium channel. He selects an action flick and recounts his Friday night fling with Red Delicious.

The women Jacoby play with have no idea he's a late blooming wild-child from a loving two-parent household, determined to live out every minute of his twenties with adventures that will develop into legendary stories. Professional by day, nasty by night. Tasha and I love the morning-after tales. We're vicarious listeners, shielded from the abuses of terrible one-night stands and pointless club hopping.

"All I remember is lace, stilettos, and handcuffs," he says, "and I can't wait to do it again. Matter of fact, I'm calling her tonight. That apple bottom was so good I've got to bite it twice. I—"

The thump of approaching footsteps cuts him short. I take a personal bet on who will strike first this time. Jacoby is 2–0 to date, so I use my better judgment and prepare to police my friend.

I assume Deidra is leaving because of the massive purse in her hand, but she rounds the corner of the loveseat to sit beside me. She kisses my cheek and says, "Haven't seen you all day."

I feel weird about the display of affection. With the exception of Tasha's house party, we haven't interacted or touched in the company of others.

"Oh, my sister said hey," she says.

"Juanita's being nice to me?"

"It's tax season. She's nice to everyone during tax season. Anyway, how you been, Jacoby?"

"A'ight. You?"

Their forced cordiality leads to small talk about the movie we've barely watched. The exchange is headed in the right direction until Jacoby says, "How's the job search going?"

Sometime last week, I casually mentioned to Jacoby that Deidra is unemployed, but she continues to bring in money—

though not enough to live on her own yet. Her clientele is grow-ing, and she's pretty much turned my guest bedroom into a spa. We're friends, and friends talk. I wanted him to know things *were* going well. But now, his question makes it seem like I've been running my mouth or complaining. Deidra hasn't expressed to me any desire to work for someone else.

She glances at me with narrowed eyes and says to him, "Why do you ask?"

"I know folks at a few places in charge of hiring. At some point, you gotta work."

"And what makes you think I need your help?"

"You're living here."

"By choice."

"So why didn't you choose to use some of that money Pat left you and get your own place?"

Deidra slides closer to him. "I don't know what Nia has told you, but I didn't ask her for anything. She offered, arms wide open... legs, too."

"Hey," I say. Their rising animosity is making me uncom-fortable. "Both of y'all chill out." I'm quickly learning that these two should remain in separate spaces, or I should fit them for restraints. A leash for Deidra and a muzzle for Jacoby.

"He can rock the boat," she says to me, "but I'm good." She grabs her purse to leave.

Jacoby keeps his eyes on Deidra as she walks out the front door. "She's got a bad attitude," he says. "And that deep-ass voice irks the shit out of me. She sounds like my little brother."

His criticism of her lower range makes me laugh. He doesn't know how much I like her voice; it riles the freak in me. He also doesn't know that I'm laughing to take the edge off my own sudden observation. I can't determine whether I missed or ignored it before, but the sexual tension between my friend and undefined housemate is crystal clear now. It's like they're aiming to squabble just so they can look at and interact with each other longer. I know Jacoby's behavior is all a cover. He likes a challenge and prefers feisty women. "Easy pussy," he often says, "ain't fun." If the opportunity ever arises for him to proposition Deidra, he will snatch it in a millisecond. Deidra, however, I'm unsure about. The breadth of her capabilities and behaviors are a mystery.

I rise to my feet and walk to the stairs. "Don't leave before you sleep that hangover off."

Hours later, just before dusk, I go downstairs again. My home is empty. I check my phone to see an hour-old text from Jacoby: *I'm out.*

I have the house to myself all night. At random moments throughout the next day, I think about Deidra. I wonder whether I cross her mind this easily. Then I wonder with whom and where Deidra is spending so much time. Does she know another woman with a spare bed?

# 23

I SPEND THE FIRST PART of Valentine's Day at work and the latter with Tasha. We meet at a new downtown sports bar to debrief over wings and margaritas, raising our glasses to life's pleasures in spite of bad dates, failed relationships, and some-timing lovers. After the toast, Tasha says, "So what did you get her?"

"Not a damn thing. I haven't seen her in three days."

"Have you talked to her?"

I sip my margarita.

"Was our toast in vain?" Tasha asks. "Why aren't you making the most of the situation?"

"Who said I should?"

"I don't understand you. You're at the starting blocks, but you don't want to sprint." A simple analogy from a high school track star. "I'm starting to believe you self-sabotage."

"Look!" I respond, raising my voice over the rowdy men across from us. "I'm not a hopeless romantic like you."

"You were before Kay—" She waits until the men kill their game cheers. "Kayla and those other bad seeds messed you up. But that's okay. I'm gonna get you on the right path."

"I appreciate the optimism, but I don't wanna talk about this right now."

The following night, I need a hefty dose of Tasha's hopefulness when Deidra returns to home base. I'm at the microwave heating leftovers when she steps in the kitchen. She's holding a different purse and a shopping bag. Apparently, she comes back to change clothes and do whatever else while I'm at work and then leaves before I make it home.

"Where you been?"

She tilts her head at my demanding tone.

"You fucking somebody else?" I ask.

"Not yet. Since we're being nosy, what else have you told Jacoby about me?"

"That you have really nice breasts and perfect oral rhythm."

"What's with the attitude?"

I slam the fork in my hand onto the counter. "I'm trying to understand why you think it's okay to sleep in my bed one night and then disappear for three."

"It's okay because you *let* me. If you want things to change, you'll act accordingly. Until that happens, I will babysit my sister's kids and spend as much time as I please with my family and whomever I choose. *They* have defined roles."

The microwave beeps but I don't remove my Chinese take-out. "You want a role? How about a label? Your ass is shifty! I won't formalize anything with a woman who's hiding shit. And don't tell me you're not 'cause I see it in your eyes."

"You're right," she says, cool, calm, and collected as usual. "I am. But for good reason."

"Old secrets and new relationships can't be companions."

"When you get serious with me, I'll open up to you."

"So we're gonna build a foundation on quid pro quo?"

"No, our foundation was built on deception. Remember?"

I roll my eyes. "That's water under the bridge. I agreed to not hold your marriage against you, and you agreed to wipe my slate clean."

"I have, but I'm unclear about my role. Am I a boarder? A friend with extreme benefits? I can't decide if you asked me to stay in Memphis for the sex or because you don't like to be alone at night. We don't do anything outside of these four walls. I only exist in your world, *here*. I'm a real-life blow-up doll that you pull out at your convenience. And that's partly why Jacoby outright disrespects me."

"He would do that regardless."

"It's unacceptable."

"You want me to put him in his place?"

"I can do that myself."

"Then what's your point?"

"The point is you want fringe benefits in lieu of a formally accepted position."

"You haven't worked in years. What the hell do you know about fringes?"

Her insistence has gotten under my skin. I want clarity on our status, too, but I'm irritated that she faults me for her disappearing acts. I open the microwave as she pulls a red gift box from the shopping bag and tosses it on the counter. She holds her tongue and leaves.

I ignore the box and eat alone, unsure what to do next. Maybe it's time to give Deidra an eviction notice— to put our meeting, the sex, the concealment and revelation, the Will, and our living together behind me. If the bullshit I experienced with Kayla is a genetic flaw, who's to say Deidra doesn't carry the same trait?

I lock myself in my bedroom to watch TV while deciding a course of action. After two hours of reality TV, I haven't reached a decision. I pick up my phone to text my closest cousin and friends for direction.

I write: *I'm stuck between a rock and hard place with Deidra. What should I do?*

Tasha replies: *Does she want to be with you? Try her out. Nothing wrong with a trial run.*

Ebony: *Be patient.*

Shonda: *Use lube.*

I delete her text. She never takes my concerns seriously.

Jacoby is last to reply: *Kick her wack ass out!*

I opt for Tasha and Jacoby's advice. I'll talk to Deidra to determine where we stand. If we have a fruitless conversation, I'll kick her out.

There's a hint of light at the bottom of the guestroom door, so I know Deidra is home. But I can't knock before opening the gift box she left me. It would be a slap in her face to ignore the gift and start our talk on bad footing.

I untie the white ribbon and remove the top of the gift box. The box contains two Mason jars. I lift a jar and cringe at the contents. My second reaction is laughter. A pickled pig's foot floats inside of it. I place the pink, fleshy foot in the box and pull out the second Mason jar. I tip it left and right to study the brownish, powdery matter inside. I untwist the lid and sniff. The scent of dirt tickles my nose. Red dirt. I'm flattered that her gift connects to our first phone conversation.

Deidra doesn't seem upset when she opens the bedroom door for me. I expected her to be standoffish, but she welcomes me inside without hesitation. She clears shuffled newspaper pages from the bed to sit with me.

"Thanks for the gift. It was very thoughtful."

"It's not much. I just wanted to make you laugh."

This moment will turn extremely awkward if Deidra expects me to spring a V-day gift on her. "I didn't get you anything," I say to squash expectation.

"I know."

I've heard this tone from her before. Sometimes, she speaks like she has extrasensory perception. At least she isn't disappointed. "If you don't mind, we need to put some things on the table.

I really need to know why you're here. Because it's free?"

"I'm here to transition in peace *and* because I like who you are. You're a giving person, and I like that your actions speak louder than your words. You can't help but to be yourself and I like transparency. Don't underestimate yourself, though. It's not a becoming characteristic."

"What am I underestimating?"

"Your position in this half-assed, sham relationship."

"Well you've been living here and in this half-assed relationship for almost three months. What are you waiting on?"

"I haven't put things on hold for you. I'm not waiting to see when you'll come around. In the meantime, I'm here. You can choose to know me beyond your bed if you want."

"Honestly, I want more if you do. I'm willing to try. That means getting to know you. It's my fault I don't know more about you by now. Do you feel like you know anything about me?"

She smiles. "Small things. You eat breakfast before work once in a blue moon. You mix clean and dirty dishes in your dishwasher. You balance your temper like you're on a tight rope. There are no pictures of you anywhere because you don't like to take them. You love specialty bath soaps. You don't like to be approached from behind. You rarely check your mail. You could sleep through a bull run. You prefer pads to tampons. And you're married to Dr. Pepper."

Damn. "You definitely pay attention."

"I try. What about me?"

Aside from my intimate understanding of the nooks and crannies of her body, I only know one peculiarity about her. "You're addicted to the local news, like a soap-opera type of addiction. You almost chewed me out when I walked in front of the TV the other day."

"Mmm." She blinks a few times, probably disappointed with

my brevity. "I also know you were in a relationship with Kayla."

I drop my eyes. "I've been meaning to tell you about that."

"I guess bad timing is a habit. Lucky for you, I don't care. Clean slate, right?"

I shake my head with appreciation. "It's cool that you make an effort to notice my quirks, but do you know how much I cared about and miss your mother?"

"Pat was…" She exhales.

"Don't censor yourself."

"If any amount of hate exists inside me, it's there because of Pat. You can share your love for her with anyone but me."

Her bitterness bothers me, but what can I say or do? For now, I have to respect this boundary.

We're quiet and staring in opposite directions until she says, "What do you want from me?"

The question incites a wave of memories and an emotion that scares the shit out of me. It's a raw feeling, like I'm missing several pieces of armor. Because she's honest with me I return the courtesy. "I had a friend in seventh grade who lived next door to me. I had a little crush on her mother, Mrs. Gina. My dad was always out and about sleeping around, and I couldn't stand being around my mama during those times. So I was more than happy whenever I got invited over.

"This one night, after my friend fell asleep, I decided to sneak out the house to check on my mom. I was always scared she would hurt herself or something. I had to go through the living room to get to the front door, but Mrs. Gina and her husband were on the couch. I dropped to the floor to spy on my crush. She was lying in his arms, talking and laughing. And they were holding hands and rubbing each other. I'd never seen a couple touch like that. You know, with love.

"I crawled away and got back in bed where I was supposed

to be. Mrs. Gina peeped in and saw me watching TV. She walked over, pinched my cheek, and called me a night owl. I've been waiting for my own Mrs. Gina since that night."

Deidra considers my answer before speaking. "I've learned that a relationship is no greater than what you put into it."

I appreciate the insight but wonder whether she will hold herself to the same counsel she's giving me. To find out, I ask, "What did you fail to put into the relationship with your husband?"

She chuckles. "I got a big fat F on good judgment, which led to some mistakes. And I wasn't honest. I shouldn't have married him, but I didn't have the courage to stand up for myself back then. I let society and crappy experiences shape my reality. Those experiences made me doubt the world and most of all myself, just like you."

"You think I doubt myself?"

Her gaze intensifies. "If you want your Mrs. Gina, you have to become her. You would've changed years ago if you believed she actually existed."

I stand from the bed. I've heard enough about me. "Is there anything highly important I should know about you before I go?"

"Of course. But in due time."

Satisfied with our conversation, I leave for my room. I lie in the dark and stare out the window, replaying my talk with Deidra. These thoughts force me to catalog my wants along with my worries.

It's hard to separate my jumbled feelings, but one feeling emerges. I want to know what it's like to evolve with Deidra. I want to make this the last night I sleep in my bed alone or single.

# 24

JUST WHEN I BELIEVE we've turned a new leaf, Deidra withdraws again. Yesterday, she left to watch Juanita's kids, so maybe she decided to spend the night with them. I didn't hear from her this morning, though. And now I'm home from work and still no word from her. I could contact Deidra, but I don't want to feel like I'm chasing her.

I'll give her a one-day pass, but if her absence presses into a forty-eight-hour period, my patience will roll into anger. Irritation chips at my tolerance the more I think about it. Reading, television, snacking— nothing eases my impatience, which mounts with each passing hour. I'll give Deidra one more hour to walk through the door or contact me.

Time passes quickly as I text, iron, and bathe. I marvel at the power of a sixty-minute time limitation when I exit the bathroom to a ringing phone. She has finally decided to call me. I clench the bath towel at my chest like it's shielding my anger. I answer and wait for her to speak. She owes me an explanation.

"Sorry it took so long for me to call. I'm just getting a chance to stop and think."

I hold the phone.

"Are you there?" she asks.

"You forgot how to text?"

She sighs. "You're right. Again, I'm sorry... I didn't know I'd have to fly to Virginia last night."

For what reason would she go to Virginia other than her husband? What's next out of her mouth? 'I'm sorry, but I can't be with you. Thank you for everything. I hope you find someone special and have a wonderful life together.'

"I thought you weren't going back to him," I say.

"I'm not here for him."

"Have you seen him?"

"Yes, but it's not what you think."

"Then why would you see him?" I'm eager for the justification— ready for her to defend why she fled to Virginia for a man she allegedly doesn't love.

"Because my daughter was rushed to the emergency room."

For a moment, I'm relieved her departure wasn't due to him, but the relief is short-lived. The next moment, 'daughter' slams my ear. I hold the phone unsure what to say. The silence is over-bearing as bitter thoughts fill my head and spill from my mouth. "It's kind of ironic I had no idea that Pat had you and now you have a child. What kind of maternal shit is that?" I'm on the verge of spitting bullets with no consideration of the collateral damage. "Is this a joke? A fucked up Carter joke! Why the hell are you just now telling me you're a mother?"

"Yes, I kept her from you, but I need you to..."

I wait but she doesn't speak. I figure she doesn't want to express vulnerability or ask for sympathy, so I fill the silence. "To what? What else do you want from me? I'd be a damn fool to give you anything else. You're not worth the baggage."

I'd also be a fool to believe that Deidra is still listening to my rant. She ended the call somewhere between 'worth' and 'baggage.'

## 25

SOMETIMES, I EXPERIENCE a short, distinct moment that demands a split-second emotional decision. The moment always feels like this lucid, recurring dream where I'm watching myself, keenly aware of my movements and spatial limitations. In this very moment, I can stop in my tracks and avoid Deidra. After all, she's here one day, gone for three, and then back again like magic. Except the trick isn't entertaining.

I should leave the parking lot and return to work, but what will I tell my coworkers? I'm hiding from the flaky woman that lives with me? I can't allow personal issues to cross into professional territory. So I step forward, too aware that each step moves me closer to her, too aware of my shoes scraping the asphalt. I stop a few feet away from my car. Deidra is barricading the driver's side door.

"I got back this morning. I haven't been to your house. If you don't want me there, I won't come back." Her voice is soft, as if we're treading on thin ice. Her crossed arms and bowed head are apologetic. It's unlike her to not yield a strong presence.

I drift into my home, observing each room and the objects that occupy them. Every accent of color and piece of furniture has more purpose with Deidra there. She makes the mortgage more meaningful, too. Though I feel silly attributing my desire for her to objects, I'm not ready to admit how much I long for her. A harsh rebuttal would release the bit of resentment I hold for her absence and secret, except I've expended too much energy maintaining a hardened stance. I want to touch her, so I do.

Within seconds, I'm lost in the sanctuary of her arms, no longer attentive of the people scurrying about the medical district or the rush-hour traffic surrounding us. She tightens her embrace, my chest sinking into hers as she whispers what I want to say: "I missed you." She loosens her embrace enough to kiss my lips. "I'm sorry."

Her sincerity is welcomed, but I've already forgiven her. I'm tired of secrets: hers, others, and mine. I'm willing to give her the chance to push the concealments aside and step into the light with me.

I invite her inside the car and we're silent for a while, allowing the close proximity to heal our wounds before she explains what happened in Virginia. I knew she was hiding something from me. I never imagined she was hiding a child.

"She's sixteen," Deidra says, transforming my image of a little girl with pigtails to a teen with flowing tresses.

I fixate my eyes on the windshield but my thoughts rapidly shift. Then a sharp yellow pencil freezes all my thoughts. Deidra is like a heavy-leaded pencil, pressing hard against the world, leaving markings the Carter family could never completely erase—writing lasting impressions that have captured me since the first day I saw her. But she was misplaced and unaccounted for by her mother and maternal family for years. She knows about erasure. So why would she hide her daughter's existence?

"Are you okay?" Deidra asks.

"I don't know." I don't know whether the pencil comparison makes sense anymore. I search for another inanimate object with dual meaning until she touches my arm and distracts me. I look to my right, the first movement I've made in five minutes.

"What's wrong?"

"Nothing." I find my focal point on the windshield again, except I keep my mind present. "Does anybody know about her?"

"Are you asking whether or not Pat knew about my daughter? Yeah, they all know about her."

I sigh. The Carters don't care for Deidra, so I'm sure they don't give a damn about her offspring. "I'm shocked Kayla didn't spill the beans."

"That bitch ain't crazy. She won't cross into this lane."

*This* is the Deidra I missed. I take hold of her hand and attempt to wrap my mind around the idea of Kayla practicing restraint. "Why didn't you tell me?" I finally ask.

"I protect my daughter at all costs. I won't let my actions or your distrust of me spill into parenthood. I won't blur those lines until it's necessary, and we haven't reached the point of necessary."

I can't dispute a word she's said. "Well... you're back in town. That means she's okay?"

She looks at me affectionately, as if no one outside of Virginia has ever expressed concern for her daughter. "Yeah. Shannon is fine. Her asthma attacks come and go."

"How does Shannon feel about you being so far away?"

"She understands. I prefer us to be together, but I can't force her to leave her school, family, or father."

I clear my throat. I almost forgot about him. "So, where did you stay?"

She grins. "I stayed with a friend, and I slept alone."

She doesn't ask the same in return. She knows I don't have a standby cuddle-buddy on speed dial.

"Where's your stuff?" I ask.

"At my sister's."

I start the car and head south for a quick pick-up.

# 26

THIS PROBABLY ISN'T THE BEST TIME to ask Deidra about her sexual orientation because we're in the midst of a date. A cozy table by a wall fountain type of date. I'm wearing makeup, a revealing dress, and I'm footing the bill type of date. But, I think my efforts should be rewarded. And right now I'm in the mood for honesty, so I have to ask. "Are you bi?"

"I left my phone on the nightstand so we can have a romantic evening without interruption," she says. "You call that romantic? Why in the world would you wait until now to question my sexuality?"

"I'm not trying to spoil anything. And I'm not questioning you. You've skirted around this for months."

Deidra places her fork on her grilled vegetables platter before leaning back in her seat. When she looks past my shoulder, I wonder whether she's concocting an answer or thinking about why I feel like she's been evasive. She leans forward to continue the conversation, the lantern between us dancing in her eyes. "I'm fluid when it comes to sex. When it comes to my heart, I'm a born-again lesbian."

I don't understand why she wasn't direct prior to today. I know how opinionated some folks are about bisexuality. But have I said something that suggests I would judge her unfairly?

"I didn't broach the subject," she says, reading my thoughts as usual, "because my history, my fluidity, is inconsequential to where I am now. To who I'm with now. What we want for each other today and moving forward is all the matters."

"Are you coaxing me?"

She smiles. "I'm answering you. And you didn't answer me. Why now?"

"They were talking about folks with bi partners on the radio yesterday, so I figured I would ask. That sounds silly, but hey. If I had an issue with your history I wouldn't have waited to address it. I'm not concerned with labels either. I don't care who you do until you start doing me... When did you experience this rebirth?"

"Two years ago when my husband arranged a threesome."

I contort my face as if the air has turned foul. I appreciate her frankness, but she could exercise discretion. "I'm a product of your husband's fantasies?" I push my plate to the side, no longer interested in savoring steak or lobster macaroni. "What's his name?"

"Eric, why?"

"I can dislike him more with a name."

She gives me a moment to relish my disdain for him. "Listen, I liked women before the threesome."

"Then why'd you have a baby by a man at sixteen and marry him at eighteen?"

"The baby was an oops. I married him because I had to. I was living in backwoods Mississippi in *poverty*," she stresses, "with a father and grandmother who didn't have much time for parental guidance. Eric was my out. It took a while, but the threesome helped me realize it was time to start making my own decisions and being honest about some things."

The waiter appears and inquires about dessert. "What's the sweetest thing on the menu?" I ask. I need it to mask the sour taste in my mouth.

As soon as the waiter departs our table, Deidra says, "You're uncomfortable with what I said. You're forcing your facial expressions."

"I just discovered my first pet peeve with you. Stop observing me so much."

"I can't help it. I care about the way you feel. So, why did you break up with Kayla?"

My jaw falls open.

"You opened this door," she says.

I sip red wine and consider whether I want to venture into memories of regret and resentment. Then I take another sip to prepare for the following: "I thought my bottom line was cheating, turned out to be psychological abuse." Deidra raises an eyebrow, eager for me to continue. "The guilt trips. The emotional manipulation. The ego! Nothing's worse than a woman with an ego. 'You'll never have a woman better than me.' 'You should be glad I'm with you.' 'What would you do without me?' " I say, mocking Kayla's squeaky voice. "She'd never admit to flaunting an air of power. And she always threatened my livelihood, especially when it came to my job." I pause to sip. "I'll never forget the time I had to go to work but couldn't find my car keys. So she drove me to work but found the keys before it was time to pick me up. It took about a week before it struck me that my keys were never misplaced. The fact that she hid them scared the shit out of me. And the fact that I couldn't smell the manipulation anymore even though it was right under my nose… Anyway, that killed our relationship and my faith in future ones." I exhale and finish the glass of wine. I feel like I've just purged to my work buddy, Maria.

"That's messed up, but I hope that's not the case."

"I'm working on it," I say as we stare into each other's eyes. A rich moment of understanding. And I remain understanding for my next question: "Is Eric providing for you?"

"You know the answer."

I do. "Be specific."

"I have health insurance and access to the bank accounts. And he's paying the bills. I'm moving toward self-sufficiency, but it's going to take a little while to get there."

Deidra doesn't seem like a woman who would let a man take care of her. I lean back in my seat as my mind drifts. I can't imagine her feeding him the first bite of a meal prepared by her hands as she so sweetly does with me. Or inching her hands up the back of his shirt after a stressful day of work, caressing away the complaints of employment. Eventually, I focus to ask, "He's paying what bills?"

"I rarely use the credit cards. He pays the cell phone bill every month."

I couldn't care less whether Deidra is taking advantage of him, except I take major issue with the cell phone service. Arguably, the cell phone is something *we* share. He shouldn't be a part of it. "Is it a shared plan?"

"It is."

"Good thing you're free tomorrow to shop for new service."

She laughs.

"I'm serious. And let me be clear. From this point forward, if you need something, come to me… What does he get in return?"

"I play nice in return. I let Shannon stay with him. I haven't filed for divorce yet. I haven't acted immaturely by wiping him clean, airing his dirty laundry, running away with one of his overrated cars, or pawning the wedding rings. Not that I care, but he sleeps with whomever he pleases."

"Deidra, I didn't just fall off the turnip truck. You're on marital hiatus and he's providing for you because he expects you to come back."

"He has false hope."

"What happens when he realizes he's wrong?"

She fixes her eyes on the approaching waiter. After our dessert is placed on the table, she answers, "Hopefully, Eric won't come to that realization before Shannon graduates. And you're right: he thinks this period of separation will get us back on track. I can't pull away as much as I want right now. If I do, it will affect Shannon."

I don't like that she's stalling, but I try to respect the choices she must make for her daughter right now. "Okay. I get it."

"Good. And speaking of failed relationships, did you ever love Kayla?"

"I mistook love for Pat as love for Kayla."

Deidra usually groans or rolls her eyes whenever I mention Pat, but this time she gives a sympathetic nod. It's a deliberate effort in honor of our date. I pray to heaven she will honor my next question: "Did you ever love Pat?"

"I despised her."

I stick a hunk of chocolate caramel cheesecake in my mouth, letting the cool gooeyness occupy my tongue instead of reacting to her words.

I must have another forced expression across my face because she looks at me and says, "I'm sorry. I..." She eats her dessert, allowing berries and vanilla bean ice cream to sweeten her response. "I don't know...It's hard to have that kind of emotion for someone who had the means to raise me but no capacity to love me. Pat never completely withdrew herself from my life. She called on my birthday and she never missed a Christmas gift. I associated the tangibles as love because I wanted her to love me. There were so many nights that I begged God for her love, that I begged for her to rescue me. But when I got pregnant, she disappeared. I guess pregnancy marked the end of my childhood and her obligation. It's a betrayal words can never give justice to."

That's hard to hear. We feel a light-year of difference about the same woman. I nearly lose my composure when a tear rolls down Deidra's face. She quickly wipes it away and drops her eyes. "And now my emotions are betraying me," she says. "This is why I don't drink." She pushes the wine she's barely touched to the center of the table. She only ordered it for me. Only because I wanted to see her sexy lips on the rim. And then I would lean forward and taste them.

I reach for her hand. "As much as we hate it, emotions are loyal companions."

She caresses my fingers and smiles. "Okay, can we shut this door now?"

Gladly. This get-to-know-you-session has become too much for public display anyway.

~ * ~

Taillights, horns, and music liven the downtown cityscape as we walk with entwined arms under the midnight sky. The night is still young. The cool April air is suitable for strolling. I, however, want to cut the dillydally walk short and head home.

Deidra disagrees. "We look too good to be alone right now. We should strut down Beale Street." She playfully pulls at the hem of my backless dress. "You did all this to eat and go home?"

I indeed put a lot of time and energy into our date by shopping for a new dress and permitting Shonda to press my growing hair. She sent my teeny weeny Afro on vacation for the weekend. Playing dress-up for two hours has been thrilling, but Deidra's titillating dress— with keyholes along the torso— is steering me to a one-track mind. I'm ready to go home and have her to myself— ready to be the only one stealing her attention and sneaking peeps her way. She doesn't mind accompanying me back home after I pull her close and reveal what I really want for dessert.

When I pull into the garage and kill the ignition, Deidra caresses my thigh. "Follow me." I meet her at the door and we lock fingers as she leads me upstairs and to the bedroom. It isn't like I need a guide. Instead, she's showing me that I'm in store for a night we have yet to experience. She pulls me along, allowing me to revel in her lemon-scented perfume and the sway of hips coated in skin-tight fabric.

She keeps the lights off when we step into the bedroom. She lets go of my fingers and opens the shutters to illuminate the shadows on our faces. I love the combination of moonlight and Deidra. The soft beam transforms her curves to rolling silk. And it makes her skin different, like she's airbrushed in brown. She looks flawless, as if a divine hand transformed her right before my eyes. She's a goddess now. This is exactly why I wanted to come home.

She takes my hand again, pulling me closer to the bed— our final destination. She wraps my arms around her waist, leaning her head back to rest on my shoulder. The mango-infused Shea butter in her hair delights my nose. Our faces meet and she whispers, "Do you want me?"

"This is exactly why I wanted to come home," I say with my fingers inching up her spine. I unzip her dress to unleash the sights and sounds I've been waiting to experience. My palms fall down the phoenix tattoo I noticed the first day we met; the ink masks a scar from a childhood accident; fingertips falling to the small of her back; palms, again, tracing the valley that leads to her hips as her dress travels south.

Lately, I've noticed a shift in the sex. It's starting to resemble lovemaking. She's craving the experience as much as the act, and she's beginning to trust me. She lets me lead more, but I can't linger or do as I please with her body for too long— a sign of a woman who spent too much time under a man who selfishly touched her. I never let images of him piercing the canal I love to explore taint our intimacy. But sometimes, I wonder whether I truly satisfy her. Do my kisses satiate her appetite for affection? Do my hands quench her thirst for intimacy? Do I cradle her, lift her, and fill her as much as she needs?

"Yes," she whispers. I pretend she's responding to my inner thoughts, though she's answering the question I spoke into her ear: "You want this?"

"Mm-hmm," she moans with melody. So I continue to provide her with what she desires: a steady tongue as she slides her clit to the gates of ecstasy. She cups the back of my head to draw me closer and intensify her mounting happiness, her hips dancing to the rhythm of our lips.

I push my hands beyond her thighs and onto her stomach, feeling the slow rise and fall of her belly in tempo to her aching moans— a plea to gain entry to the city of orgasmic bliss. I have unilateral power to grant her admission, but I choose to deny it. Instead, I rise from my knees and close her legs as I join her in the bed.

She continues to lie on her backside— enjoying the residual sensation of my tongue play. I stretch out next to her and stare into her eyes. She smiles, knowing it's time to return the favor. She unzips my dress and laughs when she realizes there are no undergarments to follow. "You never cease to amaze me," she says and nudges my waist. "Turn over."

I roll to my stomach and rest my head on crossed hands. The smile on my face exposes my impatience. Deidra climbs onto my ass, her slick pussy gracing my skin. She leans forward, pressing her goodness into me even more as she massages my shoulders and traces her skilled hands along my waist.

"Please don't make me wait," I say.

She teases me, her fingertips tickling the contours of my torso, all because I robbed her of an orgasm.

"Please," I beg.

Finally, she rises from my body. When cooler air meets the wetness lingering from my oral play, chills race down my spine, inducing goose bumps along my arms. She leans forward and rests her full breasts on my neck. Their radiant heat makes me draw a deep breath.

"Now or later?" she asks.

"Now," I order.

Slowly, slowly, just as I like, she slides her velvet bosom from my neck to the edge of my back. "Damn," I say when she gradually rubs in the opposite direction. When she reaches my neck, she saturates my lips with kisses and repositions her breasts to do it again. And again.

I love this shit but prefer that it's short-lived, which gives me something to look forward to during the week— especially given I've asked Deidra to save special massages for weekends.

Now that I'm satisfied and spoiled, I want to explore the new bounds of our lovemaking. I'm ready to give her full citizenry to cum-land. I slap her ass and she assumes an all-fours position, arching her back to relax her abdominal and vaginal muscles in preparation of my entry. I adjust her a little so she can't maintain the arched stance. I want to constrict her muscles as I insert more fingers than she expects. I know from experience that it feels better when it hurts a bit. The lustful sounds of her crying out to a higher power and interjecting my name... *This* is exactly why I wanted to come home.

# 27

I'M AWAKE IN BED alone with suffocating thoughts. Never in my life have 365 days passed by this quickly. I can't believe I haven't talked with Pat, vented with her, or broken bread with her in a year. She's a missing slice of my pie that hasn't been filled by my friends or Deidra. Thankfully, the anniversary of her death didn't land on a workday. I have the refuge of the weekend to grieve.

I stare at the closet door reflecting on last Saturday. Deidra and I were weaving through a crowded music festival at the river when Pat's voice caught my ear. I felt an urge to scan the faces around me and identify the source. Although the familiar, raspy voice emanated from a stranger, the experience was comforting.

I want to drift asleep and summon a dream that will bring her voice to me again. I wiggle into a comfortable position to slow my thoughts and compartmentalize my sorrow. I'm floating to celestial realms, seconds away from dreaming when Deidra bumps my leg. I flinch.

"You plan on sleeping all morning?" she asks.

"I want to," I mumble.

"I want to go out for breakfast."

Fully conscious and past the point of no return for sleep, I sit upright and kick my feet out the sheets. "Where?"

"Your choice."

"I don't care, as long as we go to the cemetery first."

"Cemetery?"

Deidra is usually perceptive, though now she's offensive and oblivious. I shake my head and sigh with disappointment, my reaction a clue to her omission.

There's nothing she can say to take back the emotional jolt of her response. So she humbles herself and says, "I'm okay with that." She grabs my hands and pulls me out of bed.

~ * ~

Deidra drives east, out the city, pass the suburbs and into the sticks until we reach the small, unincorporated community where Pat rests for eternity. A narrow road off the two-lane highway leads to a dilapidated one-room church. Next to the rotting wood structure is a metal fence protecting headstones of deceased Carters. I step outside the car, the warm morning breeze promising a hellishly hot day. The rustle of leaves from the brush and trees are the only sounds in the expansive, flat country land.

I look onward at the cemetery, waiting for Deidra to exit. Eventually, I turn around and poke my head through my open door. She hasn't removed her hand from the steering wheel. "Are you coming?"

She gazes beyond the windshield. "This could quickly turn into an argument, so just let me be."

I take my frustration out on the car door and walk away.

The quaint cemetery is a stroll through history. There's a headstone for a male relative who died during the Great Depression, a headstone for a male relative born a year after the Civil War ended, and one for a female child who died during the polio years. Next to her is a slight hump in the earth where Pat is buried. The elements haven't flattened her burial plot yet.

I kneel down, running my fingertips across the engraved

letters in her black slate headstone before pulling up the weeds from its perimeter. I toss the weeds beyond the fence, catching a severe whiff of burnt paper and tobacco. Deidra is leaning against the car. She takes long, satisfying drags and blows the haze from her lungs into the east-pulling wind. I hope the light-headed effect of the nicotine rush will strip her sheltered feelings just enough for her to consider joining me. I want to hold her hand while sharing memories.

She finishes the cigarette and stays in her space. I remain in mine. I'm alone with Pat beneath my feet, regretting that I didn't call one of my friends to accompany me. The faint sound of movement sparks a bit of hope. I look back again, but Deidra hasn't moved one inch from the car. The rumble comes from the gray SUV approaching from the main road. This is Caroline's SUV. We stand motionless, listening to the continuous grind of gravel as the vehicle travels the curving path to the cemetery. Deidra retreats to the car as the wheels stop.

It's too late to avoid Caroline and whoever else is with her. So I wait for someone to exit. Caroline gets out first and takes two steps in my direction. "Well, well, well."

The middle sister peers at my windshield, shaking her head and grimacing. I've never felt such appreciation for tinted windshields until this moment.

As the youngest sister guides and supports Mama C's uneven gait, I approach the SUV. I intend on an amicable greeting and fast departure. I avoid eye contact with Kayla and greet Mama C. Her sweet eyes beam as we hug. She smells like mothballs and fried food as usual. Her lips meet my cheek at the release of her gentle embrace. "How you been?" she asks.

I answer positively despite mournful feelings.

"What about her?" Caroline says. "She too scared to get out the car?"

I wait until my mouth can deliver a fairly pleasant response. "Let's not go there."

Mama C steals the attention by taking hold of my arm and walking me back to the gravesite. I support her weight as she takes slow, choppy steps across the grass. She stops two plots from Pat's resting place. "It's good to see you, Nia. I'm glad you're here. Just wouldn't be right without you. I'm glad Caroline called you."

Caroline turns her back on her mother's words. I wish she had called to avoid this joint visit. I hold the truth and help Mama C step closer to Pat's grave. She balances her weight and releases my arm, her face overcome with grief. She shakes her head in disbelief before seizing her pain and releasing it to the winds. Then she looks around and says, "Somebody get Deidra."

We share glances, but no one budges. Is Mama C senile or insensitive? Whichever the case, someone needs to say something. "I don't know if that's a good idea," I say.

She places her hands on her hips. "You already done a lot that wasn't a good idea. Now go ahead, you hear?"

My feet remain planted as I search for more words that will discourage interaction with Deidra. Ultimately, I fall prey to matriarchal pressure and depart the cemetery. I open the driver's side door and kneel before Deidra to deliver the message. "Cora wants you."

"And?"

I touch her leg— a tender gesture in exchange for cooperation. "The situation is bad enough. Let's not make it worse."

She clasps my hand. "Baby, you don't owe them anything."

I exhale, unsure how to proceed. "Deidra," I plead. I want her to get out and face her demons. More importantly, I don't want her to embarrass me, especially in front of Kayla. I have to show the influence I have in this relationship. I have to flaunt our bond directly in her face. "Please. I'll make it up to you," I say with a merciful face.

She fights the urge to deny my request by rolling her eyes and sliding out the car.

I walk a step behind Deidra in shock, yet thankful that she's uniting with the Carter clan. The tail of her maxi dress flows in the breeze. The orange and yellow pattern demands attention for miles. Her bound hair accentuates her July-kissed skin— jewelry and makeup accessorizing her beauty. There are upturned noses, but no one removes their eyes as she approaches. They can't. Deidra is a captivating stroke in the middle of a rural canvas.

When she enters the cemetery, Kayla turns her back. Deidra joins the group, her eyes daring them to get out of line with her. I stand by her side, waiting for someone to encroach the silence.

Mama C breaks the barrier. "Thank you," she says to her estranged granddaughter. Deidra moves her sunglasses from the top of her head to the bridge of her nose. No words escape her mouth so I nod on her behalf. Kayla keeps her stance and the sisters attempt to overlook Deidra. With this mild behavior, maybe we can get through this awkward moment peacefully.

"Now that we're all here as we should be," Mama C says, "let us pray." The Carter clan connects hands and closes their eyes. The environment is too hostile to dare close mine. Deidra crosses her arms, her black lenses hiding any reaction to Kayla's repeated glances.

"Father God, we come before you with bowed heads and humbled hearts," Mama C prays like a seasoned evangelist. "Thanking you, oh Lord, for the gift of life. Thank you for blessing us with wonderful times with Pat. Wrap us in your arms during our darkest hour. Help us Father God to understand that weeping may endure for a night, but joy cometh in the morning. Help us live with the joy of Pat in our hearts every day. Thank you for bringing us here today, Father. We need you, Lord. We need you to restore this family. Thank you for bringing the lost home. Keep her close to your bosom, Lord. Bless our spirits so we can be whole. We—"

"I was not lost," Deidra says. Every eye rushes to her face. "I was not kidnapped and I did not run away. I was abandoned, and you know this."

"You got some nerve," Caroline shouts and steps forward. The middle sister quickly swings her arm out to keep Caroline from charging Deidra.

"The truth hurts," Deidra says and steps closer to Mama C. "You should be praying for forgiveness."

Caroline breaks free from her sister with every intention of making Deidra pay for her disrespectful tone and the desecration of prayer on consecrated land. "Wait a minute," Mama C shouts. Her daughter comes to a standstill. "Caroline, pull yourself together. You're too old for that."

I touch Deidra's arm to encourage her to fall back and leave with me, but Mama C has other plans. She wobbles in our direction and clutches Deidra's hand without notice. Either Deidra is caught off guard or too focused on Caroline because she doesn't object to the physical contact. Mama C leads her out the cemetery, just beyond the metal gate. I watch, hoping Deidra won't say or do anything else to incite a fight and send Caroline bolting out this cemetery.

"You shouldn't have brought her here," Caroline says, keeping an eye on her mother.

I ignore her and focus on who's most important to me.

"Life is too short and precious," Mama C says. "We can move on. It's not too late."

"Seven months ago you were gunning for Pat's estate. Why the change of heart?"

"I wanted to do right by my daughter, but we all make mistakes."

"And you have a lifetime of them."

Mama C drops her head for a moment and then speaks face to face. "I'll pray for you. I'll pray you forgive me. I'll pray you come here by yourself one day and lay your burdens down right there," she says, pointing to Pat's grave.

Deidra snatches the sunglasses from her face. "Get off your geriatric high horse. You were wrong! You failed me and you failed Pat, too. She wasn't in my life because of you. You can pray all you want, but you won't get a second thought from me." Deidra dismisses Mama C with a scowl of disgust and walks to the car.

I drive us away with haste but my thoughts stay on Kayla. Her lack of reaction during the whole ordeal worries me. She didn't speak or intervene. She watched us, quietly, arms crossed with calm demeanor— an alarming behavior reflective of a ticking time bomb.

# 28

HUMS FROM THE ENGINE and passing vehicles are the only sounds between us as I drive home. We planned for breakfast, but Deidra doesn't mention it. I no longer have an appetite.

When I pull into the garage she turns to me. "Don't ever do that again," she says. "I know you feel stuck in the middle, but you're not responsible for them."

I hate the rift between the Carters and me and the strenuous pull between them and Deidra. She could help mitigate the strain I feel, though I can't ask her to soften her heart to the Carters after so many years of forced separation. I don't know what to say once we're inside so we part ways. I need space, and I hope alone time will help her consider the possibility of reconciliation.

A light lunch, long nap, and several hours of sitcoms help the taxing day pass. When evening arrives, I leave the bedroom and head downstairs. Traces of Deidra's voice float from the guest bedroom. With a book and blanket in hand, I curl my legs onto the couch. I want to stay in this position lost in the pages of the thriller until midnight.

On page seventy-three, I hear the bedroom door open. Deidra approaches and waits until I finish the paragraph and acknowledge her presence. "I know this is a strange time to ask," she says, "but do you want anything from Pat's estate? I won't be mad if you do."

"No, I never have."

When I return my attention to the book, she accepts my answer and walks upstairs. I attempt to read, but I can't follow the story. I keep wrestling with my response. I should've mentioned Pat's bracelet. She's never considerate of anything regarding Pat, and I blew her off like the moment was meaningless.

I close the hardcover and go upstairs. When I enter the bedroom, Deidra is sitting on the bed scrolling through her phone. She puts it down when I sit next to her. "I wanted a bracelet, but I couldn't find it."

"What did it look like?"

"Double-banded. Greenish on the outside. White on the inside. Kind of looked homemade."

"Hmm. I made that bracelet back in ninety-five for Pat's birthday."

"Really? She wore it religiously."

I recall two occasions early last year when Pat wore the bracelet even though it didn't match her outfit. I also tell Deidra about the time it remained on Pat's wrist as she swam in the ocean at Anguilla. I even mention the night we got sloppy drunk during that vacation. The bracelet slid back and forth as Pat threw back shots.

I grow excited about hearing more about her birthday gift until tears roll down Deidra's face. It would have been nice to receive a warning sign before the tears. A sad tone, a shaky voice, red or watery eyes. I want us to talk about Pat, but I don't want to feel guilty about it. I move closer to her. "What's wrong?"

"Sounds like the two of you had a lot of fun. You had six good years with her. I didn't have one. Today it hit home that there are no second chances. Nia, I care about you, but sometimes I want to walk away from you because of her." She can't maintain a blank affect. She shields her eyes as sobs and gasps for air accompany her tears.

I'm motionless, afraid to speak and afraid to touch her.

She cries for a moment and gathers the breath to speak. "Sometimes I find myself being mad at you because she let you into her life but pretended like I didn't exist."

"I understand," I say to ease her sadness and my guilt. I want to apologize on my behalf and Pat's, too, for all the unforgettable times we shared. I gather the courage to rub her back. I wish I had the power to transfer all the time, laughs, and love Pat gave me to her.

I take Deidra's hand and lead us to the headboard, resting against the pillows as she reclines in my arms. Though silent, her tears roll to my arm. It's funny how I started today yearning for her empathy. But now the day is closing with tears that aren't from me. After a while, she wiggles from my arms a bit and turns her face to mine. Tears wait cautiously in her eyes. She's slow to do it, but I know she'll say something.

"That was the first time my grandmother ever touched me. At thirty-three. At a cemetery."

If she wants a response, she doesn't wait for one. She grabs my arm and inches her way back into my protective hold. I'm glad she's allowing my loving embrace to remind her that I am not the enemy.

# 29

THE FIRST WEEKEND of September brings in a major storm system with record-setting rainfall. The two-day storm causes flooding and deaths. Unfortunately, four feet of grimy water damages the first level of my best friend's townhome. Without question, I welcome Tasha into my home while she transitions to a new residence.

Tasha has too many concerns to tackle— from work demands to insurance claims— to maintain a grudge with Deidra. "The thing with K.D. was almost ten months ago. That's water under the bridge," she tells Deidra the night she arrives. "And girl, to be honest, you did me favor."

By the second weekend of September, the two are well on their way to becoming fast friends. While I'm spending my days monitoring frail hearts, they're in *my* living room watching chick flicks on *my* flat screen, dropping popcorn morsels between the cushions of *my* couch.

I walk in after a tiresome day to find them watching *Just Wright*. They've moved the ottoman to stretch the crochet blanket that *my* grandmother gave me across the rug. They're lying on their bellies in matching pink pajamas and polka dot socks.

"Y'all went shopping for that shit?" I complain. And they both have a ponytail dangling from the right side of their head. "I'm gonna start charging y'all asses rent."

They keep straight faces for a split second and then laugh

at my threat. "Baby," Deidra says, rising from the floor to look at me. "Come chill with us."

I roll my eyes and march upstairs.

Tasha moves into her new place over the fourth weekend. When I come home from work the following Tuesday, the savory aroma of home cooking greets me at the door. I almost smile. Finally, things are back to normal. I'm not surprised that Deidra is standing at the dining room table with my favorite meal plated. However, I am surprised by the bouquet of orange roses in the center of the table. She steps forward and grabs my purse. "Wash your hands and have a seat."

Whiffs of fried pork chops, rice, beans, and cornbread taunt my taste buds. She also prepared fresh brewed tea with lemon slices. "What's going on?" I can't take a bite until I know whether this is a celebratory meal or a please-forgive-me meal.

"I got a job. Eat first."

I want to rush just so I can hear the details of her announcement. But the food is cooked to perfection, causing me to savor each umami-laced bite. I even postpone the details for seconds. When I'm stuffed, I sink into the seat and say, "I didn't even know you were looking for a job."

"I know. I wanted to surprise you. I started looking a month ago... I can't let a man take care of me forever."

"He wants to."

"He won't."

"What's changed?"

"Me. I'm changing. I just want to thank you for opening your home and being patient with me."

"You thank me by making me fat?"

"And other ways." She smiles and winks. "You can actually stand to gain a few pounds, especially in the hips."

I've tried calories for curves before and it didn't work. "What's the position?"

"Marketing Coordinator. I basically assist the Marketing and Catering Manager with promotions, events, press, social media. Stuff like that."

"Social media?" I've yet to see or hear of Deidra partaking in social media. She doesn't like, share, tweet, post, follow, hash tag, pin, or comment on anything.

"I *have* social media accounts," she says. "I just don't use them. Too many of Eric's family and military cronies are connected to them. But I login sometimes to stalk Shannon." She grabs my glass of tea and steps into the kitchen for a refill. "I don't have my own office. Just a laptop and desk in the corner of someone else's junky office, but I can work from home sometimes."

"Sounds good. What's the pay?"

"Starts at nineteen an hour."

Wow! I swallow tea, attempting to swallow the pay. "There are people with legit master's degrees that ain't making nineteen dollars an hour, Deidra. How do you get a marketing position with no marketing experience?"

"You see this ass and mouth? They go a long way." She grins, leading me to think the worst.

"I don't even wanna know what that means."

"It means I wore the right outfit, said the right things, and most importantly, I know the right people. Dezza pulled some strings for me."

Nepotism. I'm relieved. "So, where she got you working?"

"Porter Restaurants. You know, the group that owns the little chicken joints?"

I know the company. It's a locally owned family chain— in the news a few years back, cited for fraudulent practices and health code infractions.

She looks eager for a response. "I went to their soul food restaurant once. The food and the people were disgusting."

"*Were*. The corporate office has relocated and restructured, and they're rebranding. Hence, me."

Deidra is finally moving toward independence and demonstrating for her daughter how to start anew. I should show some excitement, but I can't muster any enthusiasm. I prefer her open schedule, her being present, me arriving from work to a clean house and warm dinner. No doubt about it, she has spoiled me.

She leaves her seat to stand by my side, lifting my head to deliver a kiss. "Be happy for me," she whispers.

"Is there a part of you that's doing this for me? You said once that I've given you mixed messages, but baby, you know I don't have a problem being here for you financially." I wrap her hips in my arms. "You don't have to work. But, at the end of the day, I know it's your choice."

A week later, I'm forced to adjust to the changes. She's leaving for work daily, in the process of purchasing a brand new sedan, and treating Tasha and me to a spa day.

# 30

WHAT SHOULD I SAY to my girlfriend's seventeen-year-old? I can't charm Shannon by playing with her Barbie dolls or offering her money or candy. She's a teenager. She's more than capable of judging me for the slightest infraction. I stand in my closet, searching the racks for a suitable first-impression outfit, wondering how she feels about me. Am I the lesbian who's stealing her mom from her dad, the sole reason her mom won't return home to Virginia?

Chances are I'll walk into our first time meeting with two strikes against me. Deidra assures me that everything will be okay. But what mother would admit 'my daughter can't stand your ass'?

Today also marks the first time I'll ingratiate myself with Deidra's family. I've only met her sister and two high school friends. My interactions with Shannon and the larger family have to go well. I don't want any ill feelings to have an adverse effect on our relationship.

I step to the end of the clothes rack to sort through hangers, again, recalling my teenage years and how damn judgmental I was back then. That's why I have to find a trendy and appropriate ensemble. Too bad I lost my personal stylist when I broke-up with Kayla. I select a few options and thrust her out of my thoughts. After four outfit changes, I snatch the price tags off a pair of red high-rise shorts and an airy, white button-down blouse.

I inspect myself in the mirror, admiring how the sheer material reveals a hint of my red bra.

~ * ~

In my previous visits to Juanita's home, someone different answered the door each time. Today is no different. A woman around my age welcomes me inside and escorts me to the kitchen. Her low-cut, sleeveless dress bares her even brown skin. The floral tattoo across her shoulder is as attractive as her bright smile.

"By the way, I'm Courtney." She extends her hand. "You are too cute. Deidra talks about you all the time. It's nice to finally meet you."

A welcoming introduction, smile, and compliment? I don't remember Deidra ever mentioning Courtney, though the name seems familiar. I think harder and recall hearing her name during the consultation about Pat's Will. Is she the witness who signed the document? I don't know what to say, so I substitute words with a smile.

"Have a seat. I'll get Deidra for you," Courtney says and walks out the back door.

In the meantime, I stare at the relatives passing between rooms as the two women preparing food chat with me. The one in jeans is Deidra's aunt. The younger one is her cousin. After introductions, the aunt pulls me into their spat about whether green beans are an appropriate side dish with spaghetti. "I like both," I say, remaining neutral.

A woman who hasn't already made an appearance enters from the den. I can't see her face while she's on the phone and bent down to access the bottom of the refrigerator. Her yellow shorts are just long enough to safely cover her posterior. The tight fit nicely cups her plump cheeks. She flips her long hair over one shoulder, calves flexing as she stands upright. From behind, she's eye candy as sweet as the grape soda in her hand. I don't know what happened to Juanita, but Deidra has some good-looking women in her family.

Just as the soda cutie leaves the kitchen, Deidra's sister enters from the backyard. And this is the best I've ever seen Juanita. Her swooping bang flows into a ponytail. Her jeans and casual blouse are ironed, no holes or stains. Jeweled sandals, gloss on her lips, shadow below her brows. She actually looks like Deidra's younger sister today.

"Hey, lady," I say.

She acknowledges me with a nod. The makeover did nothing to improve her attitude. "It's fuckin' hot outside. If Deidra wasn't so busy bein' George Foreman, she'd have her ass in here right now. Anyway…" She swigs her beer. "You want a lil' somethin' to drink?"

"Yeah, I'll take water."

"Girl, I said to drink!"

I'm anxious about meeting Shannon. Sitting here gives me time to acclimate to my surroundings. Liquor would relax me a little, but then I'd notice that I'm too comfortable and that will make me nervous. "Just water," I request.

"Suit your damn self then."

Juanita fixes me a glass of water as Deidra steps inside with another relative. She places a foil pan on the counter before sitting with me. The scents of heat and charcoaled meat accompany her.

"Who's Courtney?" I ask.

"My cousin."

"That's surprising."

"What'chu try-na say?"

I laugh at her bad attempt to speak colloquially. "I'm saying you ain't never mentioned her."

"I do all the time. That's NeNe."

Prior mentions of NeNe fill my head. She's the elementary school teacher with two rumbustious kids; Shannon's godmother; the one who texts Deidra morning, noon, and night without considering what we may be doing. Before now, I didn't realize that NeNe is married to that guy I met at Gillespie— that *this* is the couple who witnessed and signed Pat's Will.

My mind lingers on these new connections, but I'm distracted every time a door opens. And whenever someone cuts through the kitchen, I'm looking for traces of Deidra in a young girl's face. Deidra talks about her daughter so often that I feel like I know her already.

At this point, I think I've been introduced to everyone except her daughter. "Where's Shannon?"

"She's in here somewhere." Deidra stands and crosses the kitchen to poke her head in the adjoining room. "Shannon, get off the phone."

"Ma, I have friends," Shannon responds beyond the wall.

"Your friends don't pay your cell phone bill."

"Neither do you," Shannon says as she steps into my line of sight.

While Deidra gives her daughter a stern don't-play-with-me face, my stomach sinks to my feet. Why is Shannon the "woman" with the grape soda? If I had seen her face earlier, I would have noticed the resemblance between her and Deidra, the likeness between her and Pat. And I would've kept all inappropriate glances of her ass to myself.

"You've been here for almost twenty-four hours," Deidra says, "and you've been on the phone for twenty of them."

I take advantage of each spare second to pull myself together as they bicker. If I could kick myself for gawking at a minor, I would. The mistake isn't entirely my fault, though. Shannon surely doesn't look like a teenager. She's too curvy, too stacked, and too sparsely dressed. She doesn't look like the girl from all the photos Deidra has shown me.

"Sit—down," Deidra orders Shannon, pointing to the table.

Obediently, Shannon shuts her mouth and walks toward me, plopping down in the seat facing mine, placing her soda can on the table. "Only *my* mom would embarrass me just when I'm meeting you."

Suddenly, the person I initially thought was years older transitions to years younger.

Deidra sits and stares at Shannon the way my mother often stared at me when I was a teenager. It's that so-what-you'll-live type of look I received whenever I disagreed but didn't have the power to make a decision or the freedom to open my mouth again— not unless I wanted to be popped in the mouth. It's strange seeing these two interact. Before today, Deidra was my sexy, sharp-tongued lover. Now, she's in mommy-mode, dividing her attention between Shannon and me.

"Do you mind if I go to the movies?" Shannon asks me. "She wants the three of us to hang out after this."

"Don't even try it," her mother says. "You can go out when you get home."

Shannon sighs. "Fine."

The dormant teenager inside of me feels bad for Shannon. I should help. "You're not leaving till Thursday, right?" I move my eyes to Deidra. "That's four days from now. We can get together between now and then."

"I like you," Shannon says.

I laugh. I need to laugh and relax.

"You're prettier than I thought you'd be," she adds.

Caught off guard, I don't respond. But Deidra fills my silence. "Seal your lips."

"Ma, I'm just saying. Look at that shirt. I'd rock that shirt. I thought she'd be wearing men's clothes and some played-out cornrows."

~ * ~

After Deidra warned her daughter to 'act right,' she should've found her sister and warned her to do the same. Juanita's house sits on a corner lot, and she's spent the last two minutes spouting obscenities because the neighborhood kids are shortcutting through her yard.

The family has set up two folding tables and extra chairs so that everyone can gather in the kitchen and dining room to eat. We're enjoying barbeque with all the trimmings while Juanita is nibbling, drinking, and fussing. "Them lil' bitches need to stop walkin' in my damn grass," she complains.

"What grass?" Deidra asks between bites of potato salad.

"That's my damn point. I can't get the shit to grow 'cause these bad-ass kids 'round here too damn lazy to walk on the sidewalk."

The family members around the table of eight ignore Juanita's ranting. Deidra, however, is annoyed. She keeps placing her fork aside and cutting her eyes at Juanita. "You need to watch your language around these kids," Deidra says.

"Girl, they sittin' all the way over there," Juanita argues, pointing with her fork to the kids' table in the corner of the dining room. "I'm gone pop some shots at they lil' asses and I bet you they stop then."

Deidra mumbles under her breath and then sits her fork down again. "I need a moment of silence from you."

"Then go outside."

Deidra shakes her head. "Of all the problems you have inside this house, you're sitting there worried about a yard full of weeds?"

They exchange verbal jabs before their aunt intervenes and ends their sisterly spat. We finish the meal in peace, but Juanita continues to drink.

She doesn't even sit the beer can down when we gather in the den to play charades. We split into four teams of three with Deidra and Shannon as my teammates. During round one, I learn I'm on a competitive mother-daughter team. Round two, Shannon takes her position before the fireplace.

"Come on Shannon," Deidra says and claps. "You know I hate to lose. Let's get this one."

Shannon considers the word on the game card and springs into action. She waves her hands through the air with one foot raised off the carpeted floor. I have no idea what she's interpreting but that doesn't stop Deidra from yelling out possible answers. Thirty seconds later our time runs out, and we still don't have any points.

"I need to teach you how to pantomime," Deidra says when her daughter returns to her seat.

"Did we not miss the first one because of you?" Shannon reminds her.

"I did it perfectly. Y'all are just slow."

When my turn comes, I pray for an easy word or phrase. If I don't do a good job, Shannon will probably blame me for a lack of points and Deidra will attack my intelligence. I stand before the fireplace and think of the cleverest thing I can do. I extend my arms to maneuver like an airplane and twirl one finger above my head. Two seconds later Deidra shouts, "Helicopter." I return to my seat and receive a congratulatory kiss from Deidra and a pat on the back from Shannon.

The next half hour goes well. Our team wins by four points and Shannon takes advantage of Deidra's high spirits to garner permission to leave for the movies. When the house clears out, Deidra, Courtney, and their aunt stay behind to cleanup and put away leftover food. Juanita doesn't feel obligated to pitch in.

I really want Deidra to come home with me, but she opts to stay the night with her daughter and family. Before leaving for home, I head to the bathroom, running into Juanita as she staggers down the hallway. She steps close to me, the stench of beer almost backing me into the wall. I can't advance left or right without bumping into her. I shield my nose and wait for her to step away.

"You're wastin' your time," she says.

"Excuse me?"

"With my sister," she clarifies.

I glance back. No one is in sight. I hope the beer isn't tempting her to get a little frisky. It's time to leave this awkward run-in, even if I have to gently push her out of my way.

As soon as I move my feet, Juanita opens her mouth. "Deidra fucked up her marriage 'cause she couldn't keep her panties on. And she gone fuck you over, too."

"Really, Juanita?"

"I'm drinkin', but that don't mean my mind ain't right."

"Why are you telling me this?"

" 'Cause she think she better than everybody in this damn family. She always tryin' to be like them damn richie-rich Carters and they ain't never wanted her ass. But really I'm tellin' you 'cause you too good for her."

"We all have our issues," I remind her, glancing at the beer can. "Give your sister some credit. She left Shannon and her stability behind to start over and become the woman she wants to be."

Juanita steps closer and I move backward. I press my back against the wall to keep our chests from touching. "Deidra didn't leave behind shit! She didn't come back to Memphis for Pat, my kids, or nobody else. She came back 'cause she got pregnant by another man. I'm the one who took her ass to the abortion clinic. And then she begged me not to tell nobody 'cause she don't want folks to know she dirty. Hell, she don't wanna walk or talk like nobody in this family but always expect me to put up with her shit. That's why she was stayin' here. Where the fuck else was she gone go?" She laughs and waves her finger in my face. "Didn't take long before she found a sucker to shack-up with.

"Look, I'm a bottom-bitch on her totem pole, so she don't mind me knowin' the truth. And I'm gone tell it: Deidra will lie and fuck her way from point A to point B. Save yourself while you can, honey." She grins then walks away with pep in her step like we had a friendly conversation.

Sweat tickles my underarms. I'm unsure whether Juanita has conned me into anger or threw me a lifeline I didn't know I needed. If Courtney or anyone else in the family had told me the exact same thing, I would have reacted differently. I would have immediately believed them. But this shit stings coming from Juanita. In less than two minutes she's created a wave of uncertainty.

I decide to skip the bathroom and leave. I try to bind my irritation before entering the kitchen and seeing Deidra, but my restraint is a second too late. "Something ruffle your feathers?" she asks. "Come on, I'll walk you out."

"Stay inside," I say. "I'll see you tomorrow."

# 31

I'M GRATEFUL for work today. I need something to occupy my time and thoughts. I'm tired of stressing over Juanita's allegations. During lunch, I sit alone in the cafeteria and emotionally prep myself for today's outing with Deidra and Shannon. I don't want to ruin the rest of Shannon's time with her mother. Once we're together, I hope Deidra will do or say something that helps erase all the negative sentiment her sister has created.

I meet Deidra and Shannon at a pizza buffet. Juanita's eldest kids accompany them. We talk and laugh and joke with the kids, challenging each other to taste pizza with odd topping combinations. The entire time, I remind myself of all the things I appreciate about Deidra. I like her confidence; her sometimes sweet, sometimes salty demeanor; her commitment to the kids; her ability to bring out the best in me; the way she lets me experience her emotionally; the influence of her vulnerability.

I go back and forth over the pros and cons of our relationship. Without question, the good outweighs the bad. I never felt Deidra deliberately misled me. She has good intentions. So, I feel bad for allowing Juanita to incite my skepticism. At the same time, I can't ignore the possibility that Deidra has kept the origins of her transition to Memphis confidential— just as she concealed her husband *and* daughter.

We leave the pizzeria with full stomachs and head to the park to let the kids roam, yell, and play. Deidra, Shannon, and I sit at a picnic table, keeping our eyes on the kids while chatting about Shannon's last year of high school and her possible move down South.

"I've been talking to my friends about doing something memorable before graduation," Shannon shares while texting. "Something like skydiving."

"Uh-uh," Deidra says. "That's too dangerous."

Shannon lifts her head. "So is your driving, but I'm alive."

"I skydived once," I share.

"Here?" Shannon asks.

"No, about four years ago in Cancun." I jumped from a plane during a weeklong summer vacation with Pat, Loca Tres, Kayla, and three additional relatives. That was the same week Kayla and I admitted we had feelings for each other, stealing time to sneak around and have sex in random places. I keep that tidbit of information to myself. "I'll never do it again, but I'm glad I did it. You only live once."

"Exactly!" Shannon says. She looks at her mother, expecting her to refute us.

Deidra only smiles and says, "It's your choice." Then she leaves to push the kids on the swings.

Now I have a chance to ask Shannon some of the questions floating in my head. "How does it feel to have a young mother?" I begin.

She chuckles and releases the cell phone from her hand. "It's cool. Sometimes we like the same songs, same clothes. But sometimes I wish she was ten years older."

"You want more of a generational gap?"

"Yeah. Are you close to your mom?"

"I was when I was younger. When I got older, our differences pushed us apart."

"I can't wait until I'm older so she'll stop being so anal. She needs to chill sometimes."

"What?" How can she overlook Deidra's easy-going disposition or the traits that make her a lover and friend? It's just like a teenager to not see beyond the role of mother. "My mom was strict. Your mom is low key."

She laughs. "When?"

"Give it a few years. You'll understand her better. So, do you really wanna come to Memphis? I know it's October and you've got time to decide, but you don't wanna go to college with your friends?"

"They're staying in the DMV. I wanna do something different. If I get into school here, I'm packing up and leaving. Can I ask you something?"

I nod.

"Do you want kids?" she asks.

That's a question I didn't expect. "Yeah, one day."

"With my mom?"

"It's possible," I say to spare her feelings.

Shannon stares at me, as if she needs a moment to sense my thoughts. I feel just as uncomfortable whenever her mother probes me with lingering stares. She glances at her mother and says, "She really likes you. I've never seen her look at my dad the way she looks at you."

I exhale. Why are the words from Juanita and Shannon's mouths so dissimilar? My emotions slip again, though this time they're sliding toward regret. I regret that I allowed Juanita to rile me. And I hate that I can't fit into Shannon's shoes to imagine longevity with Deidra. Her sister and daughter— two people that know her intimately— are toying with my feelings.

I keep my composure, but I have to address these strained feelings tomorrow.

~ * ~

Although Deidra dropped Shannon off at the airport just before noon, she waits until I leave work to return home. She's inside less than two minutes and has already kicked off her shoes and pulled me to the couch for my undivided attention as she shares her thoughts about Shannon's visit and possible move. "And why in the world did you encourage her to skydive?"

"Why'd you move to Memphis?"

She withdraws from my arm. "We've talked about this."

"You said you needed change. From what?"

"I was unhappy."

I sigh. "Deidra, I have very little patience for vagueness right now. I know how much you love Shannon. I've seen that love with my own eyes. So I need to understand why you're not with her right now."

"Are you saying I'm a bad mother? I feel guilty enough being away from her. I don't need you beating me up about it. I do that every single day on my own."

"No! No, that's not what I meant. What happened that was so bad that you'd be apart from her?"

"You don't care about why I left. You only want to hear about my mistakes. I'm not stupid, Nia. I can only imagine what Juanita has managed to tell you. Yes, I've done some unspeakable things, but that's in *my* past. Leave it there."

I shake my head. I desperately wanted her to deny everything. I hoped that she would tell me that Juanita's words were nothing but intimidation and straight-up bullshit.

"I don't trust you," I admit, calmly. If I allow my actions to mirror my emotions this will turn into an argument. "You want me to have this unyielding faith in you that you don't deserve. I'm not going to give you the chance to wrong me. You don't deserve the chance to wrong me." My words dishearten her. She won't look in my eyes anymore.

"Where is this coming from?" she asks.

Coming from? Has she forgotten about the secrets? Her ambiguous sexuality? Her alleged promiscuity? "Are you genuinely attracted to who I am, or is this relationship convenient?"

At eight months into this relationship, I've reached the point where I have to open my heart and move forward, or protect myself and pull away, avoiding disappointment and bitterness. I hate struggling with this— especially given my twenty-ninth birthday is a week away. I should be gearing up to celebrate, not feeling like this.

She doesn't answer. She stands up and steps away from me. I can't see her face, but I know she's struggling. When she crosses her arms, I'm sure she's wondering whether or not this relationship is worth fighting for. Maybe she's hopeful. If not, she'll keep her back to me and walk away, letting me have this short-lived race.

I rise from the couch and wait a few more seconds. The least I can do is give her a moment to decide.

She turns around and approaches me, staring me squarely in the eyes. "You're scared of loving me. You're using my past as an excuse to walk away because you won't let go of your own."

"Let go of what? This is about protecting the rest of me I have left to give." I've experienced too much selfishness and bad communication and too many ulterior motives. It isn't until this moment— standing midway between the living room and the pathway leading to my refuge upstairs— that I acknowledge that I don't trust Deidra to be any different from those in past relationships. "Things are good now, but what about later?" I won't go down that road again.

"What have I done to hurt you? How is recounting every

mistake I've made going to help you? I had a life before you, Nia. Why is it your job to make me pay for the choices I made last year or the year before that one? How do things that had nothing to do with you affect us?"

She doesn't wait for me to respond. It's too late to renege on what I've already done. I've pushed her far away. We haven't exchanged many words, but what I've said is enough for her to know that we've reached our last terminal; enough that she grabs her purse from the dining room table and walks out the door.

# 32

WHEN DEIDRA FIRST LEFT, I wasn't sad or upset, and I didn't take my romantic misfortune out on coworkers or patients. However, it's day four and my confidence is wearing off. I don't like coming home to an empty condo. I don't like the TV or iPod keeping me company. I don't like sleeping alone or cooking or self-pleasuring again. Loneliness is beginning to settle in the middle of my chest. And it's dense and inescapable.

After work, I stop by the gas station and spend twenty-three dollars on chips, candy, and soda. I drive home for a weekend of junk food and tear-jerk movies. I make sure my cell phone, laptop, and tablet are turned off and left on the kitchen counter. I head upstairs, preparing to ignore all incoming communication— just as I did after Pat's funeral. Then I climb in bed and open my first bag of salt and sour chips.

The hibernation is going well until my doorbell starts ringing over and over again. Sixty seconds later, the shrieking ding-dong induces a headache. I storm out of bed to scold whomever is interrupting my solitary weekend. It's Saturday, so I won't be surprised to see a pair of religious fanatics at the door.

As soon as I unlock and crack the front door open, Tasha pushes her way inside. "Why didn't you come to breakfast?" She examines me from head to toe. Her eyes pause on my frizzy hair; on my oversized tee shirt; on the crumbs on my chest. "You look a mess."

I feel a mess. I sit on the couch to relieve my lazy feet. My junk food orgy provides little energy.

Tasha sits by my side and says, "You need to get some Folgers in your cup and answer me."

"Is it a crime to stay home?"

"It is when you're AWOL. Where's Deidra?"

"Did you come over here for her or me?"

"Both of y'all. Neither one of y'all answering the phone. What's going on?"

How diplomatic of Deidra to ignore calls from my friend. "Don't contact her again. We broke up."

Her eyes widen. "Why'd you break up with her?"

"Who said she didn't break up with me?"

"You're the idiot," she says and punches me in the shoulder.

I grab my shoulder to soothe the throbbing pain.

"She cares about you," she adds.

"Tasha, what the fuck do you know?"

She raises her fist but my reflexes are too slow to guard against her punching me in the same sore spot. I brace my tender shoulder and gasp from the rush of pain. She needs to learn how to keep her damn hands to herself when upset. "If you hit me again, I—"

"You'll what?" she yells. She leans closer, daring me to punch back.

I stare at the window, lending us a quiet moment to calm down a bit.

"What are you waiting on?" she asks. "The perfect woman? If you are, stop! It ain't gone happen. You need to get out your head and into your heart and realize that Deidra will love the hell out of you. That's the type of perfection you need, dumb ass."

I close my eyes, too sluggish to respond.

"You know I'm right," she says. "I'll be honest with you.

I've had some heart-to-hearts with Deidra. She's a good person who ended up doing the wrong things for the right reasons. And... I told her to hold off on telling you some things."

I hear the hint of apology in her voice, but I don't care. "And why in the world would you do that?"

"Because she has to deal with the consequences of her actions. Not you. Those are her fuck-ups. You don't know how to start from today and move into tomorrow. You're always worried about yesterday. Even when yesterday don't have a damn thing to do with you."

She crosses her arms and waits for my response, but this sugar slump has me too fatigued to refute what she said.

Tasha sighs. "I wish I could muster up all this good advice and find me a good one." She opens her arms. "Come here."

I slide closer and wrap my arms above her shrinking waist. The consoling hug and strengthening words inspire me to say, "You're a good friend."

"Wonderful friend."

I release her and laugh.

"Ooh, Lord," she says and pinches her nose. "You *really* need some deodorant." She stands and moves away from me. "Go upstairs and take a bath, and when you get out, call Deidra. I already talked some sense into Jacoby, so we'll shoot for breakfast next Saturday."

After Tasha leaves, I go upstairs to clean my room. I grab shoes and scrubs off the floor and vacuum crumbs from the bed before making it. I iron an outfit for today and scrubs for Monday. Then I light a candle and descend into the bathtub. The green apple aroma and warm soapy water help me clear my thoughts and consider my haunting faults.

As much as Tasha's chastising irked me, I know she's right. I also know she was holding back. She didn't mention how I'm rarely optimistic and how I blame other folks for the relationship I want but don't have, or like Deidra said, how I won't let go of bad experiences. Now that I think about it, I don't understand what 'let go' means. Admit my fears? Accept the past? Live in the moment? Trust Deidra? Realize Deidra is not Kayla? Whatever the meaning, I'm tired of dating and the emotional rollercoaster that accompanies it.

By the time the murky bath water is too cool for comfort, I've stared at the tiles long enough to decide that let go means 'do not repeat past actions,' which really means stepping outside of my comfort zone.

Like Tasha said, I'm not the forgive-and-forget type. That's how I've always been. I was a kid who had to write my letters correctly the first time. If I made a mistake, I didn't flip my pencil over to erase it. I balled up the paper and grabbed another wide-ruled sheet to start again. I didn't correct the error. I was a teenager who ended a friendship if a girl looked at my boyfriend too long. I didn't wait for an explanation or apology. I'm a woman who dates with a three-strikes-and-you're-out policy. Once they're out, I hold on to their transgressions.

I admit I have a serious problem with second chances.

I leave the bathroom and grab my phone to call Deidra. She doesn't answer but immediately texts: *What do you want?* It takes twenty minutes of wrangling through texts before she agrees to meet at the McDonald's near her sister's house.

I wanted to meet beyond the drive-through for privacy, but Deidra arrived before me. She's parked at the entrance under a bright light. I park beside her car and flip my headlights off. When I step outside, she unlocks her car doors and I take my place in her passenger seat, causing the cherry air freshener on the rear view mirror to sway a bit. Soft rhythms flow from the speakers.

There's no reason to postpone so I say, "I'm sorry."

"For what?" she demands.

I dismiss her tone. "For not giving us a chance to talk and work things out."

She turns the radio off. "The truth is for Judgment Day. Until then, there's more than one side to every story. Some people have a bad habit of adding extra players, drama, and bullshit. So whenever you want my version, come to me. Comprende?"

I nod.

"Do you have anything else to say?" she asks.

"I'm tired of this."

She looks at me for specifics.

"I'm tired of the fallout," I explain. "A good time here, a little hope there, then the shit hits the fan. A good three months here, the fan. An okay seven months there, the fan. I ended us before it got to that point."

"So, why am I here?"

"Because I want this time to be different. I can be different."

"What am I supposed to do the next time you place an arbitrary expiration on our relationship?"

"Punch me in the arm," I suggest and laugh.

Her sharp look curbs my laughter.

We take our eyes off each other and I stare beyond the restaurant windows, noticing all the commotion inside, but never settling on anything particular.

After a long moment, one that allows me to consider all the words that influenced my twenty-four hours of self-loathing, she turns to me. "Can you deal with me? Everything I am? Everything I've done? If not, be mature enough to say it. I've already done the until-time-drives-us-apart thing and the until-you-make-a-big-enough-mistake thing. I need maturity and understanding. But most of all, I need a woman who's ready."

She wants to know whether I can pardon her indiscretions

and not let the weight of her blemished past contaminate a promising future. Do I recognize that the things that made her wrong yesterday are the same things that will keep her loyal moving forward? Am I ready to accept that my doubts about love have nothing to do with Deidra?

She stops gazing into the franchise and turns to me for an answer.

"Come home."

"Home?" she asks.

"Home," I assure her.

## 33

THE SIZZLE OF MEAT and clink of dishes function as a background melody while I scan the Cherry Street menu. I consider my options, though I always default to the same plate. Jacoby and Tasha kick off breakfast with the usual conversation. What have you done? Where have you been? Who's pissed you off? The latter leads to a cathartic bitch session with each of us competing for the spotlight until someone steals the moment with a captivating comment.

"My baby was stolen last night," Jacoby says. He's great at dwindling down my life-shattering problems to welcomed boo-boos. I peer out the window for his monstrous SUV. "I know who took it," he adds, drawing my attention back inside.

"Then it wasn't stolen," Tasha says.

"She took it without my permission."

Tasha and I haven't met *she*. We stopped meeting Jacoby's bed buddies about two years ago because it's a waste of time. The women come and go quickly.

"Did you call the police?" I ask.

"She can have it."

Come again? His prized SUV is a late-model custom edition purchased brand new with good credit and a hefty down payment from a reputable dealership. More importantly, he would never let someone have anything— especially not a vehicle. I know Jacoby is far from innocent, but like a good friend, I lend my support by verbalizing thirty seconds of expletives about *she* and the "stolen" vehicle. Jacoby isn't satisfied with the verbal assault until Tasha refers to the thief as "that no-good bitch." He starts to eat again. We turn our attention to Tasha's troubles.

She gripes about Sabrina, a friend with benefits not abiding by the rules of friends with benefits. "She called me while I was at work yesterday," Tasha whispers to sensationalize her news.

"For what?" Jacoby asks.

"Nothing. And the other night she didn't leave after you know what. I was too tired to make her leave so she slept over. And last night she called to ask if I would go to a concert with her and some friends 'cause they got an extra ticket."

"She's out of bounds," Jacoby states.

"What's wrong with that?" I ask. "I thought you wanted something serious."

"I do, but not with her."

"Then reel her in," Jacoby says. "Don't go to the concert. From here on out, fuck in her bed. And if you really wanna avoid this problem, don't sleep with old women. Old women always want more."

Such bad advice. "No," I speak up. I know Sabrina in passing. She's sweet, *mature*— not old— and has lots of potential. Tasha is reluctant to shift gears because Sabrina is a felon. This, however, has no bearing on her profession or lifestyle. "What's wrong with giving her a chance? She obviously wants more. Go to the concert and hang out with her sometimes. If there's no chemistry, at you've tried."

Looks like my words are bouncing around Tasha's head. She waits a few more seconds and then accepts my advice. Jacoby and I approached from two different angles, but we helped our friend find a happy medium.

"How's Deidra?" Jacoby asks to shift attention to me.

I cut my eyes at him. I know damn well he didn't ask out of concern. He dislikes being out of the loop. Tasha is the friend with seniority, and he hates when she keeps better tabs on me.

I sip apple juice and try to think of something that's bothering me. Really, I can only complain about sex deprivation. Deidra has been out-of-town for three days. She filled my tank before departing for Virginia. My fuel, however, has rapidly depleted and I'm persisting on a fourth tank of erotic memories. I tried to fill-up when Deidra called last night. I missed her and wanted more than her voice. I suggested we video chat.

So she hangs up the phone and calls me back on my tablet. I prop up the tablet on the nightstand as she teases me with her bulging cleavage. She recaps a part of her long day before the conversation turns naughty.

"Take off your pants," she commands. "Panties too." I slide my bottoms from my waist, happy to let air grace the tingling between my thighs. "Your turn."

"Shirt," I request.

Without hesitation, she draws her camisole over her head. She removes the clip from her bound hair and tosses her head left-to-right, hair concealing the bra straps across her shoulders. She never lets her hair down during foreplay. This new element of playfulness sends me over the edge. I move to the center of the bed to ensure my knees are within the video frame, spreading my legs so she can see my eagerness.

She's happy to watch me self-pleasure and I want to see her do the same. So she rests on her back, slowly moving her phone downward, the camera panning along the brown skin I love to tickle, resting on the pussy I'm missing and can't taste.

Her fingers start to dance on her clit and mine do too. But the more we tango, the less I view. "Baby," I say to stop us. She raises the phone to her face. "Get the phone out your hand."

She follows my order and searches for something to brace the phone while I stare at the ceiling of her room.

"I'll use my purse." She steadies the phone and asks whether the angle is acceptable.

Finally, I have a full view of her hips. "Perfect," I say. So she opens her legs and delights herself again. I firmly massage between my lips and begin to reach the point where I want to throw my head back and moan with my mouth open until her camera goes black.

"Baby," I say to garner her attention.

"Shit!"

She picks up the phone and attempts to prop it in a steadier position, but I tell her to forget it. The interruption douses my flame. We remain clothes free and video chat until we almost fall asleep.

The thought of how good Deidra looked with her hair down and legs wide open is arousing. I try to take my mind off that by eating a bit of food. Then I answer Jacoby. "She's good. Just working and getting ready for her daughter's graduation party."

"Oh, when's the graduation?" Tasha asks.

"Tomorrow."

"When did she get a job?" Jacoby inquires.

"Last year!" Tasha answers.

"She's stripping?" he asks.

I tilt my head.

"That's a legitimate question."

I exhale and stare at him until he apologizes.

"Okay. Who is she staying with up there?"

I place my fork aside. I shouldn't hold a fork while he's pressing my buttons. Deidra is staying with a friend, a detail only I need to know. "I could have sworn it was my turn to vent."

"You didn't say anything."

I turn toward Tasha to officially vent. "What do you do when your best friend only talks shit about your woman?"

"Pick up your fork," she says.

I do as instructed.

"That shit ain't funny," Jacoby complains.

"You're not funny!" I stab the fork in my hash browns instead of his hand. Then I take another bite to focus on something other than him and my frustration.

"Anyway," he says. "What's next for the kid? School? Job? Travel the world?"

"Memphis," Tasha informs him.

"For real?"

This is another small thing Jacoby should've known already. A few weeks ago, Deidra persuaded Shannon to attend UofM. Actually, 'persuade' is an understatement. Deidra bribed Shannon. Deidra mailed her daughter a box full of school paraphernalia and promised her a gently used car if she comes to Memphis. She even pulled me to the phone so I could brag to Shannon about how much I enjoyed attending UofM.

"She's gonna stay with you, too?" Jacoby asks.

I ignore his snide undertone. Though Shannon is welcome in our home, Deidra wants her to partake in the complete collegiate experience. "No, she won't be a commuter anytime soon."

Jacoby stops prying, but I'm still annoyed by his attitude. I'm happy with my life and the new additions. Why isn't he happy for me?

I'm putting mistakes and distrust behind me. I've moved on, and he's overdue for moving on, too.

# 34

DEIDRA AND I have full schedules for Memorial Day weekend. We don't have a lot of time to prepare for her daughter's visit or complete neglected chores. I've been occupied with volunteering for the hospital's telethon, and Deidra is constantly traveling throughout the tri-state area for promotional events, working ten to fourteen hour days. She clears just enough space in her Thursday afternoon to get Shannon from the airport to the house. After that, she's off to her next site. Now, I'm rushing home from work to clean up. I promised Deidra I'd have the guestroom ready, except I'm too late.

"Hey," Shannon says, staring at her phone. "My mom said she'll be back around seven."

"How was the flight?"

Her index finger repetitively swipes the screen of her phone. "Too long and too crowded."

I pull off my shoes. "You ready for tomorrow?"

Her finger freezes. She sits up on the couch and smiles. "Oh yeah! I already set my alarm and picked out my clothes."

Shannon flew down for UofM's annual Freshmen Friday, a day of touring and indoctrination for incoming students— a significant event for Shannon because it's her first campus visit.

"What do you look forward to the most?" I ask and sit on the loveseat.

"Seeing the dorms. You lived on campus, right?"

"Freshmen and sophomore year. By junior year I was bound to kill a roommate, so I moved off campus with my friend Tasha."

"Can you talk my mom into letting me live off campus next semester?"

"Ha! I doubt it."

She smiles at her effort.

"Well," I say, pausing to yawn. "I need to wash the sheets in the room."

"You don't have to. You look tired."

My eyes are heavy and I desperately want a nap, but the bedding hasn't been washed since Tasha occupied the guestroom after her home flooded. I've lived with Tasha before; God knows what happened in those sheets when Deidra and I weren't home.

I toss the first of two loads into the washer and clean the entire first level of the house. Shannon is sitting on the floor feverishly texting when I walk into the room with an armful of warm laundry. She giggles at an incoming text. I throw my armload into the wingback chair next to the bed. I pull the sheets from the entangled stack and she stops her fingers to help me stretch them across the mattress. Afterward, I grab the comforter from the chair. I accidentally sweep the nightstand with the bulky material, which knocks her purse to the floor.

I quickly retrieve the contents that slid out of her purse as she hurries to my side of the bed. She snatches a box out of my hand just as I realize it's an open box of condoms. "Please don't tell her you saw these," she says with worried eyes.

I smile a little. She thinks I'll tell Deidra about the open box. Hell, who am I to snitch? When I was seventeen I had sex whenever I could and sadly in too many God-awful places. At least she carries protection. I was too naïve about my sexuality at seventeen, trying to prove to my boyfriend that I loved him while also trying to prove to myself I could be straight by having sex without condoms. And I was stupid enough to trust him with the pullout method.

I know all too well what it's like being seventeen and sexing, luxuriating in risk and immaturity. But, I'm an adult now and feel I should at least say something to her. "You...you know how to use those?"

Her eyes remain downcast as she grabs a pillowcase. "I've had sex ed from school, church, my dad, and Aunt J."

"Juanita?" I stifle a laugh.

"The last time I was here, she threw that box in my lap and said 'don't be like me.' Then she said some stuff I don't ever wanna hear again."

"How thoughtful."

"Right. And your girlfriend made me practice on a banana when I turned fifteen, sixteen, *and* seventeen. And she gave me female condoms and dental dams and made me watch a bunch of YouTube videos. So, I'm good."

I grab the last pillowcase, wondering whether she plans to put any of that banana education to use in Memphis. Why else would she fly here with condoms in her purse? I resist asking and leave for my bedroom.

Deidra arrives by the time I'm finished with chores. I run her a bath and head downstairs so she can unwind. I rest my feet by lying on my favorite end of the couch to watch a new movie. Eventually, she comes downstairs to spend time with her daughter. Near the end of the movie, Deidra slides between the couch and me, wiggling her head until she finds a comfortable spot between my arm and shoulder. I'm glad she's next to me, but I can't miss the best part of this movie.

"Let's go upstairs," she whispers.

"Maybe later," I say, hoping she'll stay quiet for just a few more minutes.

We haven't been intimate in five days because Deidra refuses to have any form of sex during or immediately after her period. Apparently, she's ready now, though I'm hesitant to make love with Shannon in the house because her mother has a tendency to get too damn loud. Heavy breathing leads to moans that lead to profanity at the top of her lungs.

Deidra tries to convince me otherwise by moving my hand to her back and leisurely kissing my neck. The soothing tongue play forces my eyelids closed, causing me to miss a significant scene in the movie. I reach for the remote to rewind, but she grabs it from the ottoman and tosses it to the loveseat.

"This movie comes on every other day. Record it," she says and nibbles on my lips.

She knows the teasing kisses aren't enough to fully unleash my sexual urges. She pulls her maxi dress up and shifts her hips until sitting in my lap, pinning me between her thighs, treating me to slow, deep kisses.

"I'll use the new toy on you," she whispers on my lips.

I don't budge. She can wait until after this movie.

I try to sit up but she sinks into my lap, rubbing the core of her body along mine while teasing my mouth. Then her lips graze my ear as she moans. Her moans always get me. She knows a soft, lustful moan full of yearning will lure me to intimacy. I intently listen as the sweet sound and her gliding hips cast a spell on me, leading my hands down her back to softer, rounder areas of her body. I completely change my mind about seeing the rest of the movie tonight once my hands realize that her dress is the only barrier between her flesh and mine.

I'm on the verge of directing us off the couch until I hear footsteps in the living room. Deidra releases her lock on my lips and I let go of her ass. We adjust to appropriate positions.

"Where do you think you're going?" Deidra asks.

"Ma, we just talked about this. I told you someone was picking me up around ten."

"Don't start with that 'someone' crap, Shannon."

"Out with Phillip. We're friends. You know him. He used to live next door to Aunt J."

"Next door? Shannon, there's a different family in that house every year."

They go back and forth about the details of going out with Phillip. I hope Deidra will cut Shannon some slack, for both Shannon's sake and mine. I'm relieved when Deidra says, "Change clothes first."

"Why?" Shannon objects. "He's outside waiting on me."

"So? Only a fool would let you walk out at night dressed like that." I silently agree that the shorts are too small and tight as Shannon storms out the room.

I take Deidra's hand. "You ready?"

She pulls away like I'm interrupting her. I roll my eyes and rest against the couch. I'm so horny now that waiting only agitates me. Shannon marches back into the living room wearing black leggings. She stops in the center of the room for her mother's approval.

"Tell him to come inside," Deidra says.

"Mama, are you serious?"

"Now!"

Shannon looks at me as if I can save her at the last second. This battle is between her and her mom. When I cross my arms, she sighs and walks out the front door.

I cannot believe Deidra is being so difficult with her college-bound daughter. We were in the middle of something, now she's stalling. If she's this guarded with Shannon's social life now, Lord knows how she'll react once Shannon is a freshman.

Shannon returns with her date. He steps into the foyer, quickly speaks to us, and waits as Shannon closes the door behind them. His baggy hoodie, new J's, and shiny watch don't match the nervousness across his face.

Deidra approaches him. "I'm Ms. Jamison. How old are you, Phillip?"

"Eighteen."

"Is that your car outside?"

"Yes, ma'am."

"Do you have a license?"

"Yes, ma'am."

"Let me see it."

Shannon bites her lip as Phillip fidgets in his back pocket. The wallet slips from his fingers and she helps him pick it up. He passes his license over and hides his hands in the hoodie pocket. Poor young man, his hands are probably trembling. I wonder whether he's met Juanita. If so, he probably thinks Deidra is as crazy her sister. I shield my mouth to keep from laughing.

Deidra gives the license back. "Happy belated birthday. Where do you live?"

"On campus."

Shannon drops her head. Phillip is so timid I'm sure he didn't think twice about lying about his residence. By now, Shannon may be thinking the same thing I'm thinking: Deidra's ruining the night for all of us.

"Do you have roommates?"

"No, ma'am. I'm in a one-bedroom."

What an idiot! I stand up and walk to the kitchen. Now that Shannon's staying, I tune them out and pour myself a glass a wine. This merlot will be my only pleasure tonight. I take a long sip and refill the glass. Then I return the bottle to the refrigerator and step to the living room for more of the sad spectacle.

To my surprise, Mr. Goody-two-shoes is promising to have

Shannon back by 1:00. He opens the door and Shannon steps outside. Deidra locks the door behind them and smiles at me.

"You ready, love?" She walks over and removes the glass from my hand. "Your mouth won't have time for this."

"Who said I still wanna have sex?"

She laughs. "Drop the act and come on." She slaps my ass and pushes my hips toward the stairs.

"You know where they're going?" I ask.

"The movies. Why?"

"Aren't you worried about him doing to her what I'm about to do to you?"

"Baby, hush!" When we reach the top of the stairs, she covers her ears. "I don't need to hear that right now."

"Okay, but earlier Sha—"

Deidra pinches my lips shut. "Don't make me gag you with my panties."

Moments later, I hear a car pulling out the driveway as I'm lifting Deidra's dress above her shoulders. Instead of letting my conscience interrupt us, I focus on the succulent breasts before my face.

## 35

MAMA AND HER SIBLINGS host a family gathering over Memorial Day weekend every year. Too many first and second cousins and grandchildren are absent from year-to-year to call the poorly planned gathering a family reunion. After years of sparse attendance, I assumed someone would step-up and coordinate an official reunion with tee shirts, activities, and a firm itinerary. But taking the lead also means accepting the risk of expenses.

So, a fraction of the family meets at my parents' house for a Saturday of catching up and picture taking. And with Mama in charge of the menu, there's always enough food for seconds, thirds, and to-go plates. I purposely selected this occasion to introduce Deidra to my family. One of my closest aunts and cousins are beginning to think she's a figment of my imagination. Today, I can bring her into the fold without being the center of attention.

With Freshmen Friday completed, Deidra concentrates on the day ahead of us. She wakes me up at a quarter till six so I can come downstairs and keep her company.

"Why are we up so early?" I complain. "We're not leaving till noon."

"I can't go to your parents' house empty handed. I need time to make a sweet potato casserole and get myself dressed."

She makes breakfast first and places a plate of food in the microwave for Shannon. To stay alert, I gather the casserole ingredients and help peel the potatoes. By 8:00, I'm back in bed, happily wiggling my toes against the cool sheets as my head sinks into my beloved memory foam pillow. I intend to fall asleep and reclaim the two hours Deidra stole from me, except she won't stop talking. She goes in the bathroom to apply hair removal cream to her legs. Once her legs are coated, she steps into the closet for something to wear.

"Do your parents know about me?" She steps out of the closet for my answer.

She wants assurance that her presence is expected, so I oblige her, again. "We've been together for fifteen months, Dee. Of course they know about you."

"What do they know about me?"

"They know that you care about me and that I'm serious about you."

"How?"

"Because I didn't bring you around too early. Shit, I've broken a family record."

"Mmm…What number am I?"

My eyes pop open. "Does it matter?"

"You're damn right it matters. I don't want your folks looking at me like I'm girlfriend of this year."

I lift my head, grinning at what I now realize is nervous chatter. "I can't believe my confident, no-holds-barred girlfriend is worried about meeting my family."

She rolls her eyes and disappears into the closet. I hop out of bed and follow her, poking my fingers at her underarms until she giggles.

"What's the rush?" I ask. "It doesn't take three hours to get dressed. And you didn't have to make anything."

She wraps her arms around my neck. "Excuse me for wanting to make a good impression."

I show appreciation for her consideration with a kiss. She releases her embrace and darts to the bathroom to wash the cream away. I want to join her in the shower so I can fondle her wet breasts. But, there's nothing sexy about the smell of lye or loose hair and cream being flung all over the shower and my body. I'll just enjoy the few minutes I have alone to close my eyes in bed.

A quarter past eleven, we drop Shannon off at Juanita's house and pick up Tasha before heading to the gathering. Tasha tags along every year to eat and gossip with my cousins. When we arrive, Mama is standing at the stove with her two sisters, too focused on mixing spaghetti sauce to pay any attention to Deidra or me. She gives Deidra a fast "hey" and a weak "thank you" for the casserole. She's cooking, so we leave the kitchen.

This year's gathering is smaller than ever with about twenty-five people in attendance. I greet my family and introduce Deidra to those who show interest. Big Ma is ecstatic to see us. She pulls us to the dining room table to talk and show-off her new flea market capri set and jewelry. Then she complains that her daughters are too slow in the kitchen. "If I was in there," she brags, "y'all would have full stomachs by now."

She voices more complaints before complimenting Deidra on her pretty smile. "How your family doing?" she asks. "I pass by the funeral home every Sunday on my way to church. Y'all keep the grounds so nice and neat."

How does my grandmother know that Deidra is kin to the Carter dynasty? I'm two seconds from questioning her when the obvious hits me. Her chattiness makes it easy to forget her dementia. "Big Ma, this is Deidra… not Kayla."

"Okay, baby," she responds. "Let me go in this kitchen and see if they need my help."

Big Ma shuffles along and I apologize. "Her mind comes and goes."

"That's okay. I guess that ex of yours made a lasting impression, huh?"

"Anyway, come with me."

Deidra follows me to the backyard to meet Daddy. He's sitting down but managing the grill, drinking beer with my uncle and male cousins. He gives us welcoming hugs and pulls up two additional chairs. Then he turns his attention to Deidra. "Put a ring on it, quick," he says.

"Daddy!" I say as everyone in earshot laughs.

"This young lady," he says, pointing with the bottle, "has made me a believer. She's a keeper." He tips the bottle to me. "But I can't expect you to make the first move."

"Amen," Deidra says.

I'm well aware that a little over a year ago, I was content with being single— that I abandoned the possibility of love. But he doesn't have to slap the past in my face or embarrass me before multiple people.

I could probably stand a few more of his playful remarks if my whorish second cousin wasn't salivating over Deidra. He's standing around, inching his way closer to where we're seated. "Okay, Daddy," I say and escort us away.

In the house, I part ways with her and head to the kitchen to snitch on Daddy. I know my parents well, so retaliation is easy. "Mama, your husband is way past his limit."

"I'll take care of it." She drops her oven mitten and marches to the backyard.

Satisfied, I join Deidra, Tasha, Shonda, and two more of my cousins in the living room for a round of margaritas until the food is ready. I sit quietly— unhappy about the way this first meeting has already panned out— as they dish about coworkers, friends, and family. They're telling so much of other people's business that Shonda and Deidra find out they have a mutual friend.

"How do you know her?" Shonda asks.

"We went to high school together," Deidra explains. "But she wasn't trans back then."

"Nia, you remember Marsha when she was Marshall?"

"Mm-hmm," I answer and sip.

"What's wrong with you?" my other cousin asks.

"Girl," Deidra says, "she's mad because your grandmother thinks I'm Kayla."

My cousin laughs. "Ooh, I couldn't stand her high-yellow, uppity ass! That's what you get for paradin' Kayla 'round here like she was the best thing since sliced bread. Now our old loo-ny-ass grandmother is gone keep rubbin' her in yo' face. Thank God you dropped her and upgraded 'cause ain't nothin' worse than a black bimbo ruinin' your day. Damn, I hate I missed that conversation."

My cousin and I haven't shared an amicable relationship since middle school. I haven't been in the mood for her big mouth for over fifteen years, and I surely won't build a tolerance for it today. I head to the bathroom to avoid confrontation. If she has anything else to say about the matter, she is free to say it behind my back.

I didn't think my time here could get any worse until we gather to eat. Mama forgets to place Deidra's sweet potato casserole with the spread.

"I thought it was dessert," Mama says in her own defense.

"What? Everyone who lives on this side of the Mason-Dixon Line knows that sweet potato casserole is a versatile dish." I disregard her sudden ignorance and warm up the casserole while everyone else fixes plates and begins to eat.

I can't pinpoint everyone that ate some of the casserole by the time we're done eating, but I know for sure Mama didn't taste one bite of it. And if I collected ten cents for every cold look she has shot Deidra since we walked in the house, I would have an extra $1.70 in my wallet. I hold my tongue, though. I don't want to shed light on something Deidra probably hasn't noticed.

When Mama walks toward her bedroom I follow her. She rests in her lounger and takes the clip off her salt and pepper hair. She removes her flats and says, "Grab my house shoes."

"Did you try the casserole?"

"You know I don't experiment with food."

"Mama, I'm too old for this."

She narrows her eyes.

"You know what I'm talking about," I say. "I'm too old for you to ignore who I am. I'm too old for you to ignore my relationship. And I'm definitely too old to go through this with you year after year."

She exhales and looks at the dresser. Our framed family photograph hasn't departed the left corner since it was taken in 1998. My brother and I are standing behind our seated parents. We're color coordinated. Red tops, dark bottoms. Smiling. Together. That's the last year we were truly a family.

"What do you want from me besides the life and love I tried my hardest to give you?" Mama asks.

"I want you to act your age."

"Hold up! Don't get beside yourself, Nia. I'm the mother."

"Then act like it." If Mama thinks I'm excusing her behavior for the sake of maternal privilege, she's wrong. "I don't have room in my life for people who don't respect who I am or who I love. I know that sounds harsh, but it's a truth I live by."

Mama drops her head for a moment. "Why does it have to be all or nothing with you?"

"That's the way you raised me," I remind her and hand over the house shoes.

Mama stays clear of us for the next hour or so but makes an

effort to say goodbye before we leave. "It was good to meet you, Deidra."

"You too, Mrs. Ellis. The food was delicious. Thanks for cooking. I know it's exhausting."

Mama leans back on her heels as surprise surfaces on her face. "I can't remember the last time somebody stood in my house and thanked me for cooking."

"Did you like the sweet potato casserole? It was my first time making it."

"It was good," Mama says with a smile. "And the more you make it, the better it will get."

Mama isn't in the running for parent of the year, but at least she ends our visit with a cordial goodbye to Deidra.

Once home, I kick off my sandals and fall to the bed as Deidra searches her iTunes playlists. She selects a Neo Soul artist and stretches across the bed with me. We could have gone out with Tasha and my cousins, but I didn't feel up to more interaction with people. Thankfully, I have a girlfriend who doesn't mind staying home on a Saturday evening to keep me company.

She strokes my back for a while and says, "It's over."

"Praise God."

"Your mom was throwing some deep, dry shade my way."

"So you noticed?"

"Am I blind? Were your exes that bad?"

"It's not them… or you. My mom just struggles with my sexuality. She even blames Jacoby for turning me lesbian."

"Was the sex that bad?"

I laugh.

"You don't disappoint in the bedroom," she says. "He knows this, and he's jealous that I get to have every bit of you to myself."

"Ugh! That's history. You know I don't wanna talk about sex with Jacoby."

"You don't want to admit that he misses that pus—"

"Baby!"

"Okay. But seriously, he's in love with you, Nia. That's why he's always attacking me."

"That's not true," I counter.

"What's not true? That he's always attacking me, or that he's in love with you?"

"We've never had those kinds of feelings for each other."

"Are you sure?"

"I'm positive."

She lifts an eyebrow. "Anyway, what's the root of your mom's struggle? Religion?"

"Not really. She's still holding on to the fiancé-wedding-child-picket fence-life she envisioned for me."

"A mother should want more than a hetero fantasy for her child. I can testify that the reality of that fantasy is full of deception and displeasure. I'd never want that for Shannon. I'd never want her to live parts of my life. A mother should hope that her daughter can live the majority of her days in happiness, no matter who she's with. In this world, that's a lot to ask."

We fall quiet and let an orgy of drums, horns, and guitars titillate our voyeuristic ears. The sounds weaken my defenses. I know Deidra's feeling the same way when she wiggles closer to hold my hand. The moment is a seamless prelude to lovemaking, but I want more than her body. I crave her emotionally. So I open my mouth after three songs to ask, "Why did you stay with him so long?"

Her eyes shift to the wall. "When I got pregnant, I didn't expect to be a single mother. I was in love... and hopeful. But Shannon's father— and I use that word lightly— decided in my last trimester that he could delete us from his life. I haven't seen or heard from him since he made his decision. I met Eric when

Shannon was two weeks old and he's been her father ever since.

"By that point, I was sick of my dad and grandma shuffling me back and forth year after year. I didn't want my baby to experience that. I wanted a better life for her. I knew Eric would do whatever he could to give us everything we needed and more if I legally committed to him. So, the day after my eighteenth birthday, I married him. The next day, he joined the Navy. We left Memphis and I acted like I was happy with him for thirteen more years because I believed I owed him a fair share of my life for taking care of us." She pauses and rubs her eyes. "Before I left with him, I had never traveled past Memphis or either side of Mississippi. Relocating means a lot to a girl with nothing but a baby. Things were good at first, but a woman should never feel indebted to a man... It goes against the natural order of things."

I reflect on her words. They give insight into the woman she was with him, as well as the woman I've fallen in love with. I'd never hold her love hostage. I want her to love me according to her terms— not obligation.

Another song plays before I ask, "Does Shannon know?"

"No," she whispers.

God. I'm speechless.

We listen to a song with lovesick lyrics before she speaks again. "I also stayed with him because my idea of motherhood was doing everything opposite of Pat. I had to give Shannon everything Pat never gave me. I had to raise her and love her and provide her with a two-parent household and stable family, his family. I tried so hard not to be like Pat that I lost myself. And whenever I thought about her living a happy life when I was sometimes miserable, I hated her.

"You know, when Pat called and told me about her diagnosis, I smiled. I literally smiled. And then I thought 'payback.' She got cancer because she didn't raise me. She got breast cancer because those are the same breasts that should have nourished me. My thoughts were crazy because I couldn't think past the anger. I can laugh about it now, but in the moment, it drove me temporarily insane."

She exhales and I do too. She drops her head on her arm and allows the music to soothe her spirit. A few minutes later, she says, "Do you think Pat used you?"

I close my eyes for a moment. It's my turn to purge. The possibility has crossed my mind a few times. I refused to confront it until now. "The Pat I knew wasn't neglectful or selfish. But the more I get to know you, the more I think that she exploited our friendship. I don't feel like it was beyond our friendship for her to be open with me. So I don't understand why she didn't tell me about you."

"If Pat had told you about me, she wouldn't have been able to use you as a substitute."

I let go of her hand. Her words bother me, but what can I do about it?

She places her arm across my stomach, staring in my eyes to make me accept the likelihood of 'substitute.' "You're the daughter I never had the chance to be," she says.

The weight of her secret, the weight of the truth, and the weight of my role in Pat's life are overbearing. So I bring Deidra's lips to mine to initiate what we're both prepared for; something we control and desire; something no one else influences or uses. Lovemaking to lustful tunes eases the burden of past troubles and confirms everything I hope for in our future.

# 36

I EASE OUT of bed just after 6:00, before Deidra drifts out of her sleep. Early morning rising brings out the grump in me. Cooking in the morning seems like more of a chore than a necessity. I, however, keep the annoyances at bay because today is a special day. It's Deidra's second birthday with me.

She comes downstairs to fresh-cut fruit and hot food that suits her pescetarian diet. Her birthday begins with a long hug and sweet kiss. As she eats, I nibble.

"What do you want for your birthday, baby?" I've asked this question for eleven consecutive days. Last year, I treated her to a weekend of pampering in Atlanta. This year, she's stubborn.

"This is more than enough."

"This is something I wanted to do for you. What do you want for yourself?"

She sighs and pushes her finished plate away. "I appreciate this, Nia, but August second is not significant to me. It only reminds me of consolation gifts and broken promises from you know who."

"Well, today is like any other Saturday. What do you wanna do? Where do you wanna go?"

She smiles. Something I said delights her ears. "You can take me to Mississippi."

"You want me to meet your dad?"

"No time's better than the present."

I'm not excited about going down to good-ole Mississippi and being in the middle of nowhere. But now that I have a working understanding of her family history, I want to meet her father. Her father and grandmother are really the only family members I haven't met.

As Deidra drives south, I recall the day she opened the lid on the Rosses. It was last year on a late September day. The entire summer, we shared walks along the riverfront. We attended indie concerts and community fests. Deidra drew energy from being out and about in the world— a trait of a Leo— and I loved being with her.

Every weekend, she treated me to movies and restaurants I would have never considered. I enjoyed sci-fi and Vietnamese more than I had expected. She switched my dial to a mode of continuous anticipation. The more our interactions diversified, the thinner her armor became, exposing me to her infectious strength. She became more complete. The highlight of my day. And she started to trust me. She placed trust in my words, intentions, and presence.

My past relationships never embodied a welcoming dependence. Those wasted times were like business relationships with emphasis on cash flow and material resources. Deidra has challenged me to build a courtship on raw desires.

Our desire for emotional intimacy flourished that rainy September day. After catching a midnight movie, I wanted to culminate the night between her legs. She had other plans.

We relaxed in bed with tangled limbs as a single lavender candle lit our faces. "I had a good time." Though dim in the bedroom, her eyes beamed. "You're a fresh breath of air," she said, smiling. "My grandma's White."

I untangled our arms and propped myself up on an elbow. Given that we had watched a historical drama set in the South, saturated with horrific race-relation scenes, her statement didn't really strike me as odd. In true Deidra-style, however, she spared details about her family until an offbeat moment. Maybe the influence of the movie and the shadows in the room made it easier for her to venture into her grandmother's life.

I settled down and said, "Okay."

"My grandmother's parents were working-class, law-abiding, non-discriminating White folks, until their unwed eighteen-year-old daughter gave birth to a half-black baby in Mississippi in the mid-sixties. No surprise, the baby daddy mysteriously vanished and she was disowned. She ran to the nearest city and landed a job at the oh-so-wonderful Carter Funeral Home, the cornerstone of the community.

"She became their good-White-folk poster child until she hooked up with the wrong man and tried to silence her demons with prescription narcotics. When she was clean, she worked.

"Anyway, to make a long story short, my folks stayed connected with the Carters. My dad was a mischievous, poor mixed boy with a trashy mother. So they let him work odd jobs after school. But all hell broke lose when he became sweet on Pat and got her pregnant. I guess your 'Mama C' was too conservative to let Pat have an abortion. A few years ago, my dad drank too much whiskey and told me that they paid him and my grandmother to take me from the hospital and disappear. He said Cora wouldn't touch me. That's why they left Memphis and moved back to Mississippi." She exhales. "He didn't mean any harm, but I wish he would've kept that information private. That's all I really know about what happened. The rest is bad history."

I gently traced her face. "There's nothing bad about you."

She smiled and pulled me closer. Her lips ushered a passionate night of intimacy.

Today, it will be satisfying to pair a face with James Ross;

the young man Pat told me she once loved but could never marry.

~ * ~

Deidra exits the interstate onto a highway that leads into the belly of the Deep South. The two-lane stretch cuts through acres of green crops that transition to The Magnolia State's legacy. Long rows of white cotton bolls cover the land as far as my eyes can see. About four miles into the fluffy sea, the fields recede to grassy plains. As we approach the town, a short wooden sign welcomes us to a turn of the twentieth-century municipality with a whopping population of 1,202 people.

Deidra slows the car and turns onto a road leading to civilization. We pass a high school with a colossal gymnasium, a dollar store, and a four-pump gas station. She turns left at the gas station and heads down Main Street. The deserted business district showcases old storefronts suitable for the set of a low-budget zombie movie. At the four-way stop, we turn right onto a residential street lined with poverty. Shotgun houses and trailers rest on square plots and cylinder block foundations. Senior citizens relax under porches and shade trees. They wave as we drive by. The street dead-ends into a church parking lot. She drives through the lot and veers into the grass, following tire tracks that lead to a house in the distance. She pulls into a gravel driveway and parks beside a late-model Cadillac. The luxury sedan looks odd beside a decrepit shack.

We get out and step onto a porch adorned with chipped blue paint and dozens of cigarette butts. Seconds after Deidra knocks, her father unlatches the screen door. He greets me and holds the faded door open as we enter a room with a partial ceiling and mismatched furnishings. Molded dry wall, cigarette smoke, and natural gas irritate my nose as we cross linoleum that squeaks and slopes along the interior.

Her father grabs a newspaper off the couch and says, "Have a seat."

I sit with Deidra on my left, trying my best to avoid the stain on my right, also trying my best not to stare at the roach creeping up the dusty wall behind her father's head. He sits in the recliner and reduces the volume on the tube television set so he can talk with less distraction.

I sit small, keeping an eye on the surroundings, particularly my feet, barely listening to their conversation, wondering how long this visit will last.

"Where's Nana?"

"Who knows?" he replies.

"What woman is sending you flowers?"

I've been so focused on the critter invasion that I didn't notice the bouquet of pink roses and lilies on the end table beside Deidra.

"My women know better than to be sending me flowers. They for you."

"You wait until I'm thirty-three to acknowledge my birthday with a gift?"

He winks at me as Deidra pulls the enclosure card from the arrangement.

With my attention no longer divided, I notice his curly hair and pale skin. He's light, bright, and damn-near white as some folks say. Remnants of handsome youthfulness linger in his face. And despite missing a great deal of teeth, he enunciates well.

Whatever Deidra read on the card erases her surprise. She turns it face down and tucks it in her purse. She changes the topic of conversation and I go on watch again.

"Don't mind the house," he says, catching me staring at the

rat droppings in the corner. My eyes move from the poop to him. "Ain't nothin' but a mirage. This a kingdom."

I nod and grin to mask my discomfort. I glance at the TV show and ask, "Are you a fan of reality court shows?"

"Faithful," he says and tells me all about the judges on the TV circuit. "They got some new blood comin' up, but one thang ain't changed. All the black judges got white bailiffs, and all the white judges got black ones. Only on TV. That shit don't happen in M'ssippi...Y'all want something to eat? Got some neck bones and greens."

"Jimmy," Deidra says. "We didn't drive down here to play sleep-and-eat with you."

He laughs and stands from the recliner. His faded shirt and worn jeans don't match his brand new sneakers.

As soon as he exits the room, I whisper, "Does he live here? This place is inhabitable."

"Just enough to claim residence."

"And what did he mean by kingdom?"

"He meant the land. It's worth thousands."

"Millions!" her day says.

I close my mouth and she rolls her eyes in disagreement.

Her father returns with a plate and explains to me, "A Jap'nese corporation wanna build a distribution center right here. Me and Mama inherited this land and they can have it for a million a acre...This good." He points to the food with his fork. "Y'all sure y'all don't want none?"

"No, thanks," I say.

"You know I don't eat meat," Deidra replies.

He swallows a bite. "Ever since yo' Mama died, you been on a health kick."

"I have to be. I'm trying to live way past forty-eight."

I look at her, astonished that her "Mama" is the basis of her restricted diet.

"Then stop smokin'," he says. He looks at me. "All them cigarettes on the porch ain't mine." His eyes return to her. "If you got cancer in yo' genes, you don't need nothin' flarin' it up."

I agree. "Tell her again."

"Time to go," Deidra says, rising to her feet. "I don't need my daddy and my woman tag-teaming me."

I say goodbye and follow her out the door. "What about the flowers?"

"Leave them. They're the nicest thing in that house now that we're gone."

We go home and opt for a lazy day, lounging in socks and pajama pants. Bras, but no pajama tops. We nap for hours and order delivery. With the exception of birthday wishes received by texts and phone calls, this is an ordinary day for Deidra. One birthday wish, however, sticks out like a sore thumb. It isn't the hour-long conversation with her daughter or the quick chats with her sister or friends. It's the card in her purse. The card has pestered my curiosity since we left Mississippi.

I wait until nightfall when Deidra showers to sneak into her purse. I pull the card from the side of her wallet. I can't believe what this shit says. *I miss you like crazy. Happy Birthday.* The card is signed with a single letter: *E.*

I put the card back the way I found it and return to the bedroom as if I never left.

Seconds after I sit on the bed, Deidra comes out the bathroom wearing an untied robe. She sits in my lap, her warmth and sweet-smelling skin toying with my senses. She caresses my arm and waist, expecting her sensual touch to arouse me to the point that I'll touch her in return. Instead, I push her thighs from my lap to the comforter.

"I thought you told him that you're in a relationship."

She closes her robe and stares into my eyes to access my thoughts. "I did. The flowers are meaningless."

"Nothing's meaningless about a man who's still vying for his wife's affection."

I don't know him or what he's capable of doing. My only means of protection is the distance that separates us. We don't talk about her husband. The only time he's somewhat mentioned these days are during conversations about Shannon. And those mentions are rare. He doesn't exist in our world, but I need clarification. "How far would he go for you?"

"I don't know."

Her answer seems more safe than honest.

"I know you're stalling on a divorce because of Shannon," I say, "but you need to set the record straight with him. This is *my* territory."

~ * ~

I wake up early to get dressed for church because I promised to join Mama for Friends and Family Day. Deidra is awake but lying in bed. We're both surprised when her phone rings because no one ever calls this early on Sunday. The call must be important. I hope nothing's wrong with Shannon.

When Deidra rolls her eyes, I know the call isn't urgent. She sighs out of frustration with the caller. She presses a button to lower the volume and conceal the caller's identity, but it's too late. The tenor voice is a dead giveaway. Less than twenty-four hours have transpired since she received his flowers of yearning, and now he's following up with a phone call. Any other time he just texts.

Deidra exchanges pleasantries. "Yes...I'm fine...You?"

I open my jewelry box for a pair of earrings, but I keep my

eyes on her through the dresser mirror. I should've known this would happen. After all, it's their anniversary. Makes me wonder whether he called last year while we were in Atlanta. Did she have flowers in Mississippi when we returned from that trip? Whatever the case, too much time has passed. He doesn't care about boundaries. Deidra isn't supposed to be here with *me*.

"Eric, what do you want? This better be about Shannon." They go back and forth, her voice growing louder with each passing second. "What did you just say to me?" She sits up and cuts him off. "Don't ever threaten me!"

He yells in response.

"And what the hell are you going to do when you get here?" she fires back. "Shoot her?"

He yells again.

"No," she argues. "Keep your ass in Virginia and take care of Shannon. *She's* your priority. She'll be moving here in three weeks, and then I'm absolutely done with you."

She ends the call and walks into the bathroom, slamming the door behind herself. I wish she had de-escalated the heated exchange before hanging up on him. The last thing I need is for her fuming husband to come to Tennessee to snatch her up, harming me in the process.

I place the backs on my earrings and knock on the bathroom door. She opens and says, "You're leaving?" Her voice and face are relaxed, as if the argument didn't happen.

"Do I need to flee the country?"

She smiles to turn off my alarm. "He's all bark, no bite. You don't have anything to worry about, baby."

Another safe answer.

She comes out the bathroom and straightens the collar of my suit jacket. I haven't been to church in nearly a year. This will be the opportune visit to pray for safety.

# 37

AROUND 8:00, I awake and drag my feet downstairs, hoping Deidra has prepared breakfast as she does most Saturday mornings. I'm sleepy and hungry, but no tasty aromas waft from the kitchen. She quickly hugs me and goes back to the foyer. I curl on the couch to watch her lift and stoop and move about preparing for move-in day. She's been antsy all week, bursting with joy and anticipation of Shannon's arrival. She stacks a few boxes and organizes several bags of groceries.

"How do I look?" she asks.

I inspect her from head to toe. This is my first time seeing her in a tee, boot-cut jeans, and baseball cap. She never dresses this casually.

"I can't go to campus looking like Shannon's friend. I'm going for a cute big sister look." She looks at me for a response.

"You landed on soccer mom."

She smirks and turns her attention to the task at hand.

I'm happy for Deidra. She's ecstatic about Shannon living

in her proximity again. No more texting or phone and video calling to keep them connected. They'll have the luxury of seeing each other face to face. "What are you gonna do when Shannon is too busy for you?"

"What do you mean?"

"She's a freshman. She'll have a demanding social life. Parties, friends, step shows, events, organizations, maybe a campus job. She's moving to a lively city. She'll find something to do every weekend."

Deidra empties her hands of canned vegetables and squints at me. She's open to welcoming Shannon into adulthood, but she isn't prepared for the realities of college. Mommy time will be the last thing on Shannon's mind.

"Your baby will be somebody else's baby by the end of next month," I add.

She picks up a roll of paper towels and throws it at me.

After I hurl the roll back, Deidra goes into the kitchen to raid the refrigerator and cabinets for more groceries. She's already confiscated all four of the mini orange juices I purchased two days ago, in addition to my unopened bag of black bean tortilla chips. I don't mind though. Her move-in day jitters amuse me.

I watch Deidra stuff more of our food into grocery bags. She's completely disregarding Shannon's mandatory meal plan. My mother didn't put forth half of this effort when I went to college. She drove me to the dorm and left within the hour. I smile when Deidra unpacks the groceries, rearranging the food until each bag stands neatly upright.

"Do you really think she'll be too busy for me?" she asks, filling the last bag.

From what I was told, Deidra barely graduated from high school, and college wasn't an option. Her focus was marriage and motherhood. *A Different World* shaped her ideas about collegiate life. Sadly, the majority of her paternal family hasn't accomplished anything beyond a low-paying job or felony. This is new to her and she trusts my first-hand experience. "She's got a place to live, an arsenal of food, and a shit-load of options to keep her occupied every day."

Deidra leaves the foyer and joins me on the couch, resting her head on my shoulder.

"I didn't mean to dampen your spirits."

She accepts a consoling kiss on the forehead and takes my hand. "It'll wear off," she says.

And it does. As soon as her phone rings, she leaves the comfort of my shoulder and reverts to move-in mode. From the call I can tell that Shannon has reached the metro area. Soon, Deidra will remove dorm room essentials from the foyer, ushering her daughter to the starting line of a new journey.

When Shannon steps inside, her mom gives her a moment to chat and admire her new belongings before handing her an item to carry— starting with the cool ass storage cubby I purchased as a graduation present. I want to take things outside, too, but I park myself on the loveseat to prevent crossing paths with Shannon's dad. I see him through the blinds leaning against his truck, waiting for something to load. For Shannon's sake, I will avoid him.

I really didn't want him to come by here. Deidra has coached and coaxed me all week in preparation of his arrival. "He's going to swing by here and pick up Shannon's stuff. You don't have to come out and he won't come in." And yesterday, "I won't have time to talk to him. As soon as Shannon's unpacked, we're parting ways." She actually prefers that I participate. She talked for days about how she wanted the weekend to unfold: father, mother, and mother's lover happily launching daughter together.

"Are you sure you don't want to come to campus after orientation?" Deidra asks once the foyer is clear.

I'm fond of Shannon and appreciate Deidra's desire to have me by her side, but I'm not open to being around her husband— no matter how estranged they are. I walk to the door, offering a hug before saying, "You can tell me all about it later."

She accepts my decision and leaves.

I don't look forward to spending the day at home by myself so I call Tasha to hang out. She's single, bored, and free— three reasons to join me for retail therapy. I pick her up and we head to the mall to curb my craving for China Express. Tasha craves eye candy.

"This is the best time to go to the mall," she says. "Mature women with jobs shop early."

# 38

TASHA LEADS THE WAY, skipping the stores with low-price points, dipping into the ones with clothing and accessories for professional women. I follow her, combing through racks for blouses and slacks that catch my eye. She waits while I purchase a low-cut top that will nicely accentuate Deidra's cleavage. Then off we go to Victoria's Secret. We haven't even crossed the threshold when Tasha spots a cutie checking out panties. She goes inside and I scan the walkway for the nearest bench.

I sit beside a senior citizen reading the city newspaper and text Deidra for an update. *Still at orientation* she replies. She wants to skip the activities and presentations and get on to dorm room decorating. I text back *Patience baby patience.*

Tasha sought teddies and ladies for a shorter period than expected. Either something went really right or really wrong. I hand over her shopping bags and ask, "What's the verdict?"

"I'll call her, but I'm tired of closeted bitches. I mean damn, am I not charming?"

"Very," I answer, hoping we're finally making our way to the food court. I can't imagine resorting to prowling the mall for potential dating material. "Maybe you're trying too hard. Some things should happen naturally."

She stops walking and glares at me. "You ain't never had to find somebody to date. You just get the girl who's already connected to you. We all can't find love at a damn funeral."

"Actually, it was Chuck E. Cheese's."

"Who cares?"

I sympathize with her frustrations. She has explored traditional courting, internet hookups, and blind dating. Flawless makeup, fashionable outfits, and dating decorum pan out to nothing more than one-night stands or texting buddies. And here I am in a solid relationship with a married woman while Tasha can't land anyone gay or single.

I proceed to the food court and she follows. "You have to be content with being alone. The universe will bring you someone when you least expect it," I encourage her, speaking personally. "Bad experiences can create low expectations, but you're not cursed. Things will change."

"Shut up!" she says. "You sound like a fucking horoscope."

She's closed off, so I seal my lips and step into the China Express line. I give her a minute to herself while thinking about my own experiences.

I know all too well about low expectations with relationships. Those initial butterflies I felt when dating always turned into foul creatures that devoured the possibility of a functional relationship. Because of those experiences, I'm addicted to failure. But I strive hard for sobriety. I don't want skepticism to cause me to relapse with Deidra.

After eating, we head to the car. Deidra calls with an update as we're leaving the mall parking lot. "This apartment is filthy," she says. "I cannot have Shannon in this nasty-ass room. She'll be in the hospital again."

"Is there mold?"

"That, rust, dust, and mustiness. We're not moving one thing in here until it's clean, but I need my crate." Her trusted cleaning supplies are in the milk crate in the laundry room. "It'll take almost an hour to drive home and back."

I listen, paying more attention to merging onto a crowded expressway.

"Anyway, where are you?" she asks.

"Out, shopping with Tasha."

"Well, you can run home and bring it to me?" The question sounds more like a demand than a favor. It also seems like a last-ditch effort to lure me to campus until she says, "Can you meet me halfway?"

Though that is a much better option, my conscience nudges me. Why should Deidra waste time with meeting me when I have an open schedule? This day will only happen once in her lifetime. I need to help eliminate the challenges and make the day memorable.

The matter is settled. I'll run home and deliver the crate.

~ * ~

The interior campus streets are jam-packed and slow moving with no access to street parking near Shannon's dorm complex. The traffic officers direct all incoming cars to the parking garage, which is annoying because I only have one thing to deliver and will have to travel by foot on a humid August day. Tasha stays in the car with the air and music blasting.

Nostalgia hits me as I walk from the garage to the dorms. The engraved quotes in the sidewalk, manicured landscapes, charming redbrick buildings, and palpable energy are so familiar. I miss the fervor and newness of freshman year— a time when real-world responsibilities and complicated relationships were non-existent.

Shannon's apartment is three blocks from the garage. I head west in search of DOOR 212, stopping shy of DOOR 208. I sit the crate on the ground to call Deidra. At this distance, I can avoid the heart of activity and still see her walk out the second-floor apartment. Shannon steps outside and waves at me as Deidra proceeds down the stairs.

"You didn't have to walk over here," she says.

"I don't mind. How's it going?"

"Slow."

There's no need to postpone progress, especially after the door opens and Shannon's father strolls outside. I grab the crate and hand it to Deidra.

"No goodbye kiss?" she asks. I move forward like her lips are magnetic, relishing the moment to remind him that Deidra's with me. As people pass with armloads and dollies, we share a nose-touching kiss and separate. "I'm sure Shannon didn't like it either." We laugh and kiss again, like first-year students craving attention and reputations.

I walk out of the complex feeling like I've relived a moment of freshman year. I'm glad that I pushed my reservations aside to make the delivery. The smile on Deidra's face was definitely worth it. Students, parents, volunteers, and staff stroll along the sidewalks, feeding my positive energy.

I stop at the corner with a swarm of strangers, waiting for the traffic officer to direct our crossing. My eyes wander in all directions, not expecting to see Deidra's husband in the distance. Where is he going? With two blocks to go, I glance back to gauge whether he's following me. At first glance he's there. The second time I check, nothing.

In the garage, I bypass the group huddled at the elevator and head to the stairs. Footsteps and voices trail me, but no voices that I recognize. It's unlikely that I've parked on the same level as him given my late arrival. I exit the stairwell on level four and hesitate, awaiting memory and sense of direction to kick in. When I step forward, a deep voice shouts my name.

Of course I know who it is. I look back to survey the distance between us. He's quickly approaching me, so I stop walking. I have to keep my eyes on him. I keep my stance loose in case I need to sprint in the opposite direction. He stops two cars away, though he's close enough to charge forward and grab me.

It's sunny out, though the shadows of the garage are deceiving. I have my phone, but by the time I attempt to make a call, he'll snatch it away. Tasha had the music so loud when I left the car I doubt she'll hear my muffled screams. No one else has entered or exited this level of the garage since he stopped me. I have no idea whether the security camera by the elevator is under surveillance.

Before I let these thoughts trigger any degree of panic, I should assess this situation. "Are you parked on this level?" I need to know whether his presence is coincidental or deliberate.

"I'm on two."

"Then what do you want?"

He steps forward and I step backward. I rub my pants pockets, realizing they're empty. The only thing I can use to defend myself is more distance.

"You're a major player in Shannon's life now," he says. "We should at least meet."

"For what? I'll never see you again."

He stares at me hard. "Listen, I know my wife. I know why she went to Pat's funeral. Payback. And I know why she's bumping pussies now. Payback. You actually think she switched teams for you?"

He flashes his million-dollar smile, a complement to his tall, dark, chiseled stature. He knows he's a catch. He takes a step closer. Then he squares his shoulders, bringing his hands together in front of his crotch. Cocky.

"I'm still her refuge," he says. "Don't forget, not too long ago, Deidra was on her back with her legs around my waist, singing me praises and begging me to go deeper."

That's a hit below the belt, but I don't flinch.

"She's a rebel with a short-lived cause," he adds. "When the dust settles, she'll find her way home."

The animosity is intense, but I'm over his posture and intimidation. From what he's said, I know exactly what I'm dealing with: a man with a bruised ego. There's only one thing left for me to say. "How true, Eric. Tell Deidra I'll see her later."

# 39

LATELY, MY COMMUNICATION with Jacoby has consisted of lengthy texts and video messages. We haven't watched *SVU* in months. We see each other in passing at work and rarely have lunch together anymore. So I'm not surprised when he calls after work to suggest we get a bite to eat. We haven't talked in days.

Deidra is lying in my lap watching the evening news. I place my free hand on her arm. "I'm not alone," I inform him.

"Okay. She gotta eat, too," he says.

Is this a roundabout invitation? Skeptical, I ask, "Are you sober, Jacoby?"

He chuckles. "I'm serious. There's a new Mexican restaurant not too far from you."

I've already been there with Deidra. The food doesn't warrant a return visit. "Nah, what about that place down the street from you?"

"Cool. They got good wings."

As soon as I end the phone call, Deidra says, "You sure you want me there? You can bring me something back. I don't need him spoiling my day."

"It's fine. Let's get out the house." Though I enjoy lounging in undergarments for extended periods of time, I'm restless now. I need to put on a little makeup, leave home, and interact in a different space. Last week, Jacoby agreed to be cordial with Deidra on a full-time basis. So I expect him to dine in good spirits.

~ * ~

At the restaurant, there are no slick comments as we're escorted to the table. No eye rolling as we order. No dismissive hand gestures as we eat and talk. Jacoby is loquacious as usual. He doesn't use Deidra's presence as an excuse to spare details from his scandalous tales.

"Sometimes— for about two seconds during the big reveal— I'm thrown off when a woman is straight on the top and nappy on the bottom," he shares.

Deidra laughs. "And then you recall relaxers and flat irons?"

"Right!"

The more they talk, the more lewd the conversation grows. I just sit back, half listening, watching the NFL kickoff game on the nearest flat screen. They're getting along and need the practice. No need for me to interfere.

Their conversation catches my ear when Deidra says, "I prefer some hair. Hairless is too juvenile for me."

That's good to know because I planned to do more than trim the hedges this weekend. I had every intention of unearthing them. I divert my attention from the game to see what other tidbits of useful information I can gain.

"On top of that," Deidra continues, "hairless women are kind of lazy."

"Come again?" Jacoby says. "You making a judgment based on the carpet?"

"That's been my experience."

"You sound like a woman with mileage."

I freeze, waiting for his remark to wipe the grin from Deidra's face, but her amused expression doesn't change. "From what I've heard so far," she says, "you have thousands more than me."

He laughs. "Let's toast to oil changes."

As they salute with tea and Sprite, I think about the few cars I test-drove before Kayla. Deidra eventually admitted to me that she jumped in the driver's seat of two pre-owned cars during her marriage. But we are *Driving Miss Daisy* compared to Jacoby. He's a reckless speed demon who crashes and burns weekly.

"You got a preference on the texture?" he asks.

This is how they should have interacted from day one; mature and amicable without brief undertones of sexual tension. They have more in common than they realize. Folks that sit in the middle of a restaurant speaking openly about pubic hairs with people in earshot deserve to be friends. Hopefully, their newfound similarities will propel them forward.

My optimism is tested when the waiter brings the bills. He places one before Jacoby and the other before me. Jacoby pays close attention to who will pay for our meals. If I grab the ticket, he'll hold his tongue. Then tomorrow, he'll send ranting texts about how Deidra is using me. Without discussion, Deidra grabs the ticket and Jacoby breaks his gaze.

"What are you doing this weekend?" I ask.

"My weekend started yesterday. Matter of fact, when I leave here I'm swinging by the house then I'm off to see some females who keep asking to double-team me."

I have no words, but Deidra has a passing thought. She looks out the window and disapprovingly shakes her head.

"If you weren't with Nia," he says, "you'd be in line, shoving your way to the front for this wood, too."

"Agreement!" I remind Jacoby. He's way out of line. Apparently, he has an hour grace period before the fake smiles and forced cooperation expire. "Seriously?" I roll my eyes and exhale to curb foul words.

The reprimand is effective. He shuts his mouth and they both slide cards from their wallets across the table with the tickets. However, as soon as the waiter retrieves their payments, Deidra breaks her silence. "A man who brags on his dick in public has a short attention span in private. But, despite your shortcomings, a quick fuck would be worth breaking you in."

"The only thing you'd get from me is a sore back," he says.

"Please. I know your type. You crave attention. You like when women coddle you. That craving translates to being my bitch in the bedroom. I just need a thirty-minute hall pass."

I tap my fingernails on the table. At this point, what's the point of intervening? If I open my mouth, profanity will fly out. And then I'll get so mad about losing my cool and attracting unwanted attention that I'll say something just to push Jacoby's buttons. "Don't act like you don't know about being versatile in the bedroom," rests on the edge of my tongue. "I know you missed your calling, but it's not too late. You're still young and virile enough to join the porn industry. You're good; gay-friendly talent is in high demand. You might as well get paid for nutting every fucking day." We both know his closeted ass doesn't like to be reminded that he's hiding behind a steel door. And undermining his profession is like shitting on his manhood. The thought of saying those words to him is so enticing that I'm salivating. But if I blurt that out, he'll crack. He'll verbally assault me and Deidra will unleash all hell on him. Then we'll all leave this restaurant in handcuffs.

I clench my lips. Eventually, they'll reach a dead-end road.

"Damn," Jacoby says, "who's doing who? Nia, I thought I taught you better."

Deidra is capable of fighting her own battles, but I can no longer sit quietly— not after Jacoby has disrespected my rela- tionship, again, by referencing our short sexual history. Before I can form the statement that should fire from my mouth, Deidra places her hand on my leg. "I yield to her touch," she says. "Unlike you, I don't have a problem relinquishing control."

"Really?" Jacoby asks. "Then shut the fuck up. Wait…On second thought, keep your mouth open. You'll finally put it to good use once you're on your knees."

Deidra's face is unreadable. I don't know whether she's on the verge of snapping or stalling to form a rebuttal. She turns to me, eyes begging for permission to go toe-to-toe with him.

"End of conversation," I say. And I mean it.

She drops her head, seeming to struggle with whether she'll surrender or declare war with Jacoby. After a moment, she places her hands in her lap and avoids eye contact with him.

The waiter is taking forever to return with their cards. I keep forcing myself to avoid Jacoby's face. But the same frustration that makes me turn away also makes me want to look at him again. I don't know why I expected him to look somewhat dejected. He's not. He glances at me and pinches the grin on his face. I just know he's itching for the opportunity to provoke Deidra. I'm tired of waiting and being in the midst of this tension. When I grab my purse to leave, Jacoby turns his attention to Deidra and says, "You're paying the bill, *today*, but you know what you were doing. You were serving burnt out pussy for meals and a place to live."

"You've got some nerve."

He ignores me to savor his dirty words. "You have a job, *for now*, but you're still a lying, married whore on the come-up."

I point at him. "Stop!"

"Let him finish," Deidra says.

"Be glad you chose Nia. I would've fucked you and dropped you off on the nearest corner. You wouldn't have deserved the ride there, and you damn for sure don't deserve anything she's done for you."

I ease my hand to Deidra's knee, but I'm not afraid of an explosive response. I'm touching her to restrain myself. She doesn't speak or blink. I can barely tell whether she's breathing. She's expressionless with her chin atop her fingers as if Jacoby no longer exists. Her detached reaction helps me retain my composure. My heart is pounding and I want so badly to pick up whatever's left on this table to shame and scar him for his insults.

Finally, the waiter returns with their cards and receipts. Deidra signs the merchant copy and tucks the other copy in her purse. "Let's go, love," she says. She's willing to walk away. I'm eager to retaliate.

"No," I say. I take a deep breath to keep my hands under the table. I've been sitting here until I can open my mouth without physically attacking him. "You got a problem with me?"

Jacoby tosses a tip in the middle of the table. "What are you talking about?"

"This bullshit boils down to the fact that I cheated on you with a woman. You insecure motherfucker. And till this day, I *don't* regret it. Thank God I'm not like you. Thank God I'm not sleeping with random women to give my asshole a break. Grow up Jacoby and get the fuck the over it."

He fixes his eyes on the opposite side of the restaurant.

"Admit it!" I demand.

"You're wrong," he says.

"No, you're wrong for not wanting me to be happy because you couldn't keep me." I notice heads turn in our direction. People are staring now and I'm starting to feel self-conscious about our confrontation. I glare at him before rising from the table. "The next time you come for her, I'm slapping the taste out your mouth with the first thing I get my hands on."

Jacoby smiles a little. He knows I'm dead serious.

Once Deidra and I are in the car, I still need to vent. I can't drive with all this pent-up, volatile energy. I push the gear to park and turn the ignition off. "Did you have to go there with him?" I ask. "Do you really think it was appropriate to say all that shit?"

"Yes, I did. He needs to shut up or be shut down."

"It's Jacoby! He has a big mouth. But you didn't have to disrespect me, too."

Deidra unbuckles her seatbelt and shoots me a piercing stare. "I respect you," she yells, pointing in my face. "I respect that you're a grown-ass woman with the competency and liberty to make your own decisions. I don't question your desires. I recognize you're the captain of your ship. But Jacoby treats you like a fucking deckhand and he treats me like a filthy pirate! And he believes he's standing at the bow with a gold compass. Just like a man to think he's running some shit— especially when he's given a primetime seat in the lives of two lesbians. I've been putting up with his shit for too long. You've waited until tonight to finally revolt and push his bitch ass overboard. I'm glad you're finally putting his pompous ass in his place because I'm tired of doing it for you. But, don't get in this car acting like you've done something. You don't get a metal for being too— damn— late."

Two things shoot to the forefront of my mind. One, she has some nerve trying to blame Jacoby for her insensitivity. Two, I don't need my girlfriend of a year-and-a-half telling me that I've mishandled my friend of eight years. Ignoring her will piss her off more than disputing her. So, instead of delighting her with an argument, I start the car and drive away.

The problem with ignoring Deidra for twenty minutes is the quiet time. It gives us time to reconsider our words and actions— time to level her head, time to soothe my temper. By the time we pull into the garage I need to apologize. We can't go inside and treat each other like strangers in the home we share.

"Look, Deidra…you're right. I should've demanded that he

stay in his lane a while ago."

"Well, I only say certain things to him because he'll take the bait and completely disregard you. But there were times I had to defend myself. You can't fault me for those times."

"I know. I don't think we'll have this problem anymore." I reach for her hand and she rolls her eyes. "What?"

"You're talking like it's over. Like his feelings for you have magically disappeared."

"Why do you have to go there?"

"I'm not going to just sit here and overlook the fact that he mistreats the woman I love just because he's jealously in love with her."

"He's *not* in love with me. He acts like that out of...I don't know...he's protective."

"I agree. His exterior is messy, immature, and deplorable. But when you peel back the layers, his core is simple. He's simply protecting the woman he loves. Baby, I'm not asking you not to be friends with him. I would never do that. I have no problem sealing my lips and letting him steal the show because I'm not invested in his cheap theatrics. But he's important to you. That means he should care enough to change. Tonight, you drew a line in the sand. Plenty of people witnessed that. So now, he's responsible for his change. From this day forward, you have to hold him accountable."

# 40

I KNOW SOME PEOPLE that refuse to answer unknown or private phone numbers. "If it's important they'll text or leave a voicemail," they say. I wish I were more like them. Instead, I answer unfamiliar numbers sometimes without thought and other times out of curiosity— like today.

"Hey you."

My brain stalls a second before identifying the caller's voice. I drop the phone from my ear and immediately end the call.

Seconds later, my phone buzzes and the same number as before appears on the screen. This time around, I answer to stop the unwarranted contact. I'm in the bed in my favorite pajamas watching my favorite sitcom. I don't have time for this. "What is it, Kayla?"

"Hello to you, too."

"Why the hell are you calling me?"

I expect her to match my snappy tone except she pleasantly replies, "I'm calling to invite you to lunch. I just want to talk. Are you free on Saturday?"

"Talk about what?"

"I'm trying to right a wrong."

A remorseful Kayla? That's an oxymoron. Intrigued, I consider the reasons I should probably lend her a few minutes of my time. A quick conversation could ensure she no longer aims to single Deidra out or that her family isn't huddled somewhere scheming another legal attack. And sometimes, it's safer to abide by the 'keep your enemies close' rule.

"Why wait?" I ask. If she's seriously apologetic, we can talk now. "I'm listening."

"If it's not too much to ask, I'd prefer in-person. Just food and light conversation, an hour tops."

I hesitate, unsure whether I should accept. Deidra has to attend an annual expo this Saturday, so I'll have most of the day to myself. I don't want to hide anything from her. But I also don't want to bother her with someone like Kayla.

"What restaurant do you have in mind?" I ask.

~ * ~

Come Saturday morning, Deidra rises early and I stay in bed until whiffs of breakfast tickle my nose. I fight sleepiness and roll out of bed, shuffling my feet to the bathroom for my morning pee. Deidra has a habit of calling my phone now instead of walking upstairs. I head to the kitchen before my phone rings. She's lifting bacon from a sizzling cast iron skillet when I step in the kitchen.

I sit at the table and notice all she's prepared as she loads our plates. She's pairing thick cut bacon with an omelet, hash browns, baked apples, biscuits, and gravy. She opens the microwave and removes a plate of pancakes.

"Deidra, this is too much."

"I want you to have a good breakfast. I feel like I'm neglecting you."

We've reached the edge of summer and her job continues to rob us of couple's time. Her weekends are spent at festivals, conventions, and other largely attended public events. I appreciate her thoughtfulness and the big breakfasts, but if I keep eating like this love handles will surely surface.

I hold my peace and treat my taste buds to the morning feast. And the feast is heavenly. Deidra cooks with the knack of a woman twice her age. "Your cooking is almost on par with my mom's," I say.

She grins. "And you almost complimented me."

I offer to clean up the kitchen. Deidra has a spare hour and I don't want her to spend any of it on dishes. She decides to spend the extra hour visiting Shannon. Once she's gone, I look at the leftovers and dirty dishes and figure that for a Saturday morning with a stuffed stomach it's only fitting to retreat to the bedroom and fall asleep again with the TV as a lullaby.

Fifteen minutes past noon, I drive to a café in Midtown to meet Kayla. To my surprise, she's at the hostess station waiting for me. When I approach, she steps forward like I'll accept a hug Is she crazy? I dodge the hug by turning my head toward the parking lot like something or someone else stole my attention. After we're escorted through the cozy café to a two-seater table, Kayla asks about my week.

"It was good." I'm determined to keep my words brief. I'm not here for jovial conversation. Kayla does her usual by pairing my one sentence with forty.

I barely listen as she complains about the family business and some other particulars I didn't catch. My eyes wander between her and other patrons. On one landing, I'm reminded that Kayla spares no expense on her appearance. Her sculptured eyebrows, stiletto nails, and diamond-sweep earrings embellish her denim jumpsuit. She has a keen eye for chic flare that rests between trendy and excessive. I don't like hair weaves anymore, but extensions are cute on her nonetheless. As a whole, she's undeniably sexy— a perk I never overlooked or undervalued. The physical was never an issue for us. Our chemistry was effortless. Chemical reactions, however, ruined us.

"You know what you want to order?" she asks, breaking into my thoughts.

I'm not hungry due to breakfast. But, I need a dish to keep me occupied for the duration of this lunch. I scan the menu for something light and inexpensive and settle on the house salad. Kayla pauses her rambling to order a Panini. With the orders placed, she rambles on again. "We're shooting a TV commercial next week."

"Are you starring in it?"

"God, no."

"Why not? This commercial could finally launch your modeling career."

She smiles. "You got jokes."

Her smile forces my memory to the brief time we were happy; when we first moved in together and cared about nothing but spontaneous sex and splurging; a time when I believed that maybe, just maybe, I had found "the one." How shallow of me.

"I think it's a waste of money," she says.

"I'm sure you won't complain if the commercial boosts profits and lands in your pockets."

She smirks and changes the subject by asking about my family. When I respond, I realize that much hasn't changed. My mom still finds solace in cooking. My dad still roams the streets. My brother still hopes he'll be released from prison soon. Shonda still calls near the end of every month to borrow money for whatever bills she didn't pay the previous month.

"Okay…and how is Deidra?"

I eat cucumber rather than answering.

"Does she know you're with me?"

There's only one answer. "Of course."

"That shit wouldn't fly with me."

"That's why I'm not with you."

She rolls her eyes. "So, how are things going?"

"She's amazing, but I'm not talking about our relationship with you."

"You got something to hide?"

"Why do you care? You decided we aren't worth vindication? Since the day you threatened me, I've been waiting on the almighty, unforgiving Kayla to swoop in and wreak havoc."

"Damn, is that how you feel about me?"

Duh! I lean back in my chair and stare at her.

Kayla's disappointed but quickly clears her pouty face. "You know how I get in the heat of the moment," she says. "I say things I don't mean."

"Since when?"

She takes several bites before replying. "I'm trying a different approach. Some people say kill 'em with kindness works."

"Works to gain what?" It's time to find out why I'm here.

"To gain closure on a number of things."

"Like?"

"You and me for one. And—"

"Wait, wait," I say with a raised hand. "We closed things a while ago. I dealt with my shit, recognized my wrongs, and moved on. And I was woman enough to accept the consequences. I bit the bullet and lived with my parents while I got my money in order and detoxed from the fucked-up relationship you dragged me through. Your hang-ups don't have anything to do with me."

She looks around. "Well...there should be some closure around Pat's estate."

A string of profanity races through my head. "I'm not going there with you."

"Hear me out. It's been almost a year. I've tried to give you and her some space, but enough is enough. We need to deal with this. She needs to do something with the estate. Is that too much to ask? It's like she's torturing us."

"Torturing you?"

"Yes! Have you forgot how it feels to lose someone you actually love?"

"Don't patronize me."

"The difference between me and you— you and us— is that we haven't been able to truly move on because of the bullshit called Deidra. If Deidra would grow up, deal with her mommy issues, and stop holding the estate over our heads, we could all move on. It's time for her to make some decisions."

I motion for the waiter so he can expedite my check and I can move on from lunch. This conversation is officially over. As soon as I reach for my wallet, Kayla says, "All I'm asking you to do is talk to her. Apparently, you care about her so I assume she cares about you."

I ignore the attitude and pull a twenty-dollar bill from my wallet. My ticket is $8.51 but I only have the twenty. I leave the bill on the table and warn, "Don't ever call me again."

I can't believe that Kayla and her family still thirst for Pat's money. Old news has once again become a thorn in my side.

# 41

MONDAY ARRIVES SWIFTLY and is uncompromising as usual. In the last hour of my shift, I'm asked to stay at work for two hours of overtime. In the last thirty minutes of it, a patient vomits on my arm. I doubt she did it accidentally. After scrubbing my arm, I toss my uniform top and head home, hoping that after a shower, Deidra will grace me with a home-cooked meal and one of her sensual back massages.

I'm relieved when I walk into the living room to see her beautiful face. She's sitting on the couch in my direction waiting for me, but something is wrong. Her eyes are cold. Does she have a bone to pick with me, or is she irritated that I've interrupted her during the news?

Whichever the case, I don't sit next to her yet. I stall by placing my purse on the loveseat and kicking off my shoes. "Hey, baby," I say to sense her mood. Her eyes stay on me as she picks up the remote. The TV screen goes black. At least ten minutes of the news broadcast remains. Something is definitely wrong.

"Why did you go behind my back and get together with Kayla to discuss Pat's estate?"

Shit. I can't let a guilty look to wash over my face. Like any couple, our relationship isn't perfect. We have our battles and commemorative scars, but we champion our commitment and cherish this relationship. She knows my expectations and boundaries, and I'm well aware of hers. Anything Carter related is a violation. I won't lie, but I have to say something to lessen the blow. I sit on the arm of the loveseat to keep space between us.

"That's not exactly true. I had lunch with her, but I didn't go because of the estate. I just…I knew you'd stop me if I told you that she wanted to meet."

"I sure would because food is spiritual. Food is a measure of good faith. Food goes hand-in-hand with camaraderie and can signify the extent you care about someone's wellbeing. So why in the world would you meet-up and eat with her? You know I wouldn't even want you at her funeral. I'm in this relationship *partially* because you assured me that her being your ex was a nonfactor. You know I don't give two-shits about the kinship. Therefore, she has no business in our lives."

Though my intentions were good, I knew the dangers of meeting with Kayla. So, instead of trying to plead my case, I let her lead this conversation.

"It's messed up to get a call from someone who despises me and have her throw information in my face that should've come from the woman that claims she loves me."

"I know you're mad, but don't question my love for you."

She drops her head.

"What did she say?" I ask.

"That both of you agreed enough time had passed and I should reconsider signing over the property; that I'm selfish for not doing the right thing; that you were with them when they met with a probate lawyer. Why would you consult a lawyer and then beg me to stand my ground with the estate? I don't understand why you can't be upfront with me. If you want something, say it!"

Shit. I don't know what to say. I should have known Kayla would do this. I should have finished my salad and amicably parted ways with her instead of fleeing the scene. I should have remembered that if I didn't play nice she would retaliate and re-sort to the vengeful person she's always been. I need to clear the air with Deidra, but I hate to backpedal for the sake of convincing her of my loyalties.

"Deidra," I say, low and even-toned, "Kayla twisted the truth. I was at that meeting with the lawyer, but not for that reason. And no, I don't want anything from you."

"Then why'd you meet with her? Because you wanted to?"

So far, we've avoided an argument, so I keep my mouth shut and reflect on the past year. I've waited for Kayla to rain hell through slashed tires and broken windows, or something sinister like interfering in Shannon's affairs. I expected fire and brimstone, but all Kayla did to fuck me over is make two phone calls. I guess she wasn't lying when she said 'I'm trying a different approach.'

Kayla is clearly wrong, but I am, too. Nothing I say will justify my actions. And regardless of the bullshit reasons I came up with on Wednesday to convince myself to have lunch with her on Saturday, ultimately, I had lunch with her because I wanted to. I wanted Kayla to see how much better I am without her.

Deidra slides to the edge of the couch and stares at me with troubled eyes. "I gave too many years of my life to a man who only wanted to me to stay home, raise our child, and look nice for him. A man who felt it was his God-given prerogative to sleep with any woman he damn well pleased. And when he made me feel low enough..." Tears glimmer in her eyes. She inhales to control the emotion. "...I slept around because it was the only way to get his attention. I degraded myself because of his sel-fishness, because of his I-wanted-to attitude. So please don't tell me you wanted to."

I consider lying, but two wrongs won't make this right. "Deidra..." My words fall short. "I'm sorry." That's all I can say.

She shakes her head and stands from the couch. As she walks

past me, I grab her hand. "Dee," I plead, looking up into her tired eyes before standing to meet her face to face. "Kayla called out the blue and I needed to know what she was up to. She's a snake in the grass. Seeing her was a way to protect you."

"Protect me from what? I'm not scared of her. Her family doesn't threaten me. There are only two people in this world who can hurt me, and I can't stand to look at one of them right now." She drops her head. I pray tears won't follow. "I don't want to be around you right now." Her weak, sorrowful voice is heartbreaking. I've broken the stronghold that roots our love in trust.

I let go of her hand. I can't force my will and make her stay. She proceeds upstairs. I hope she won't come back down and leave me alone tonight. I sit on the loveseat and strain my ears to follow her movements. The house is quiet until footsteps scurry down the steps.

"I need some time to myself," she says, avoiding my gaze. "I'll call you later."

I nod. I can't force forgiveness. She walks into the kitchen carrying her purse and a matching duffel bag. After she slams the door closed, I hear the garage door open. Then she pulls out the driveway, leaving me until who knows when.

# 42

I'M WOUNDED, but I try my best to give Deidra the space to forgive me. She's been gone since yesterday and I'm already tired of her absence. I need to hear her voice. I want to get out of bed, drive to her sister's house and bring her home, except I don't want to cause a scene. I'm sure Juanita would show sisterly solidarity just to act a fool with me. I call Deidra and she doesn't answer, but when I text she replies within seconds.

*When are you coming home?*

*I don't know.*

*I miss you.*

She doesn't reply.

*Is this necessary?*

No reply.

Her distance pisses me off to the point that I need to channel my frustrations. Still holding my phone, I think about the core of this problem, the prime reason I don't have Deidra in the bed next to me. I open my contacts, press *C*, and scroll to my target. Though nearly midnight Caroline promptly answers my call.

"This is unexpected," she says.

"If you got something to say, you can say it to me."

"Excuse me?"

"Your family doesn't jump until you tell them how high, so I know Kayla called us because you ordered her to."

"Listen, *girl*. I can speak for myself. You need to teach Deidra how to do the same."

"Teach? You're the only one who needs to learn how to do something. So learn how to fall back and realize that Deidra doesn't want shit to do with you. After that, learn how to move on because you won't get a damn thing from Pat's estate. Leave us alone!"

I end the call and stare at the closet door. I feel strange about my nasty and aggressive tone. I once had so much respect for Caroline. She was Pat's sister, my extended family. But now I can't believe her actions and their ongoing chase for Pat's money.

My moment of remorse doesn't last long. Now that I've vented, I feel so much better, even a bit hopeful. So I lift my phone to text Deidra again.

*Baby.*

*What?*

*How can I get you home?*

I wait so long for her reply that I fall asleep.

~ * ~

The next morning, I'm overwhelmed with sadness. It's a sadness I never felt before falling in love. This kind of love makes me care deeply. In the depths of love, the smallest things matter. And they matter immensely while sad.

The routine workday helps lift my spirit, but after work I need to talk to someone. Too bad Maria is on vacation. Jacoby isn't an option, and neither is Tasha. She's too friendly with Deidra, too biased. So I contact Shonda while driving home. I monopolize the conversation by explaining why Deidra hasn't slept by my side the past two nights.

"Dang," Shonda cuts me off. "Is it that serious? You didn't fuck Kayla— again." She chuckles. "All you did was have cheap-ass lunch with her. Deidra should be glad you went 'cause now y'all know where the Carters stand."

I exhale. I understand Shonda's viewpoint, but she's never been *in love*. She hasn't learned that lovers can argue or separate over anything— no matter how large or small the infraction.

"Buy something she likes and take it over there," she suggests. "You know we like to be spoiled. We like to be chased, too. So do it today."

"Deidra does things in her own time," I explain. She also likes simple pleasures. Cooking. The local news. Quality time with family. Going out every now and then. The last thing she'll appreciate is some expensive or perishable gift. I thank Shonda for the suggestions and then focus on getting home safely.

Being home only exacerbates my loneliness. Rather than sit around and drive myself crazy, I seek company. When Tasha doesn't answer my call, I reach out to Jacoby. He's tamed his aggression toward Deidra since the blow-up at the restaurant. Two days after the episode, he called with an apology. As soon as I answered the phone he said, "Are we cool?"

"What? You better come correct."

"Okay…I apologize."

"Apologize for what?"

He laughed. "Damn, you my mama now?"

"Bye," I threatened.

"Okay!" he said and listed his wrongs.

Since that conversation, we've been on good terms again. I established some rules and boundaries, and he continues to abide by them.

"You still at work?" I ask.

"Nah, at home. But I'm headed out. You should come with me. I'm going to this networking event type thing."

I don't have anything to do, so I throw on a simple gray

dress to accompany him. Hopefully, the trip will help ease my loneliness. Jacoby picks me up and twenty minutes later we reach The Winery II— a restaurant/venue I've passed many times but never visited. We enter a Tuscan-themed foyer and two women at a registration table greet us.

The loud-talking one informs me this is a monthly networking event hosted by a Black professionals Meetup group. "We meet every fourth Wednesday," she says. I thank her for the clarification and she hands me a nametag and blue Sharpie. I despise nametags so I write *Vicki* with heart-shaped dotted *I's*.

"Why are we here?" I ask as we walk away to mingle and do whatever else we're supposed to do at a networking event.

"I wanna meet new people," Jacoby says.

"Are clubs and bars beneath you now?"

He grins. "I need to diversify my contacts."

I settle with "okay." In actuality, he's slept with too many people in overlapping circles. He's leaping into new and unknown territory to expand his horizon.

We walk upstairs to a large meeting room. I look around unsure what to do next. About one hundred people are mingling in mini semi-circles or chitchatting with the row of vendors. Almost everyone has a clear cup in hand. I follow the social cue, grabbing punch while Jacoby fixes a plate of finger foods. Then we find seats along the wall to further scope out the place before getting into the mix.

I'm not a large crowd or mingle with strangers type of woman, so I find the seat comforting. I prefer to chill and sip in the company of people I know. My idea of networking is calling a friend or family member to ask whether they know someone who can help me find or fix something or get a discount on this or that.

While people watching, I notice that the double-doors on the far wall open to a balcony. "Let's go outside for a minute." We start to weave through the crowd. But weaving means passing a dozen semi-circles of chatters, and in passing we're bound to interact. And not far from the balcony we're beckoned to interact.

"Are ya newbies?" asks a stout man in a black suit.

"Yes," I confirm.

"Delighted to meet ya, Vicki," he says, offering his hand.

Jacoby glances at the nametag on my chest as I shake the man's wide hand. As the three of us chat about the monthly meet-up, two ladies and another guy join us, completing and authenticating our semi-circle. Jacoby threw his plate away, but I still have my cup in hand. Appearance-wise, I fit right in. I let everyone else do the talking and learn that the two with the matching dress and tie are married. This piques Jacoby's interest. Whenever his hormone antennas fly up, he enunciates, keeping all prefixes and suffixes on his words. And he crosses his arms and strokes his chin while speaking, as if he's an intellectual and debonair gentleman.

I'm unsure whether this highfalutin act is for the husband or wife until the husband says, "What do you do?"

Jacoby replies, "I save lives."

After a few more minutes of meaningless talk and business card collecting, I pull Jacoby away to the balcony. His eyes, however, stay in the room in pursuit of that lady's husband.

Only close friends are aware that Jacoby plays on both sides of the fence. He would never admit his discomfort with bisexuality, though it shows loud and clear through his guarded actions. I didn't know he had a taste for men prior to our three-month fling. During month two, when I confided in him about my attraction to women, he disclosed his bisexuality. Through the years, I thought his friendships with women who openly love women would help him gain confidence with the spectrum of human sexuality. Fast-forward and he still keeps a death grip on his straight-boy privilege.

The September air is cool and comfortable and I'm happy to have something occupying my mind, even if for a brief time. We have the balcony to ourselves until two women step outside to chat with Jacoby. He's a well-dressed, decent-looking brother, so there's no way these women will miss the opportunity to meet a prospective eligible bachelor at a professional's event. And they swoon as soon as they start to talk and find out he's a bona fide nurse. A *male* nurse. By virtue of his profession he's a nurturing, sensitive, and dedicated man. They have no idea. Thankfully, Jacoby isn't wearing scrubs with a stethoscope around his neck. On those occasions, women don't ask his occupation. They assume he's a physician. Physician or not, the panties come off after one hospital horror story and a wink.

"Are y'all related?" the busty one asks me.

"We're friends," I plainly answer, giving Jacoby the opportunity to engage with her.

He pulls me close and squeezes my arm. He looks through her, waiting for me to continue or curb the conversation.

"Oh. Good friends?" she asks.

"*Great* friends." I rub his back to play along. But really, I'm doing her a favor.

"Well," she says, "it was good meeting you." She hands him a business card, letting her fingers linger in his hand. "Feel free to stop by any time." She smiles and strolls off with her buddy.

"Thanks, Vicki," Jacoby says. "Come with me. I need an assist with something else."

I follow Jacoby back inside and refill my cup. Then we return to the seats along the wall. We're still until he places an arm across my shoulders. "What are you doing?"

"Don't move," he says, stroking my arm. "Dude is feeling me." I peer across the room at the husband. I doubt that he noticed our return. "Men like that prefer a man with a woman. Look at me and smile."

"What?" I manage to ask before laughing.

"I'm serious. Act like I'm turning you on."

Something about this is amusing. Now I want to see whether our fake attraction will actually bait this married man. I turn to Jacoby, our faces just inches apart. Two seconds later, Jacoby winks and I lose my cool. He wipes my spit shower from his face and I continue to giggle.

It takes a moment to kill my laughter, but I pull myself together. I look forward and place my hand on his thigh. Then he leans into my ear and says, "Kiss me."

"Hell no!" I lean away from him, almost spilling punch in my lap.

"Just one kiss."

"Game over, lover boy." Though I refuse to continue with the antics, our public display of affection must have appeared authentic. Minutes later, the husband parts from his wife and Jacoby bolts from his chair.

I fill the time by texting Deidra: *I miss you.*

*Where are you?*

I reply with strategy: *Bored in bed.*

*I came by. You weren't there. So again where are you?*

"Damn," I say aloud. I press the phone icon to call her and confess. "I'm at a networking event."

"Why didn't you say that at first?"

"I wanted you to have pity on me."

"Well, I'll see you tomorrow after work. I'm babysitting tonight."

I'm disappointed with the delay but comforted by the next-day guarantee. I feel even better when she promises to answer my call once I get home tonight.

When Jacoby returns, we leave the event. I don't ask whether his private balcony session with the husband was worthwhile, and he doesn't offer any details besides "glad I came."

As we approach the boulevard that leads to a cluster of chain restaurants, he says, "You wanna get something to eat?"

"Uh-uh. I just wanna pour myself a glass of wine, get in the bed, and call Deidra."

"Call her?"

I sigh. "She's been gone a couple of days."

He chuckles. "Trouble in paradise?"

I shoot him a nasty look.

"What happened?" he asks. "She don't need you no more? She's ready to move on?"

"I didn't say one thing about you locking down a booty call on a balcony, but you trying to talk shit to me?" Here we go again. "You need to remember the definition of friend."

He turns left at the light, bobbing his head to Reggae, ignoring my words and mounting anger.

I'll be damned if he minimizes with silence. "You know something," I say. "Pull over." I'm on the verge of slipping off a heel and stabbing him in the eye so he can't look at a down-low man or interested woman the same way ever again. I need to make an immediate exit for my safety and sanity.

"What?" he asks to confirm whether I'm serious.

I unbuckle my seat belt. "Hit the motherfucking brakes!"

Jacoby veers into the parking lot of an abandoned building. When I pull the door handle, he grabs my wrist. "You can't get out a moving car."

As soon as he stops and lets me go, I push the door open. "I'm a good friend," he says to stop me.

I get out anyway and glance around the derelict lot. I want to leave, but I shouldn't wander alone on this street.

"You're doing the most. Get back in," he says.

Conflicted, I climb back inside and close the door. But we don't say anything. He's staring out the driver's side window and I'm gripping my phone. I don't know whether he's trying to figure out what to say to me, but I'm trying to figure out how I can get home. "Nia," he says, calmly. "I've been everything a friend should be and more...I'm your man."

"Excuse me?"

"When Kayla and them other bitches fucked you over, I was there for you. When you fight with Deidra and she walks out on you, I'm here. I'm always here for you."

"Okay, congratulations. But you don't have a right to fight me whenever I don't live my life according to the Book of Jacoby. I don't appreciate you being combative and shit."

He gazes into the distance. "Look, I'm tired of the double standard. Kayla fucked with your heart over and over and you gave her chance after chance. Shit, three years' worth of chances. Then you get with a married, two-faced, fake-ass lesbian with ulterior motives and claim she's the love of your life? I guess I wasn't shit! We hit a bump in the road and you left me there like road kill...But I manned up. I didn't deserve you back then, but I never walked away. I waited...for years. Where the hell was my second chance?"

I exhale. I can't remember the last time Jacoby shared his deeper emotions and pains. When Jacoby and I ended our tattered relationship, I didn't believe we'd lost anything. We weren't in love, so love wasn't lost. We didn't share money, a home, or anything else substantial. Now, I realize he did lose something along the way. He lost the possibility of rekindling our affair.

I understand his position, but he needs to recognize what I was experiencing. "I was a work in progress, Jacoby. I told you my desire for women was growing by the day. You knew I couldn't keep forcing my attraction to men…to you."

"I couldn't tell when we were fucking."

"Why does everything boil down to sex with you?"

"Because your words mean nothing. I go by your actions. You've always kept me close."

My thoughts run to all the times I needed Jacoby's help; the times I needed a listening ear; the times we hung out at each other's homes; the *SVU* episodes; the Saturday-morning breakfasts; the lunches at work. All those times were an extension of our friendship. Why would he expect more?

I quickly push myself out the SUV, leaving the door open. He jumps out and runs over to stop me. "Where are you going?"

"Just leave!" I say, stepping around him.

"Look around. It's getting dark and we're a block from the hood. I'll take you home."

I shake my head, dropping my eyes to search deep inside. Then I turn around and approach him to share my thoughts. "I'm sorry for disregarding your feelings for so long… but where do we go from here? I'm in love with Deidra and you can't shit on my relationship because you didn't get what you wanted from me. Nothing's going to change."

He steps away and rubs his forehead. The droning engine and passing cars smother the silence between us. He turns to me with defeated eyes and says, "Fine. Let's go."

"No," I say just above a whisper.

Jacoby closes the passenger door and takes the driver's seat. He slowly approaches and drops the window. "Is this how it is?"

"I don't have a choice."

I'm hurt when Jacoby backs up and drives away. I'm even more disappointed when I don't see his taillights in the distance. I keep expecting him to show up as I'm walking to the nearest establishment. I fight the urge to glance back again.

I pull out my cell phone for a rescue as I hurriedly walk the four-block trek to a fast food restaurant. Before I Google a cab company, I decide to try Tasha first. Thankfully, she's in her car and only a few miles away from me. I'm too self-conscious to stand outside of Burger King while waiting for her. So I enter the building and order a Coke. I sit near the entrance, hoping I blend in. This beverage doesn't camouflage me as well as the one at the networking event.

Nearly ten minutes later Tasha calls and says she's outside. I walk out and notice someone in the passenger seat. I wish she was alone, but I'm in no position to complain. I keep quiet and get in the backseat.

"What happened?" Tasha asks.

"Just take me home."

She turns around and pulls off. I close my eyes and rest against the seat. I'm so agitated that I feel like I'm floating. And I'm embarrassed and disheartened. All this emotional shit over the past few days is draining. After a while, I open my eyes and behave civilly.

"Hey," I say to Sabrina.

She glances over her shoulder and quickly speaks as if she doesn't want to further upset me. Funny how Sabrina was the friend with benefits that Tasha had reservations about dating. But here they are, together on a Wednesday, holding hands and happy. I'm glad to see something good transpiring.

"Tasha, I'm done with Jacoby."

She examines me in the rearview mirror. "You just need to sleep it off."

"I'm serious. Hell, according to him, we've been in a sexless relationship for three, four, five years. And I've been pretending like I'm not his woman."

Tasha shakes her head. "Girl, you need to sit back and put

your seatbelt on."

I didn't notice I'm on the edge of the seat, speaking loudly as I complain only inches from their ears. I lean back and snap myself in. "Y'all can be friends, but I'm giving us space. No more breakfasts...nothing."

She glances in the mirror. "For how long?" There's concern in her voice.

I'm too sad to tell her the possible truth. I can't bring myself to say "maybe forever."

I'm surprised Tasha hasn't shifted the subject by demanding a second-by-second account of what happened. She picked me up at Burger King for God's sake. So she knows whatever occurred is inexcusable. Maybe she doesn't want the details because details would make our severed friendship real. Instead of speaking anything into existence, we stop talking.

Once I'm home, I head straight upstairs. I kick off my shoes and seek shelter under the sheets and comforter. The middle of my bed is safe and comforting. I desperately want Deidra, but I'm too tired to call her. I pray that when I wake up, morning will end the cycle of crap over the last seventy-two hours.

## 43

*ARE YOU COMING or not?* Shonda asks.

I can't think of another place I'd rather be right now. There's nothing like chilling on the couch after dinner with my head resting in Deidra's lap. I relax and text, giving her the courtesy of silence as she watches the news, her fingers stroking my forearm at random.

*Maybe next week* I respond. I'm not in the mood for Thursday night happy hour.

I'm surprised Deidra isn't tired of my dragging mood by now. I've been laying around after dinner for three weeks, sometimes too caught up in my feelings about ending my friendship with Jacoby. I sort of feel like I've buried him alive— like the ghost of our friendship is haunting me.

That's why it felt so awkward running into Jacoby at work yesterday. I dropped my eyes to the tiled floor, following the squares to Cardiology while he made a beeline for the elevator door. Until yesterday, I've managed to avoid crossing paths with him, though Tasha speaks with him frequently. She's dissatisfied with the rift in our friendship but respects our individual feelings.

Deidra doesn't support or discourage our dissolved friendship. "The ball is in his court now." That's all she said about it.

I wanted Jacoby to meet me halfway; to acknowledge what happened and accept that we can't change past emotions or failed hope. I wanted him to reach out and show that he cared enough to move forward. But, like Deidra told me, he's responsible for his change. I let the leftover expectation fade from my heart. I have to lend my concern to other matters.

Deidra and I resolved the friction from my lunch with Kayla. I've agreed to stay clear of enemy lines, and she's agreed to not runaway during conflict. I don't intend on contacting the Carters, but I care too much for Deidra to leave the matter alone. In particular, I'm worried about the anger she carries, but there's no good way to approach this subject. I can't get her to address the hurt and rejection. These thoughts fill my head until Caroline's intruding voice alarms me.

I lift my head to see the commercial on TV. I hear Caroline's voice but she hasn't appeared on the screen. Evidently, this is the commercial Kayla mentioned. Carolyn promises "outstanding, affordable service to honor your loved ones regardless of race, religion, or denomination" as staff interact with patrons in the funeral home. The commercial ends with Caroline in a yellow dress suit delivering a service guarantee. As the image fades, I sit upright and turn to Deidra. I can't believe she watched the entire thirty-second advertisement. This means her thoughts are swimming and I aim to catch them.

I place my phone aside. "How do you feel about that?"

"About what?" she asks, drilling through the channel guide.

"About seeing them in action."

She presses buttons on the remote control instead of acknowledging me. I reach across her lap and pull the remote from her hand. She waits a long moment and says, "That commercial reminded me that something has always been missing. But nothing can fill the void, so what's the point?"

"The point is to deal with it."

"I'll deal with it the day after eternity."

"So you plan on feeling this way till the day you die?"

Her eyes fall for a moment. "What do you expect from this conversation?"

"You know that balance is necessary. They've had the upper hand in how you've experienced the world since birth. You need answers. Maybe answers will balance everything out and help you find some peace."

She crosses her arms. "You mean *we* need answers?"

I think long and hard about my response because her frustration will spark anger and anger will close her off. "Baby, I'm trying to make sure that the woman I intend to spend the rest of my life with is happy."

~ * ~

Deidra waits four days to continue this conversation with me. She makes breakfast and hands me a plate. "I understand why I need to reach out to them. But you want this more than me, so you need to call them."

I'm not going to argue with her about the accuracy of that statement. I eat while thinking about the best Carter to contact for a face-to-face conversation. This won't happen until I make it happen.

I know Mama C wouldn't speak candidly. She would advocate for "moving on," which will piss Deidra off. Caroline is confrontational. The talk would end with someone in the hospital. The middle sister doesn't do anything without Caroline. Cookie, the youngest sister, is too passive.

Actually, passive is a good match for Deidra's assertive personality. And, Cookie can possibly relate to Deidra on a peer-to-peer level because she's only four or five years older than her.

Now that I have the right Carter, I have to choose the right location. We need an environment free of distraction, suitable for flaring emotions and biting honesty. After considering a few options, I settle on our living room— an environment I can control.

The following morning I call the funeral home. I'm glad that a staff member answers rather than someone who would recognize my voice. I ask for Cookie and wait for the call to transfer. Cookie is surprised to hear from me but pleasant as usual. I cut to the chase with the purpose of my call.

"Okay... why me?" she says. "Why didn't you ask Caroline?"

"Because this has to be a hands and drama-free talk."

She laughs. "Well, at first I was mad, too. But I washed my hands of the estate and all that mess last year."

I'm relieved. I knew she was a good choice. "So, you're okay with clearing the air about your family history?"

"It don't matter if I'm okay with it. It's something we need to do."

With that said, I schedule a date and time that works for her before sharing my address.

Deidra isn't thrilled about the confirmation but has three more days to get her heart and head ready. Saturday morning comes and she doesn't mention Cookie's pending visit. She cooks breakfast, completes chores, and goes to lunch with Shannon, arriving home an hour before the scheduled talk. She goes upstairs to lie in bed until I call to announce Cookie's arrival.

When I welcome Cookie inside, she sits on the loveseat, leaving a good amount of space between her and wherever Deidra sits. I don't plan to interfere in their conversation, so I step out of the living room to sit at the dining room table. The distance permits me to hear everything with minimal presence.

Deidra is taking forever to come downstairs. I return to the living room and chat with Cookie in the meantime. I mention the commercial and we laugh about Caroline's ensemble. "I told her not to wear that loud Easter suit," Cookie teases.

Deidra comes down a few minutes later and greets Cookie, but she seems irritated by the small talk. She crosses her arms and side-eyes me. "Listen," she says at a break in our chatting. I return to the dining room so she can proceed with Cookie. "Tell your folks to forget about the estate. It's not happening."

"I think they get that now."

"Good. I'm closing the estate. The little bit of debt that Pat had I paid off months ago. So now I'm going to claim the life insurance money, withdraw the accounts, and sell the house and whatever's left. All assets will be sold. Then I'm donating the sum to charity." She glances at me and back at Cookie, whose expression is a mix of pain and astonishment.

"What about your daughter?" Cookie asks. "She…she could use the money one day. Or you can put it away for her children."

"It just tears you up to know that well over three-hundred and fifty thousand dollars will go to complete strangers, huh? A lot of people believe that family is more valuable than money. But no one ever valued me, so you shouldn't give a damn about the money. And why would I pass guilt money to my daughter or her children?"

Cookie clears her throat. "Deidra, I don't think Pat gave you everything because she was guilty."

"Then what would you call it?"

Cookie shrugs. "Satisfaction. I think she gave you everything because she finally had a choice."

Deidra tilts her head, waiting for clarification.

"You think Pat didn't keep you because she was young. There's a little truth in that. There was shame around her pregnancy, but it's more than that, too. Pat…" Cookie briefly closes her eyes. "Pat was molested by our daddy's brother. She didn't tell anybody about what he was doing to her until she found out she was pregnant. She didn't know if the baby was his or your father's." She exhales. "Madear and Daddy didn't believe in abortions, and Madear's mama wasn't having it.

"They sent Pat to live with our aunt in Florida until you were born and they could figure out paternity. I didn't know what was going on back then 'cause I was only four. I knew Pat had a baby when she was fifteen, but I was well into my twenties before I found out about the sexual abuse and everything else. It was hard on everybody, but Daddy took it real hard. Madear and Daddy just wanted to put it behind them and create a life for Pat that didn't include the pain of all that, and that meant pretending like she never had a baby.

"A few years ago, Pat told me she regretted not being there for you, but…she was human…and she was part of a family with a reputation to keep. Back then Pat didn't have a say. I think that's why she changed her Will and left it all to you. It was her last chance to make a choice for your benefit."

Cookie's words weigh heavily on my spirit. I thought I could remain quiet in my corner of the room but I'm itching for details. "Is he alive?" I ask.

"He died in the nineties."

"Was he prosecuted?"

"He went to prison. I don't know how long though."

Pat's secret didn't surface until her funeral. Then Deidra partially filled in holes I never knew existed. Now, Cookie has smudged muddy, grit-filled colors onto the gray picture I painted about Deidra's rejection. Nothing could have prepared me for the horror of Pat's youth. More questions race through my mind but I don't verbalize them. Cookie turns her attention to Deidra and I do, too.

Deidra rubs the back of her neck and sighs. "Thank you for being the first in your family to show remorse for my experience."

Cookie nods. "Is there anything you wanna ask me?"

"No, but I need a favor. I need certified copies of Pat's death certificate."

"I can mail them on Monday."

And with that, the conversation ends. I thank Cookie for coming over and Deidra heads upstairs. I keep to myself, giving her a few hours of solitude.

At dusk, I order Chinese food and Deidra eats with me. We sit in the living room and watch an on-demand movie. I wait until she's eaten half of her fried rice to ask, "Are you all right?" She's an open book once food hits her stomach.

"I'm okay."

"When did you make a decision about the estate?"

"The same night you told me I can't take a grudge to the grave."

"So...how do you feel about what Cookie said?"

She sighs. "I've always wanted to know why Pat didn't want a relationship with me. I've always wanted more than my dad's version of the truth. But Cookie she just validated the excuses. When Pat first called me about her Will, I got involved because I wanted to move past my anger. And I wanted them to stop running away from me. But... that backfired. My feelings were tied up in the estate, but I know I can't hold on to them forever. The fact is Pat wasn't there for me."

"I hear you...Baby, I think that—"

"I knew it was coming."

"You don't even know what I'm about to say."

"I knew you would say something."

"Dee, just hush and listen. Pat wanted you to have it all. Accept it. Think about what you can do with the money. Shannon can get through college debt free. Shit, I wish I could've got through school without taking out loans. Buy her a house one day. Open a business. Go to college. You like marketing. Go to school and get a degree. Do whatever. My point is that you did a lot to survive. You had to because of the decisions they made years ago. But you have to make better decisions *now*. Don't make the decision from pain."

I hope I was more convincing than preachy. We're silent until she leans over and kisses me. "I'll invest the money."

"You decided that fast?" I ask.

She laughs. "No! I've been thinking about this for a while. You've just encouraged me to actually do it. There aren't too many Black women being handed small fortunes, so I think I'll invest it. I don't know anything about investments, but that's what financial advisors are for. Shannon has never wanted for anything, so if I'm blessed to have grandchildren they can have the money. Or…you can have a baby."

Thankfully, I've swallowed my last bite to dodge choking. "We talked about this. You know I don't wanna carry a baby. You've been there and done that." A few months ago, we decided that after our three-year anniversary we would try to conceive. "*You* agreed to carry. I agreed to be at your beck and call. Right?"

She winks.

"Why'd you tell Cookie you were donating the money?"

"Didn't you see the pitiful look on her face? I couldn't resist. And if they believe it's all gone, they'll leave me alone."

I wonder whether Cookie will relay today's conversation to Caroline, and whether Caroline will make a last-ditch effort to save Pat's estate. I'll let Cookie deal with that. I'm just appreciative of Deidra's peaceful formula to end the opposition.

# 44

"IT'S LAST MINUTE, but possible," Deidra says. "The last weekend of October is still available for booking."

My birthday is two weeks from now and I don't have plans to celebrate. I've experienced enough parties for half a lifetime. Deidra, however, wants to throw a big birthday bash at some venue in Germantown. "I'm good with dinner and a movie."

She frowns. "You only turn thirty once."

I ease into the turning lane. "What did you do for your dirty thirty?"

"I went to Vegas." She smiles at the memories. "Did some things that will go to my grave. But anyway, my work schedule has died down. I can do the party. I know a DJ and I can find a bartender, and I…"

She rambles for a solid minute, attempting to change my mind. Though I'm unmotivated, I can't completely neglect her enthusiasm. "Please keep it simple," I say. "I just wanna hang out with the people I like the most." This doesn't include a long list of folks, so the coordination won't be too much for her to handle. We reach our destination and head to the restaurant entrance to have dinner with Tasha and her girlfriend, Sabrina.

During dinner, Tasha agrees to help Deidra ensure all the necessary people are contacted for my birthday gathering. They're going to make me celebrate this year. The details of the occasion were to remain secret. Except Tasha— who still hasn't mastered the skill of confidentiality— blurts out the location the day before my birthday.

"Y'all are taking me to a pole dancing studio?"

"I guess Deidra's trying to tell you something," she says and laughs. "But for real, it'll be fun." I press for more details, but Tasha won't tell me. "Let me get off this here phone before I say something else I ain't supposed to tell you."

I spend the first waking hour of my birthday responding to a flood of birthday wishes on social media and another half hour taking calls from family and old friends. While talking to Mama I receive a text from Jacoby: *Hbd*. I reply *Thx*. I stare at my phone, considering whether I should send another text to ask how he's been lately.

On second thought, I don't want to send the wrong impression. I'm okay with the separation. Until he tells me otherwise, I'll continue to assume he's okay with it as well. At times, I can't believe we're keeping our distance. Usually, we'd piss each other off, complain to Tasha, and then bury the hatchet over breakfast. But it's been over a month since I walked away from him. I miss accounts of his raunchy lifestyle and the variety he added to my sphere. But, I'm content with preserving the good times we shared and the reality of his friendship being a closed chapter of my life. I place my phone down and pick up my tablet again.

"Why didn't you tell me you're awake?" Deidra asks, peeking through the doorway. She enters the room and joins me in bed. "Happy birthday, love…Oh, I just talked to Shannon. She said 'happy birthday, old lady.' "

I laugh and touch her chin. "You feel all right?"

She sighs. "I'm okay."

I wish her mood were better, but given what she experienced this week the dull okay and heavy sigh are welcomed. The first emotional blow came right after she filed for divorce. Word of her pending divorce trickled through her grapevine of cousin-in-laws and friends in Virginia within forty-eight hours. One particular friend called to vent on Wednesday night, offended that Deidra had officially closed the door on her marriage and their close-knit naval community. This is the same friend that invited Deidra to stay in her home whenever she visited Virginia.

So I'm surprised when their conversation sours— signaled by the frown on Deidra's face. She places the call on speakerphone so I can hear the rant flying out of this woman's mouth. "Eric has done nothing but love and provide for you, and he provided for you despite your transgressions. You don't think I know you were cheating on him for years? Hell, do you know how many times I questioned leaving you alone with my husband? But I was there for you, even after you moved to Memphis and got with Miss Thing. And you know how I feel about homosexuality. My Bible says that's a sin and I still opened my home to you. I thought *she* was the home wrecker, but this mess is because of your nasty ass."

I take the phone from her hand to end the call and verbal assault. "Why does she think it's all your fault?"

"I was part of *his* circle of friends and family up there. She doesn't know the truth about what happened between us. Who knows what Eric has told people since I left."

"That's no reason for her to disrespect you."

She drops her head, bruised by the betrayal of words from her closest friend in Virginia. "That part of my life is over and done with, and so is she. I'm going upstairs."

She walked away before I could console her. Unfortunately, the stresses of life didn't stop there.

The next morning, I left home to visit my parents for a few hours. When I returned, I went in the kitchen to sift through mail. I called out my love's name but she didn't answer. Her car was in the garage so I knew she was home. I went to the bedroom to see whether she was asleep. The bedroom was empty. I went back downstairs to get my phone and call her.

"I'm outside," she says.

When I exit the back door, she's staring at the wood fence that encloses our rectangular patio. She lifts a cigarette to her lips and inhales long and hard, causing the smoldering end to glow momentarily. She drops her hand to flick ashes past her bare feet. Then she's still for a moment. Only the diamond hoops dangling from her ears move a bit.

She lifts her hand and pulls the smoke harder, as if she needs it to alleviate a pang. Deidra stopped smoking on Valentine's Day. Abstinence from tobacco was her gift to me. I'm too scared about the answer to ask what the matter is.

After another drag, she shifts her gaze and says, "Shannon may be pregnant."

My first thought is Phillip. Then it switches to Deidra. I don't need her to express the weight of her disappointment. It fills every inch of this confined space so tightly that I can't step toward her. I remain in front of the storm door until she's ready to welcome my support.

"Before Shannon moved here, I told her that men don't care about your feelings. They only care about expectations. And then I told her that my entire marriage was sex for money. I got what I needed as long as I met his expectations. But most of his expectations were around my body. The words were insensitive, and they probably hurt her feelings because I was criticizing her dad, but I wanted her to understand how easy it is for women to turn their temples into trashcans. I wanted her to know that even in marriage, some women use their bodies to guarantee keeping a roof over their baby's head and food in their mouth. I wanted her to know that…" She shuts her eyes to hold back the emotions, shaking her leg to fend off the tears she doesn't want to over-power her. "That I made a lot of mistakes with my temple, but she didn't have to make those mistakes or deal with the aftermath because I've already committed her sins."

Tears fall from her cheeks. She wipes them away and puffs again. "I told Shannon her body is a source of pleasure and this is a good thing— but sexual gratification needs to be on her terms and for her benefit because no man will treat her with any degree of respect if she doesn't exercise her right to speak and choose first... God, sometimes I wish my baby was gay," she says and laughs with tears.

I laugh, too, hoping my laughter will take the edge off Deidra's worry. She's shared with me the difficulties of being a teenage mother and the precautions she took to ensure Shannon wouldn't repeat the cycle. She wanted her daughter to experience youth and young adulthood before motherhood and to obtain education beyond high school. "I've done everything I can to make sure Shannon has the love, resources, and autonomy to live a better life than me," she said.

I hate that she feels her guidance and efforts are fruitless now. "Baby," I say at last. "Lesbians got issues, too."

She smiles at me. "Trust me, I know...I just can't stand the idea of a man mistreating her."

"So Shannon doesn't know for sure if she's pregnant?"

"No. When you left, I went to campus to take her out for brunch. But she said she was too sick to come outside. I went in to see what was wrong and she wouldn't look at me. There's only one thing she'd hide from me. So I flat-out asked 'are you preg-nant' and she said 'maybe.' I told her to walk her ass to the car so we could get a test, but she wouldn't move. I got mad at her and she got mad at me. The next thing I know she's screaming for me to leave. The situation took me by surprise so I left."

Deidra and Shannon are inseparable. They talk to each other daily. I envy and appreciate their relationship. I wish I could have experienced that kind of bond with my mother as a young adult. The pain in Deidra's eyes compels me to do something. Regardless if Shannon is pregnant or not, I can't let the altercation separate them.

I take Deidra's hand and escort her upstairs. Once she's comfortably in bed, I drive to the nearest drugstore for a pregnancy test. Forty minutes later, I'm approaching the flight of steps to Shannon's apartment. A roommate answers my knock and lets me inside their cylinder block dwelling. When Shannon opens her bedroom door, she doesn't seem a bit surprised to see. And she doesn't say anything. She just widens the door so I can cross into her dim room. I sit in her purple computer chair and she climbs onto her elevated bed. She lets out a short breath like the effort has winded her. Shannon stares at the TV and combs her fingers through her frizzy hair. Then she lies on her side and looks at me.

"I didn't come over here to give you a speech. What you're feeling could be a symptom of a number of things. But you can rule out or confirm pregnancy with this." I open the plastic bag in my lap and pull out the test. "I took one of these my sophomore year. I was living in the dorms by the Athletic Center. The common space is different, but my room was setup like this. Anyway, I waited to take it because I was too scared to look down and see a positive stick. I didn't want to deal with considering an abortion or possibly dropping out of school. But eventually, I had to know." I stand from the chair. "I'll leave this for you." I place the test beside her laptop, praying she will take it soon.

Nearly three hours later, Deidra receives a text from Shannon: *It's negative.*

After those emotional blows, I don't want Deidra worrying

about whatever she's planned for my birthday. We can have a good time any weekend. But she insists her spirits are high and reminds me that people have been contacted and things have been scheduled.

"Be ready by five," she says and rolls out of bed.

When 4:00 rolls around, I do as I'm told and dress appropriately in flats and tights. I'm ready for the pole-dancing lesson I shouldn't know about right now.

# 45

I DIDN'T EXPECT DEIDRA to drive me to the Warehouse District— an emerging downtown neighborhood with pop-up stores, trendy restaurants, and art galleries. We enter a restored brick building and climb steep steps to the second floor. The foyer opens to a wide lobby where my birthday crew is standing. I should have grateful surprise across my face, but I can't fake astonishment. Instead, I hug my guests, starting with Tasha and Sabrina; my cousins, Shonda and Raya; my college friend, Ebony; and my colleague, Maria.

After a moment of exchange, Deidra pokes my waist. "You knew about this?"

I grin, unsure what to say as she cuts her eyes at Tasha.

Deidra opens the door to a dance studio with ten gold poles dispersed along shiny hardwood floors. A lean dance instructor welcomes us and cues the music as my cousins and friends change their footwear. Deidra reaches into her purse and hands me a pair of heels I've never seen before.

"Where'd you get these?" I didn't plan on dancing in anything other than flats.

"Purchased just for you," she says.

I cooperate and slip the black heels on my feet. Everyone, except Sabrina, grows almost a half foot taller.

This is my first pole dancing experience and I'm excited to experiment with swaying hips and sexy stances. The instructor leads me to the pole of honor and kicks off her lesson with a basic around-the-world dance move. Before long, we're gap-legged and seducing ourselves through the wall of mirrors. I don't have the shoulder strength to invert myself on the pole. But thanks to gravity, I kill the spins and splits.

Sabrina is the star of the class. She's a tomboy by birth but down for the lesson and shameless in her dancing. She pulls up her baggy pants and works the pole, never skipping a challenging spin or a sensual slide.

My poor cousin Shonda, however, hasn't possessed an ounce of rhythm since she stopped playing the triangle in elementary school. She's a step or two behind the entire one-hour session. She doesn't mind though. She's content with just gripping the pole and looking sexy in bejeweled stripper heels. And she keeps the heels on after we end the class and head down the sidewalk to our next destination.

We walk two blocks east to a new restaurant with a mix of Southern and Latin American foods. It's a monotone space with minimalist furnishings and splashes of mood lighting. The host escorts us to a sleek black table in the far corner of the restaurant reserved for our privacy.

Once our entrées are placed, I garner everyone's attention. "Let's toast."

"To what?" Tasha asks.

"First, let's toast to Sabrina, who'll receive a trophy from me in about a week engraved with Pole Dancer of the Fucking Year." After the laughs die down, I continue: "To my love and bestie, for doing a great job with the guest list. To Shonda, for shamelessly announcing in the middle of pole dancing that she 'don't need rhythm to ride a mean dick.' To Raya, for not push-ing her sister off her stilts. To Maria, for letting her hair down and shaking a tail feather with me. And last, but not least, to

Ebony, for being a good friend even when I fail to uphold my end of this friendship."

Ebony is a sensitive soul. Her wine glass doesn't make it to her lips following the toast. She replaces her glass with a napkin to dab tears. I hug her and we all drift into good conversation.

Deidra doesn't say much as we eat and swap updates, gossip, and exaggerations. She sits to my right as an active listener, as if she's learning about me by observing and listening to everyone.

"What's next for the two of you?" Maria asks her.

Deidra glances at me first like she's too shy to answer. "We have a list of adventures planned between now and summer. But what I look forward to the most is continuing to grow with Nia. She's shown me the joys of a partnership, and I want to give her that and more."

"Aw," my friends sing as I blush.

"What about diapers and binkies?" Ebony asks.

Deidra and I eyeball each other, agreeing to keep the matter between us. "We'll get there," I answer.

"So y'all are for-real-for-real?" Tasha asks. Something about her question and hard stare make me feel as if she wants a vow before my closest friends and family; as if she wants me to testify about my relationship, declaring that I'll never allow challenges to diminish our bond; as if she needs me to impart hope for her and Sabrina. "Is she farting around you? Have you seen her pop in or pull out a tampon? If so, I *know* y'all are serious."

I smile at Tasha's litmus tests as Deidra laughs and turns to me for an answer. "Believe me when I say we're past the point of no return."

"Right," Deidra says. "So, I guess that's why you have no shame asking me to bring you a roll of tissue while having a full-fledged conversation and wreaking havoc on the toilet with the door wide open."

We expose more of each other's quirks through a few min-utes of embarrassing confessions and laughs. Then we leave the restaurant and walk a couple of blocks over to an urban lounge for drinks, music, and dancing. Deidra and I mingle and line dance to a song, but eventually we find our way to a sitting area to cuddle and flirt.

"Why you being so chill?" I ask.

"I can't steal all of your attention. I have to share you with others sometimes."

"Have a drink with me."

"You know I can't hold liquor."

"I won't get anything strong."

I flag a waitress and order strawberry ale. Deidra takes two sips and claims a third will make her tipsy. "These hips are no good when my head is swimming."

"Oh, that's next on the itinerary?"

She winks. "Possibly."

We remain secluded, guarding purses and drinks until clos-ing. Before parting ways, everyone promises to not wait until my thirty-first birthday to hang out again. "As a matter of fact," Tasha says, "let's get together next month. Y'all can come to my place. I'll cook, just bring your smiles and trash talk."

Deidra drives us home along the sparse streets, holding my hand as we listen to soft tunes. Once home, she closes the garage door and kills the ignition. We stay in the confines of her two-door sedan to talk. The enclosed space amplifies the distinct sounds of our voices. Our slightest movements are audible. The blue light from the gadgets on her dashboard barely shows our faces. This is our odd couple's thing and we take advantage of the intimate moment whenever we can. We usually stay in the car for about an hour, or until the air gets stuffy, or until one of us has to pee. Tonight, we're taking the time to reminisce about the highs and humors of the evening.

"Did you have a good time?" she asks.

I reach across the console and bring her closer. I give her a kiss for the entertaining birthday, another kiss for keeping everything simple, and a third for making me feel special. The smack of our lips and the lull of her moans are a symphony to my ears.

Deidra gets cold after a while, so we leave the car and retreat to the bedroom. I rest against the headboard as she changes into a tee shirt. "I know I said no birthday gifts, but I just changed my mind. I want a pole." I point to the empty corner between the wall and chaise lounge. "We can put it right there."

"I'll get one tomorrow if you promise to use it."

"I plan to watch...and tip with sexual favors."

She thumps my arm and kisses my cheek. "I actually have a gift you can open right now."

My eyelids are too heavy for anything beyond groping. I want to relax and fall fast asleep since it's shy of 6:00, but she wants to make love. When Deidra opens the nightstand drawer and pulls out a small gift bag adorned in my favorite color, I realize she has something else in mind.

"Open it."

I take the blue bag and reach beyond the metallic tissue paper. A soft fabric brushes my skin and I pull out the contents. *I love you beary much* is embroidered on the baby bib between my fingers. A fuzzy bear with a big smile is in the center of the terry cloth fabric. Though we envision a baby in our future, the premature timing of the bib alarms me. I hope this isn't a cry for expediency. I look at her for an explanation.

"Ugh, don't look so scared," she says. "I'm not rushing you. I'm ready for many more birthdays with you, for life with you. The bib is just a symbol of how I feel about you now and what we'll have in the future."

She wants a verbal reaction except I'm relieved and speech-less. My concern declines even more once I consider all the kick-ass gifts I've received in my thirty years. Very few had this level of meaning and significance. Most gifts I received prior to this moment were more expensive and immaterial— usually outdated or useless after a year or two. This is one I want to cherish. "Thanks. I like your originality. This is cool."

She hands me a small silver box.

"What's this?" I ask, masking my delight.

"Just open it."

I place the box in my lap to untie the blue ribbon as a smile takes over my face. When I lift the lid, my excitement vanishes. I freeze with my hand suspended mid-air. Hardly breathing, I can only fully manage the movement of my eyes. They dart from the box to Deidra and from her to the box again and again before I finally close them from shock and a bit of oxygen deprivation. I'm lightheaded until I force myself to inhale and resume motion.

"You're good?" she asks.

Does she want to know whether I'm satisfied with the gift or clear of a panic attack? I don't answer. I just breathe and sort my emotions. After settling from shock, I'm overwhelmed by confusion, except I take a few seconds to think before sharing my feelings. Then I shift from confusion to curiosity— a desire strong enough to end my daze.

"Where'd you get Pat's bracelet?"

"I've had it all along."

I exhale as questions rush my brain. "Why did you keep it from me?"

She looks across the room before catching my gaze. "I made that bracelet because I was begging for Pat's love. It's really the only part of me she ever had. She gave it back the day we re-corded her reading the Will. I know I'm selfish and vindictive for keeping it from you, even after you told me you looked all over her room for it. I apologize for acting out that way, but... I was too bitter to hand it over. I'm giving it to you now because it doesn't belong to me. It's rightfully yours. It's time for me to accept the relationship you had with Pat."

I can't find the words to express the gratitude and surprise I feel— not just for the bracelet, but her honesty as well. Her evolution. Her choice to forgive Pat's mistakes and grow with me. I want to tell her this, but more words aren't necessary.

She turns the lamp off and pulls my waist to hers so we can stretch out, spoon, and finally rest. I stroke her hand and occasionally glance beyond the aqua bracelet on the nightstand to the windows. The glow behind the curtains grows brighter by the minute. Dawn is cleansing and welcoming— as new and enlivened as this tide in our relationship.

I reflect on the year before last when I ransacked Pat's bedroom in search of the bracelet because I wanted something of hers to always have with me. The fact that I actually got what I wanted makes me smile. I received something from Pat before tonight, though I never imagined her death would leave something greater than the bracelet. I never cared about the value of her possessions or policies, never expected her to leave me anything in her Will. At first, all I wanted was the flimsy bracelet I'm now toying with in my hands.

Pat knew all too well how much I underestimated my desire and potential to love and know it intimately. So she tapped her celestial wisdom to give me someone that would enhance my faith, life, and happiness.

I know beyond a shadow of doubt that Deidra is an everlasting gift from my guardian angel.

### Nia
Also spelled Nyah
Language/cultural origin: Swahili/East African
Meaning: purpose

### Deidra
Also spelled Deidre or Deirdre
Language/cultural origin: Irish/Gaelic
Meaning: sorrowful; wanderer; a legendary beauty

### *Dear Reader*

~ Your thoughts are welcomed and appreciated. Write a review for *The Dawn of Nia.*

~ Share your thoughts with me via social media or email (l.cherelle@respublishing.com).

~ www.facebook.com/lcwrites
~ www.twitter.com/laurencre8s

~ Visit www.ResPublishing.com for books by other Resolute Publishing authors and Lauren Cherelle (a.k.a. L. Cherelle).

~ Like Resolute Publishing on social media to help build a community of readers and writers.

~ www.facebook.com/resolutepublishing
~ www.twitter.com/resolutepub

~ Last, but not least, I don't underestimate the power of your voice or opinions. Tell a friend about this novel.

## *About the Author*

Lauren Cherelle uses her time and talents to traverse imaginary
and professional worlds. She has published stories in *G.R.I.T.S:
Girls Raised in the South: An Anthology of Queer Womyn's
Voices & Their Allies* (2013) and the anthology *Lez Talk: A
Collection of Black Lesbian Short Fiction* (2016). She released
her first novel, *Accept the Unexpected*, in 2011.

During the week, Lauren works in nonprofit development and
administration. On weekends, she hangs up her fundraising hat
to focus on developmental editing, graphic design projects, and
personal writing. She resides in Louisville, KY with her partner
of thirteen years. Together, they aspire to open a business incu-
bator that houses a community-based mental wellness center
that serves women and families.

Outside of reading, writing, and working, Lauren volunteers as
a child advocate. She loves to visit new cities, binge watch her
favorite shows, play in her curly hair, and teach women to
explore and adore the power of intimacy.

*Website: www.lcherelle.com*

## Reading Group Guide

These questions are designed to enhance readers' conversation about *The Dawn of Nia*.

### Love

- In the Chapter 2, Pat told Nia: *I really want you to experience how good it feels when you're on the way to knowing love*. Discuss specific experiences in Nia's emotional journey that helped her know love.

- Love hurts sometimes. Love isn't always pretty. Love can be challenging. Cite examples from Nia's relationship with Deidra that would test your commitment to love.

- Consider your definition of love. What is the simplest way you can define it?
    - How did Nia and Deidra express their love for each other?

### Secrets

- A secret* is a) done, made, or conducted without the knowledge of others; b) kept from the knowledge of any but the initiated or privileged; c) something that is kept hidden or concealed.

*As defined by Dictionary.com

- Secrets are a theme in *The Dawn of Nia*. Which secrets were most memorable to you?

- In Chapter 11, Nia revealed to Deidra her association with Pat. How do you feel about the way Nia handled her secret prior to disclosure?
  - How do you feel about the way Nia disclosed her secret to Deidra?

- In Chapter 17, Kayla revealed Deidra's (first) secret (i.e. Deidra is married). Were Deidra's secrets an extension of being guarded and bruised or sneaky and manipulative?

- Have you ever learned of a family secret during a funeral? Did the revelation spark animosity or resentment?
  - Did the revelation bring closure?

## *Opinions*

- Was Nia mean to Kayla, or did Kayla "ask for it"?

- Discuss sex on the first date. Is it ever okay?
  - Can sex-only interactions develop into sustainable relationships?

- How do you feel about Jacoby's view of Deidra? Is he justified or disrespectful?

- What are your thoughts about Nia intervening in the Carter family's quest for Pat's estate? Would you act similarly?

- Can friends (such as Nia and Jacoby) with a romantic/ sexual history remain objective and supportive when new relationships arise?

- Jacoby is a character that wanted to "have his cake and eat it too." Does he meet the criteria of a down-low man?
  - What advice would you give him?

- In Chapter 34, Shannon told Nia: *And your girlfriend made me practice on a banana when I turned fifteen, sixteen, and seventeen. And she gave me female condoms and dental dams and made me watch a bunch of YouTube videos.*

  In Chapter 44, Deidra shared with Nia a conversation she held with Shannon. Deidra said: *I told Shannon her body is a source of pleasure and this is a good thing— but sexual gratification needs to be on her terms and for her benefit because no man will treat her with any degree of respect if she doesn't exercise her right to speak and choose first.*

  Did your parent(s)/guardian(s) help you develop perspective about sex and your body?
  - How do you feel about Deidra's efforts with Shannon?
  - Considering your children (or young people you influence), what would you say differently/similarly than Deidra or your parent(s)/guardian(s)?

- In Chapter 39, Nia, Deidra, and Jacoby had a verbal confrontation in a restaurant. Afterward, Deidra admitted: *I only say certain things to him because he'll take the bait and completely disregard you.* Do you agree with her combative approach?

- In Chapter 43, Cookie provided insight into Pat's youth. Considering Cookie's revelations, who was ultimately responsible for Deidra's abandonment?

### Relationships

- Every couple's journey is uniquely challenging and rewarding. What did you admire most about Nia and Deidra's growing relationship?

- Chapters 13 and 23 provided insight into Nia's past and current relationship with her parents. Her childhood experiences helped mold the foundation for romantic experiences in adulthood. Can you identify specific instances where your parents' (or family's) shortcomings affected your adult experiences?
  - How did you overcome these deficits?

- In Chapter 38, Eric told Nia: *When the dust settles, she'll find her way home.* Do you know men who would let their wives "stray"?

- What advantages would distance and discretion provide a marriage?

- Why would Eric financially support Deidra while she lived in Memphis?

- If you were in Nia's shoes, would you end your friendship

with Jacoby? If you were in Tasha's shoes, would you encourage reconciliation?

- Initially, Tasha disliked Deidra due to her interactions with K.D. at the house party. Have you ever disliked a friend's significant other?
  - Did your dislike/distrust improve over time?

- African Americans have a long history with fictive kinship. Discuss your experiences with "play" kin (e.g. play mama, play aunt).
  - Given your experiences or feelings with play kin, would you support or discourage Nia's relationship with Pat's daughter?

- Have you ever dated a married man or woman?
  - Where expectations or boundaries established during the courtship?
  - How would you handle Deidra's marital status?

### *Motivations*

- Did the Carter family want control of Pat's estate out of love and respect for Pat or for personal gain?

- As the story developed, did you question Deidra's motives or loyalties? If so, when?

- In Chapter 30, Juanita trapped Nia in the hallway. Juanita said: *Deidra didn't leave behind shit! She didn't come back to Memphis for Pat, my kids, or nobody else. She came back 'cause she got pregnant by another man... Save*

*yourself while you can, honey.* Whose interest was
Juanita serving?

- In Chapter 35, Deidra asked Nia: *Do you think Pat used
  you?... If Pat was honest about me, she wouldn't have
  been able to use you as a substitute.* Do you agree with
  Deidra's assertion?

- In Chapter 45, Deidra gave Pat's bracelet to Nia. What did
  the bracelet symbolize to Deidra?
    - Have you ever withheld a physical object due to
      emotional attachment?

## *Etcetera*

- Discuss the following characters individual (personality)
  flaws: Nia, Jacoby, Caroline, Deidra, Juanita, and Mrs.
  Ellis (i.e. Nia's mother).
    - Do you have personal experience with any of
      their flaws?

- As their relationship progressed, Deidra revealed to Nia
  her experiences with poverty, lack of parental guidance,
  infidelity, and emotional maltreatment from her husband.
  Discuss specific cultural/societal issues that contributed
  to Deidra's struggles.

- *The Dawn of Nia* is set in Memphis, Tennessee with some
  scenes taking place in rural Tennessee and Mississippi.
  Identify specific passages or references that were
  distinctively Southern.